Crystalle Valentino writes erotic fiction. She is the author of *After Hours*, *Personal Services* and *A Private View*, all coming soon from Black Lace.

After Hours

CRYSTALLE VALENTINO

BLACK
LACE

1 3 5 7 9 10 8 6 4 2

First published in 2000 as *The Naked Flame* by Black Lace,
an imprint of Virgin Books
This edition published in 2013 by Black Lace, an imprint of Ebury Publishing
A Random House Group Company

The Random House Group Limited Reg. No. 954009

Addresses for companies within the Random House Group can be found at:
www.randomhouse.co.uk

A CIP catalogue record for this book is
available from the British Library

The Random House Group Limited supports the Forest Stewardship
Council® (FSC®), the leading international forest-certification
organisation. Our books carrying the FSC label are printed on
FSC®-certified paper. FSC is the only forest-certification scheme
supported by the leading environmental organisations, including
Greenpeace. Our paper procurement policy can be found at:
www.randomhouse.co.uk/environment

MIX
Paper from
responsible sources
FSC® C016897

Printed and bound by CPI Group (UK) Ltd, Croydon, CR0 4YY

ISBN 9780352347602

To buy books by your favourite authors and register for offers visit:
www.blacklace.co.uk

Chapter One

'Would you consider cybersex?' flashed up unexpectedly on Venetia Halliday's computer screen as she sat in her first-floor office over her restaurant.

Venny did a double-take. She had just been completing the accounts and was feeling tired after Saturday night's trade, even if the restaurant hadn't been particularly full. From outside came the noises of departing patrons getting into their cars, some still grumbling loudly over the food. She knew they were right to complain. She knew that she had made a mistake when she had hired Bill Thompson two months ago. She also knew that she was going to have to do something about him, or go under.

Venny stared at the screen.

Well, would she consider cybersex?

She had considered a lot of things in her lifetime – a whole clutch of impulses had in fact been grasped at with initial enthusiasm – but mostly she disliked risk and so abandoned those wild impulses untried.

Hair extensions? No. Too much trouble, and would it look like a wig after all that fusing-on and fussing?

Quitting London for a stress-free life in the sticks? Emphatically no.

Getting a bigger, sportier car? Again, no. Getting a smaller car and saving on petrol and insurance? Yes to that one.

Liposuction to save on gym time? Nope. Too big a coward. Body piercing? Here again cowardice played a part. She wasn't worried about shocking her parents – they lived in Spain, and were rarely in touch. What worried her was the suspicion that having her navel or nipples pierced was going to hurt like hell. Added to that, she thought that tongue studs looked too gross for words, so she'd settled for having her ears done. Very daring.

If she was truthful, it was her inbred caution that had led her to this sorry pass. She had hired Bill because he had seemed like the safe option. The other applicants had seemed too go-ahead, too cocky, too likely to undermine her authority from day one.

But Bill Thompson had been different. Quiet. Chunky and dark-haired and brown-eyed. Sweet, she had thought. Attractive, but not overwhelmingly so. Not like that other one. A light frown crinkled her brow. The one with the impudent blue eyes and the shock of gelled hair and the tall angular body.

Venny sat back in her chair and considered. What was his name? Gin? Finney? Something like that. One look and she had known he was trouble. That he would be expensive, demanding, impossible, a sexual time-bomb ticking away in her kitchens, just waiting to explode.

So she had hired Bill. Steady, reliable Bill. Who had turned out to be without culinary flair and bull-headed and pedantic, so that any complaint about the unexciting food or slow service was greeted with massive bouts of sulking and a complete refusal to change a thing.

Obviously, Venny was going to have to make the changes.

She looked at the screen again.

Cybersex.

An ironic smile flickered over her lips. She had believed that hiring a chef would set her restaurant, Box of Delights, on the road to success, justifying all the angst she had suffered over refurbishments and bumpy cash flow. Cash flow was, in fact, still her biggest problem. She had to pay the staff, the suppliers, the overheads, the accountants – but she loved it. This place was her baby. She had dreamed of it winning her the prestigious Blue Ribbon award this year. After that, publicity would follow, trade would rocket, and all her problems would be solved. Then she might sell. Or she might not. She'd see.

But there was Bill, who right now was a problem and a half. Bill was admittedly sexy in his heavy, blokish way, and the other staff tended to warm to his genial charm, even covering for him when he made mistakes.

Troubled, Venny – she hated her full name, Venetia, and never used it – leaned back in her leather chair and slipped both hands behind the sweat-sticky fluff of blonde curls at the base of her neck to ease the tension there. As she moved, her tightly cut caramel-coloured suit strained tight against her prominent breasts. She liked suits. Suits were an armour-plated uniform to Venny, making her feel businesslike and invulnerable. The summer storm rattled and rolled outside, making the close city air feel sticky. Her green eyes closed and she exhaled slowly, regaining calm. It wasn't raining yet, but soon it would pour and bring relief from the torpid August heat.

She stretched again, relishing the pressure on her nipples from the silky material of her suit. This was going to be difficult. This was the bit of the job she hated. Mostly, she loved what she did. She was an entrepreneur. She'd gone straight out of university and into a series of dull dusty jobs to raise cash for what she knew she wanted to do more than anything else – set up businesses, run them and then sell them on at a tidy profit.

First she'd purchased, with the help of a knee-tremblingly large bank loan, a small faltering manufacturing company. She'd initially had a partner – a fellow business graduate – for that one, and he'd legged it when the going got tough, nearly grossing her an ulcer instead of the profit she had foreseen. But she struggled on and somehow made sense of it. Later, when it was in the black for the first time in a decade, she sold it for double what she'd paid, and her ex-partner demanded half. She'd paid him off and figured she'd learned a valuable business lesson so probably the louse had done her a favour. No partners, ever again. Then on to the second, a defunct hotel. The profit had been less overall on that one but, without an ex-partner to threaten lawsuits, she did just fine.

And now she was on her third.

A restaurant.

Venny sighed and drummed her fingers on the desk. She could have bought houses and tarted them up. She could have bought antiques and flogged them on. Why a restaurant? She wasn't even interested in food.

She opened her eyes and glanced down at her jutting breasts. Her nipples were erect, clearly visible through the thin material of her suit. That was why she did it. The buzz. The thrill.

Venny raised her hands and reflectively ran them down over the full curves. Her nipples tingled deliriously when she touched them. Fully clothed, Venny considered that she looked a bit too lush and curvy for the current fashion. But when she was naked, she looked extremely good. A real mug's eyeful. Her blonde, curly hair was long enough to just touch and conceal and tease her nipples. Her green eyes were almond-shaped, almost catlike in their appeal, and her heart-shaped face was centred by a neat, small nose. Her mouth was full, the lips flaring and pouty, promising an abandoned passion she doubted she could ever truly deliver. But God, she wished she was naked now, and receiving more enjoyable relief from her tensions from an able lover.

And there was one on offer.

She knew where the cybersex message must have come from, because this computer was linked to the one beside the till downstairs, and all the staff had departed for the night except Bill.

With her tongue trapped seductively between her teeth, she leaned forwards and tapped out on the keyboard: 'Why settle for cybersex when I can have the real thing?'

'Who says you can have the real thing?' flashed up instantly.

Venny typed: 'I do. I'm the boss, remember.'

'As if you would let me forget it,' came back – just a trifle waspishly, she thought.

Venny shut down the computer and stood up, stretching luxuriously. She crossed to the open window and lifted the thin blind to peer out. A gusty breeze scented with rain cooled her face and she inhaled deeply.

The quaint Camden side-street was quieter now as bars and restaurants closed and people began making their way home. She gazed at the half-timbered white-painted houses opposite Box of Delights, the packed rainbow-hued windowboxes dotted here and there, the heavy heads of marigolds and surfinias and geraniums dancing in the freshening breeze beneath the cold sodium glare of a stylish repro 'gaslight'. Even the shop signs were carefully vetted in this pretty, select little enclave, so that the ambience of the place was never spoiled. If you squinted a bit, she thought, you could almost be back in the nineteenth century. Except for the cars, and the fumes, and the ever-watchful traffic wardens, and the clampers. Oh, and the city noises, the shrieking of a car alarm, a police siren, an ambulance.

This city.

She loved it.

As she peered out at the encroaching night, fat drops of rain started to pelt the window. Lightning flared above the darkened rooftops and she let the blind drop with a clatter. She hated thunderstorms. They felt dangerous and uncontrolled, like an unruly passion.

Unruly passion, she thought, and turned away from the window.

When was the last time she'd felt anything even close to that?

She could imagine her friend and flatmate Dani's brisk reply to that one. Never. Because she never took risks, never took chances. Well, *almost* never. She did take the odd minimal, calculated risk in business; sometimes you had to, to make progress. But basically she was a control freak. And true passion, true stomach-churning desire, was a huge risk, one that Venny felt safer avoiding.

As she stood there in the slanting rainbow light from her fake Tiffany desk lamp, Venny found that man's face floating into her mind for the second time. The laughing blue eyes. The crackling energy he'd radiated. His mouth, curving upward in a smile full of sexual challenge.

Irritated with herself, she switched off the lamp and walked – teetering slightly on the skyscraper heels the male patrons found so alluring – out of the office and down the stairs. At the bottom was a quilted burgundy baize door. She opened it, and stepped into the kitchens.

And froze, her jaw dropping by a mile.

In the middle of the brightly lit room, which was dominated by the big stainless steel tables, ovens, cupboards and utensils of a professional kitchen, stood Bill.

He was about the same height as her when she wore her spiked heels. His body was robust and hairy as a hearthrug. The hair on his head was tidy and cut close into the nape of his neck, but if it were allowed to grow longer she just knew that it would be a mass of thick dark curls. Bill was facing away from her, idly stirring the contents of a saucepan.

He was wearing nothing except a white linen apron tied around his waist.

When Venny finally got over her shock, she admired the show. Bill had good broad shoulders, and his waist where the apron was tied was taut. Beneath the knotted ties was a pair of delectable buttocks. They were much paler than the skin on his back or legs, and there was a suggestion of dark hair between and slightly beneath them, because he stood with one leg comfortably bent at the knee.

Despite her reservations about this, Venny felt her crotch moisten. It wasn't like Bill to be surprising, but he'd certainly surprised her tonight. And it was a pleasant surprise, she had to admit that. Bill had been flirting with her for weeks now, and he was handsome and appealing, if you ignored the fact that he was a liability in business.

Venny had found herself pushing it to one side. She liked Bill. All right, she fancied Bill too. And there was more to a person than how they did their job. Even if they did it badly.

A sigh slipped from between her lips as once again she pushed that unpalatable fact away. It was, in these circumstances, easy to do so. Her thighs clenched lightly. Suddenly lightning flared, dimming the lights for a moment. Venny shivered. Well, this was passion, wasn't it? Of course it was. She deserved this, and she wanted it too.

Venny walked forwards slowly, very aware of the movements of her own body, aware of that old itchy need. Underneath her suit she was wearing a very sensible black body, but now the thin garment seemed to chafe her nipples and it felt uncomfortably damp between her legs.

'Bill?'

Bill looked over his shoulder and his conker-brown eyes lit up with pleasure as they met her more cautious green ones. His lashes were black but a bit sparse, thought Venny. And then she thought that she was being over-critical, and she ought to let herself go more, just like Dani said. Loosen up, she told herself impatiently. You're supposed to be enjoying yourself.

'Venny,' Bill greeted her, and turned back to the pot, stirring it gently. Venny could see his balls hanging down between his legs, and she imagined that she could see the tip of his cock too.

But she probably couldn't.

In fact, the tip of his cock was probably up around his navel right now, at the head of a giant erection, because the thing they had been side-stepping around for the past few weeks was finally going to happen, and he wanted it even more than she did. For her, there was regret mingled with the excitement she felt. For him, there was just the excitement.

'Feeling hot tonight?' Venny joked lightly, and then wondered if she should joke at all. Bill was notoriously prickly, and men were endlessly sensitive about women who laughed during sex. Then the fact that she was having to censor her thoughts and her speech in her own damned restaurant caused a stab of impatience, even irritation, to dull her desire just a tad.

Must be the heat, she thought. Summer in London with its mild micro-climate was often oppressive. And summer in a restaurant kitchen was always hellishly hot, in the low hundreds, and now there was a storm coming in fast, stoking up the humidity to boiling point. They didn't run to air conditioning. She wished they did, but for the moment she really could not afford it. But at least the venerable old building with its age-blackened beams and peculiarly sloping floors and walls was cooling now that the restaurant was empty.

A sudden thought occurred to her, a thought that was shocking but titillating too.

'Bill, have you been like that all night?' she asked, and

her mouth was so dry with anticipation and nervousness of what was to come that she had to lick her lips before speaking.

'Sure I have.' He laughed softly, then shook his head. 'Just joking. Of course I haven't. Although it was tempting at times, if only to try and cool down. Little Jane was so hot that I told her to wait topless on the tables. She wouldn't of course. Far too respectable. We were all a bit disappointed. She has such sexy little breasts, don't you think? Small but high. And you can always see her nipples through those sports bras she wears, like fat little buds.'

Venny declined to comment, feeling her desire slip down another notch. Yes, Jane had delightful little breasts. She would grant her that. But when a man was seducing you, did you really want to hear about another woman's nipples and how he and the rest of the male staff letched after them?

Hardly.

'Yes, it must be nice in this heat,' said Venny tersely. 'Being small-breasted.'

'Not a problem you have, though, is it?' said Bill, with an admiring leer at her front.

This wasn't going at all like Venny had planned. Every cloddish word he uttered seemed to shrivel her desire for him just a little more. In fact, every time he opened his mouth he was sticking his big foot straight in it. As a teenager, Venny had had a complex about her big tits. Hunch-shouldered and cross-armed on all public occasions, she had desperately tried to conceal them. Later, she began to see them as a bonus. And so did every man she had ever slept with. Not that there had been that many. She was cautious in love as well as business. All right, *too* cautious. But the habit of holding back, maintaining a distance, was so ingrained with her that it seemed she was never going to shake it off, even if she wanted to. And right now she wasn't sure she did.

Venny reached the hob where Bill was stirring the pot. From the front, she had to admit, he looked even better. Naked to the waist as he was, she was able to admire his solid chest with its dark flat nipples. Black hair circled them in hypnotic swirls and then feathered down the centre of his chest. His stomach, considering the huge amount he could pack away while raiding the larder after the lunchtime session, was pretty flat. And then there was the apron, which obscured her view until it reached his knees. Then his calves – thick and well-shaped and strong. He was built like a rugby player.

As she drew close she caught a tantalising whiff of his sweat, and an acidic waft from whatever he had in the pan. A blast of heat caught her, too, from the hob. She leaned a hand on the cool counter beside the hob and watched for a moment.

'So what *is* cybersex?' she said at last, wondering if he was one of those tedious closet computer nerds, and hoping the explanation was going to be brief.

Bill gave her a warm grin. He was completely unself-conscious about his near-nudity, Venny noted. She found herself wondering what his mouth would taste like.

'Haven't you been reading the articles in the press, Venny? Cybersex is hot, right now. The ultimate safe sex. Fantasy and flirtation. All in the head.'

Venny chewed that over. Anything involving computers sounded dull as hell to her. They were tools to do jobs with: nothing more, nothing less. 'All good sex starts in the head,' she pointed out. She'd read it somewhere and, what's more, it was true.

'Yeah, but it progresses to the body, doesn't it? And how can it, when one person is in, for instance, Scotland, and the other's in Tahiti or some Godforsaken hole?' Bill tutted and stirred the pot a bit. 'All these women getting hysterical about their partners getting involved with people online! That's cybersex, Venny.'

Fascinating, thought Venny, not without irony. 'They could meet,' she suggested offhandedly.

'And find each other repulsive?'

'Well, it's a possibility.'

'God, it's hot. Aren't you hot?'

'A bit, yes.' Venny laughed. 'You want me to go topless, too?'

'I'd like that.' Bill's face was suddenly earnest. He switched off the hob and turned towards her. He glanced down. 'You see how much I would like it?'

Venny's gooseberry-green eyes dipped down to the front of his apron. Below the tightness of the apron's waist-ties, his cock was forming a small tent. Her eyes flicked back up and met his.

'Well, why not?' Heartbeat accelerating, Venny unfastened the single button on her jacket and slipped the well-cut garment from her shoulders. She draped it over a nearby stool. The black body was still decorous, even demure. 'How about that?' she teased with a smile.

'More,' said Bill, his eyes taking on a glaze of lust.

Raising her eyebrows at him, Venny slipped her fingers under the body's spaghetti straps and eased them down over her arms. Shaking out her loosely curling blonde hair in a provocative movement, she pushed her thumbs into the top of the clingy fabric and in one smooth movement pushed the body down around her waist.

'Enough?' she asked, then flinched a little as thunder roared overhead and the storm edged closer.

'Nowhere near,' said Bill thickly. At least she had his full attention now.

'OK.' Venny tossed back one hank of hair, then the other; but, as she did so, she covered each breast with the palm of a hand. Now her hands covered them instead of her hair, and her eyes were teasing.

'God, Venny,' he growled, and touched a hand to his urgent, aching penis.

'Goodness, such impatience,' she purred, and let her hands fall to her sides.

Bill stared at her breasts like a man spotting a water-hole mirage in a desert. She had always suspected he was a breast man, and she didn't know what that said about him, but she suspected it meant he was a bit too macho for her taste, perhaps a tad less than super-intelligent.

Well, that was OK. It really was. Tonight, it was just fine, and she let him look, and felt pretty excited herself just by doing that simple thing. But when it seemed he might stand there all night just looking, Venny felt that perhaps it was time to move things on. She stepped towards him, intending to kiss and caress him, when suddenly Bill moved, and they collided a bit hectically, Venny unable to stifle a giggle. Bill frowned sharply at her levity before clamping his big hands over her breasts with a grip like a Sumo.

Yep, a breast man, she thought, flinching with discomfort. And he was certainly a big man, looming over her, his cock prodding at her stomach. She felt moisture seeping through down there, just above the waistline of her skirt, a tiny hint of pre-come which stirred an answering excitement in her. But Bill was busy kneading her breasts like dough.

Unsubtle technique, she thought, and then, with a conscious decision to stop thinking, she let herself get into it, absorbing the sensation of this man, these big capable hands pushing and pulling at the very sensitive flesh of her breasts. Now he was grabbing a nipple between finger and thumb, and his head was going down.

Oh! That was nice. Venny put her arms around his neck and leaned into his mouth as he suckled her. His mouth was very hot and very wet and her nipple seemed directly connected to her sex by sizzling nerve-endings. Unconsciously her head went back and her hips tilted forwards, and the urgent prod of his cock was as stiff as steel now, while her cunt seemed to liquefy in anticipation.

As Bill's mouth worked, so his hips began to move against hers. His lips sucked at her erect nipple, and his hips pushed. His whole mouth took the nipple in, and his hips retreated. Over to the other nipple now, and his teeth nipped her quite sharply so that she cried out in a crazy mingling of pain and pleasure. His hips pushed forwards. His tongue paddled over her nipple, crushing her with a weight of delight, making her legs go weak, and then his hips went back, but she placed her hands on the silky skin of his big buttocks and drew them back again to her, urgently.

In a trance of passion, Venny was aware of Bill's hands working at the apron's ties. When he tossed the apron aside, his cock, suddenly unrestrained, sprang up between them as if spring-loaded. Almost shyly Bill placed his hands on his hips and looked down at his swelling penis, and now it was her turn to look.

And wow, it was impressive. Bill's cock was directly in proportion to the rest of him. It was big, red and thick. A rug of black pubic hair framed it like velvet flung beneath a prodigious coral carving. And his balls were heavy, hanging so temptingly between his furred thighs. Venny reached out a tentative hand and touched them, making them swing lightly. Bill groaned and grabbed her hand, keeping it there. She squeezed them obligingly, feeling them start to lift and harden.

'You like it?' gasped Bill. He was still pushing his hips forwards almost automatically, and Venny was treated to the sight of his glans rhythmically pushing out beyond his foreskin like a child playing peek-a-boo.

He put a hand to his cock but quickly removed it. He was too aroused to take much more stimulation, she saw.

'It's . . . gorgeous,' Venny murmured, and felt that mad desire to laugh surface again. She stifled it, knowing he'd be terribly hurt if she let the fast-building guffaw escape. 'Really, it's wonderful,' she affirmed, frowning with the effort of suppressing her mirth.

What was wrong with her? Here he was, a perfectly presentable man desperate to have sex with her, and she was finding it very hard to let go, to get into it. Dani's right, she thought miserably. I am a control freak, and I even want to control this, and the fact that I can't is making me nervous.

She just hoped Bill handled his bread dough a little more carefully than he handled a girl's tits, that was all. She also hoped that he didn't demand she admire his baguettes on Monday, because she'd crack up.

But then she remembered the other thing she had to do tonight, and realised that would not be a problem. Relax, she told herself. It feels good, doesn't it?

And it did. It felt a little treacherous too, which didn't please her or make her particularly proud of herself, but pleasure was pleasure and business was business.

And now Bill had pushed a hand up under her skirt, and with a gasp of surprise she felt him nudge her legs apart. She wasn't wearing tights: it was too hot for that. Her eyes stared into his as he gripped the fabric of the body at her crotch, and pulled. She felt the fasteners pop apart one by one.

Grinning triumphantly, Bill pushed her legs open further with a rough movement of his hand, moistening his fingers against her with a fumbling movement. But she didn't dislike his ham-fistedness now. Sticky with heat and desire, Venny found herself panting lightly as Bill quickly freed the fastenings on her skirt. He managed it pretty easily, too; well, this was a man who could shell eggs with one hand. Surely a skirt couldn't be beyond him.

Bill eagerly pushed both skirt and body down to the floor in one swift movement and suddenly Venny was standing there stark naked except for her shoes.

Maybe it was her surroundings that were putting her off, Venny thought as he looked her over like a dog with a new bone to chew on. A nice soft bed wouldn't come amiss right now. But this was what she should do more of. Acting on impulse. Taking risks. It was probably good for her karma or some damned thing.

Now she just wished he'd get on with it, but Bill was staring at her crotch in fascination. He put out a big trembling hand and brushed it up over her little pelt of toffee-coloured pubic hair. Venny flinched and felt the sweet, hot surge of lust taking hold of her again. Her clit swelled within its silky wet folds, seeking caresses. Her stomach fluttered madly. Her nipples were outrageously hard.

'Do you shave this?' Bill asked hoarsely, having to lick his lips first so that he could speak.

Venny shook her head. 'It's called a Mohican,' she said faintly. 'The beautician waxes it so that it leaves just a strip of hair about an inch wide,' she explained helpfully. It had been agony to have done, and she wasn't going to bother having it done a second time. Pube-waxing could go in the same bin as extensions and body piercing, as far as she was concerned.

Her unexpected hairdo turned him on. Venny could see that. His breathing grew harsh just looking at it, and his cock twitched hungrily. Bill's hand reached out and stroked down over her stomach, teasing the skin there into wild tremors of excitement.

'Wow, that's sexy,' he murmured, and moved in close to her, one beefy hand reclaiming a breast with a wince-making grip while the other went lower to push his full, aching penis down and into the little runway the moist lips of her cunt provided for just that purpose.

'Do you like that, Venny?' Bill rubbed himself back and forth against her, each time slipping deeper, each time pushing harder.

God, I don't think I'm ready for this, Venny thought in panic. Relax, she told herself sternly. Get into it. 'Yes, I like it,' she murmured, kissing the salty-tasting skin of his shoulder. His skin was smooth with heavy ill-defined muscles moving beneath it. Suddenly, she felt about as likeable as Lady Macbeth. She was using him.

Yes, but wasn't he using her too?

And anyway it was too late to pull back. Far too late. Bill's mad pushing was taking an upward turn, and she felt the big stiff head of his cock nudging at her opening, felt his hands going under her buttocks, lifting her, while his legs pushed between her thighs, opening her up even wider.

Venny found herself sitting on the steel counter. She nearly yelped when her bottom struck the cold metal, and nearly yelped again when his thigh caught hers against the metal in a neat little crushing movement that caused her a brief but intense flash of pain. But there was pleasure too, and she fell back onto her elbows across the wide counter and gazed up at him, hearing her own panting breaths mingling with his.

Bill was staring fixedly at her heavy, lolling, naked breasts as he fumbled the head of his penis into her. Goodness, it was thick. But her own juices were flowing fast and hard now, and he slipped his big cock into her with remarkable ease, pushing it right up into her in one smooth movement that wrenched a cry from her.

'All right?' he panted hopefully. 'Not too big?' He was half-smiling, half-grimacing with the effort of not coming off in two seconds flat, she could see that. He was a nice man. Considerate.

Venny shook her head and lay back, idly toying with her clit. Maybe if she just closed her eyes he'd get on with it, get it over with. She closed her eyes. And oh, yes, it felt good. He was chugging away at her now, pushing, pushing, pushing, and every hard thrust he made took his cock deep into her, touching her where she was most sensitive, most responsive. She felt her orgasm begin to tweak at her as she relaxed into the feel of Bill's energetic fucking, and she thought, yes, this is great, and then he came.

He just came.

He came with a lot of noise too. He grunted and groaned and Venny opened her eyes in disbelief to see his face screwed up as if in pain. The bastard was coming already! Forced back onto both elbows, Venny desperately tried to move against his emptying cock, tried to maintain her own stimulation, but she knew it was a losing battle. And why hadn't he touched her? Wasn't every modern man supposed to know that you were supposed to touch a woman to get her ready to orgasm, not just shove your cock in and hope for the best?

'Sorry,' Bill muttered, and leaned forwards with his shaft still buried up to the hilt in her and started lapping with his tongue at her nipple in a half-hearted sort of way. Venny felt anger building instead of desire. To think she had even felt guilty about doing this.

'We make good partners,' he slurred against her breast, interrupting her line of thought. 'Don't you think we do, Venny? We could be good partners both in and out of bed, what do you say?' And he gazed at her with puppyish appeal, while his cock wilted inside her.

Venny closed her eyes again. The anger was very strong now. Partners! Unwittingly, Bill had hit on the one thing guaranteed to enrage her. She pushed against his shoulders and he drew back in surprise, groping for a hank of kitchen roll as his penis came free. Venny hopped down from the counter, and while he was busy drying off she yanked her skirt on and, not bothering with the body, pulled on her jacket and buttoned it securely. Her body hummed like a strummed guitar, and her legs felt as secure beneath her as unset jelly.

'That was good, huh?' Bill asked, dropping the used tissue into the pedal bin. 'So what do you think, Venny?'

He turned to her, his cock at half-mast, and his eyes widened in surprise to find that she was already dressed.

'I'll tell you what I think, Bill,' said Venny icily. 'I think you're fired.'

Chapter Two

When Venny got home to her Camden flat it was raining heavily. Lucky she'd brought the car today. Not that the flat was very far from the restaurant, but she didn't really like schlepping around London at night, and particularly not in the middle of a summer storm.

And this was some summer storm. Lightning strobed and needle-sharp flashes speared the sky, then thunder rolled into the vacuum behind the lightning strikes and blasted her ears like exploding mortar shells. The pavements were black and slick as patent leather, rain pummelling against them so hard that the heavy droplets bounced back into the air. Really, the weather matched her mood.

She parked the car in her precious permit-holders-only space and went inside. The next-door flat in the converted Victorian warehouse where she lived was no longer tagged with its SOLD sign. Well, these were good flats; they sold fast. They had loads of historical ambience, with the lock being right beside them. Barge owners had stored their cargoes of timber, coal and wood in these buildings, and now after a long time rotting as derelict hulks they were in full use again and the property developers were having a ball. And the warehouses were not only being renovated as flats. There were shops too, and craft studios, and live jazz and rock nearby, and the market for bargains. The canal permeated the place, wafting freshets of soft moisture and strong diesel into the air all around it. Trees, their shadowy branches dancing in the breeze, crowded on its banks like suicides about to jump.

Now why had she thought of suicides? Venny wondered. Bill was tougher than that. People moved in and out of jobs all the time, in and out of short contracts, in and out of appointments that had seemed rock-solid secure, for that matter. Like Bill Thompson's before she fired him.

He hadn't taken it very well.

In fact he had taken it spectacularly badly, and inevitably there had been the painful post mortem. Was it something he'd said or done? No. Was it his cooking? Well, yes. He wanted to cook just Italian, nothing else, while she favoured serving a more broad-based fusion-food line. And he didn't even cook good Italian. And there was his attitude, of course, although she didn't want to get into that, and flinging accusations at this point was unlikely to prove helpful, didn't he think so?

Bill clearly didn't agree.

Bill had gone right ahead and flung a few accusations.

Like, he couldn't believe what a cold ball-breaking bitch she was.

Like, she had used him tonight and then given him the finger.

All true. Venny had to admit that. He had shouted and, even worse, he had stood there without a stitch on while carrying out his harangue, his deflated cock bobbing away in counterpoint to his angry words, which just made him look ridiculous. Venny was sure she had had more embarrassing encounters, but she was damned if she could remember when.

On Monday she would have to phone the employment agency and dig herself out of the shit. She wasn't a chef. Microwaving ready meals taxed her culinary expertise to the limit. Her ignorance of food production was total. She didn't know whether the Barnsley black sausage was superior to the French *boudin noir.* She didn't care about bento boxes or *nuoc mam.* Opening a cereal packet was, frankly, an effort. As for the rest of the staff, they were just servers and choppers; none of them had the knowledge needed to command kitchens.

So this was the picture. She had bookings for covers she could not provide. She had an unbearable sexual itch. And she was going to have to crawl to her bank manager for a bigger loan.

But the only way was up, right?

Over the noise of the receding storm and Shania Twain blasting out on the stereo, Dani heard Venny come crashing into the flat. Dani was in the high-ceilinged kitchen. It had exposed brick walls and a big half-moon window underneath which cutting-edge fittings had been grafted on. She was working, but she was having fun too. Dani was dedicated to having fun. That, and country and western.

'Hold on a minute,' she said to the empty room, and turned Shania down.

She opened the door a crack and peered out at Venny through hanks of choppily cut dark hair. Where Venny had hung back from body piercing, Dani had embraced it with almost missionary zeal. There was a ring through her eyebrow, twin studs on her neat little nose, a row of silver skull-and-crossbone death's-heads parading up the lobes of both dainty ears, and Venny knew that her nipples, her navel and even her labia, under their little coat of dark fur, had all been pierced. All this, and a penchant for cowgirl boots and fringed buckskin jackets, marked Dani down as eccentric in Venny's eyes. But they suited each other, like the odd couple. The sober and the wild, thought Venny sourly. The daring and the dull.

'Thought it was you,' said Dani. 'Either that or a very noisy burglar. Bad day at the office, dear?'

'I fired the chef.' Venny dumped her bag on the hall table.

'Excuse me?' Dani half-turned and giggled as if someone had goosed her from behind. Shania was turned up again. 'Why?' she shouted, turning back to Venny.

'Because he's a lousy chef; because he's got an attitude problem,' said Venny. 'And he wanted to form a partnership, can you believe it? Anyway, I don't want to talk about it.'

Dani cast about for something to cheer Venny up. Almost immediately, she found it. 'Hey.' Dani's chocolate-brown eyes shone with delight in her sharply defined little face. 'There's a flat-warming bash next door on Tuesday. It's going to be a vampires and virgins theme party. You coming?'

'Tuesday?' Venny echoed dismally. 'I thought Tuesday was your line-dancing night at the Electric Ballroom?'

'It is, but I can skip one week.'

Venny shook her head doubtfully. 'I've got Monday to get through first.'

Venny yanked the door shut and walked on along the hall and into the bathroom. Dani shook her head. This was Venny's other problem – apart from the control-freak thing. She was always so uptight.

Not like her.

Easy come, easy go, that was Dani. Privately schooled and pot-smoking only child of rich parents, she had emerged from a superior education with a lust for life and a cut-glass accent which she had quickly dumbed down. She had grown up with everything being handed to her on a plate – and the plate was silver. She expected things to be cool, and somehow mostly they were.

Dani's parents had helped finance her mobile catering business. Parties, meetings and receptions. They'd bought her a van. Sometimes when things were tight they even helped with the rent.

And it didn't stop there.

Because of her parents she was well connected. Because she was well connected she was fully booked, with work coming out of her ears.

But she didn't have to work. She worked for fun.

She was having fun now.

'Where was I?' she asked herself dreamily, closing the kitchen door, tapping her booted foot along to 'That Don't Impress Me Much'.

She eyed the big circular cake that stood in front of the sink. It was three feet high, and a metre wide at the base. It was pretty, too. Sugar pink scalloped with white. It had taken her a troublesome hour with the tissue paper and stapler to get it looking that good.

'*Surprise!*' she shrieked.

The top of the cake sprang back on a hinged flap.

A blond and naked man with an all-over bottle tan sprang up from the cake and flung his arms apart with a grin. His cock bobbed over the lip of the cake, semi-aroused.

'Now look,' Dani tutted. 'What do I have to do to make this thing stay up?'

'Strip?' suggested Jamie.

Which was an appealing suggestion, but Dani knew that once they got going down that road she'd never get all the rest of the work finished.

But still.

Maybe if she just played along.

Whatever, she decided that she wasn't going to let him put it in, not tonight. She wasn't even going to let him cop a feel. She was a fun girl, but she had a sort of honour; when you booked a job, you made damned sure you got the thing done to the best of your ability. She had that much in common with Venny.

'OK, OK.'

Dani peeled her beige top over her scruffy dark hair and stepped out of her floral trousers. She kicked off her boots. She was left wearing a scrap of burgundy silk around her crotch, and Jamie thought she was still overdressed. She had cone-shaped breasts with edible dark-cherry nipples. Jamie was salivating like Pavlov's dog when the bell went.

'More?' he asked.

'Oh, OK.' And of course Dani was enjoying this, too; it was making her feel horny as hell in fact. She tossed aside her knickers. The hair on her mound was black against her velvety, white skin. Jamie's cock reasserted itself.

'Better,' she praised, and reached out to fondle his cock thoughtfully. 'Now, how do we keep this rock-hard on Saturday night when you jump out of the cake at the hen party? I can't be standing there in the buff then.'

'You could,' said Jamie.

'No, I couldn't. I know. Keep a men's magazine and a torch in there with you.'

'Like what? Motorbike monthly?'

Dani tweaked the tip of his cock.

'Ow,' said Jamie.

'Well take this seriously, will you? Damn! It's going down again.'

'Your fault for pinching it,' accused Jamie.

'This is the dress rehearsal,' said Dani sternly. 'It's got to be right. God, it's hot. Drink?'

Jamie nodded. Dani got two tins out of the fridge, popped the pulls and gave him one. Jamie downed the whole tin, tipping his head back and gulping it down like the guy in the Diet Coke ad.

Dani sipped hers and watched him. She liked a bit of rough, and Jamie fitted the bill just fine. Sometimes she wondered if he was just a tiny bit too hot to handle, but still she considered him one of her best discoveries. She'd spotted him months ago when she'd done a dinner for the art college. There she'd been, dishing up the baby pink salmon mousses, the bloody red slices of beef, profiteroles dripping with chocolate and cream, looking prim in her black dress and white apron. More wine, sir? Red or white?

Trying to behave as if she didn't know damned well she was turning on all those dusty academics like crazy.

And all the time, while they had been eyeballing her, she had been eyeballing the painting of Jamie, stark naked on a blanket.

Instant lust.

She'd quickly found out who he was. He was a Glaswegian and an art student. He was seriously shaggable. He was lowlife and light-fingered. He made weird planet-shaped mobiles to sell, and ice sculptures, which was useful to a busy caterer like Dani. She already had three commissions booked ahead for him: a wedding at Leeds Castle in Kent, a twenty-first at the Oxo Tower, and the Blue Ribbon restaurant awards at the Cranleigh Hotel in Piccadilly.

Jamie was permanently potless, always in need of money.

Well, she had money, and she felt sorry for him, sorry for the raw deal life had pushed his way.

They were both pleased with their arrangement and they sealed it on the first date. She'd fucked him bandy, and he'd been signed onto the payroll.

But Jamie had one big fault – the attention span of a gnat. Oh, he had pluses too, like that humongous cock of his. And he looked good, broad-shouldered and narrow-hipped, in a waiter's uniform. Jamie had the good sense to flatter old women, defer to men, flirt discreetly with the babes. So when Jamie was on the team, the tips flowed free and there were lots of happy smiling faces. And he balled the boss hot and strong whenever she wanted it. Which was frequently.

But there was work to do tonight.

Jamie tossed his can into the sink and looked at her.

Come-to-bed grey eyes and tousled streaky blond hair.

The heat and the quiet of the night thrummed as they stood and looked at each other. The rain had eased to a whisper.

Dani was stroking her throat slowly with the moisture-beaded tin.

Finally she put the tin aside.

'Well, just this once,' she said, and stepped into the cake with him.

Venny was lying in the bath, her tits half-submerged and sheeny with water and foam, when she heard them. She stuffed the end of the flannel in one ear and a hank of loo paper into the other.

She could still hear them.

Panting, murmuring, bumping and grinding.

Oh, and shrieking.

Why did Dani always have to howl like an Alaskan she-wolf when she was getting laid?

Venny yanked her useless earplugs out, lay further back in the citrus-scented foam, and thought calm thoughts. But before very long work problems started drifting into her consciousness, and then Bill put in an appearance with his wounded puppydog eyes and his big red cock. Before she knew it, her nipples were puckered above the waterline and she was rubbing them with her fingers and feeling hopelessly horny.

She stretched her legs out restlessly beneath the water and her breasts bounced as she moved. Critically she gazed down at them. She had lit candles around the tub before undressing, lavender-scented ones to soothe stress – and oh, boy, did she need that – and the soft warm glow from them highlighted her tits beautifully.

She put her hands under them and lifted them higher, and thought suddenly of Bill's dark head hovering there, of his hot mouth sucking at her. Restlessly her palms moved over her nipples, scuffing them into heightened sensitivity, and then her fingers tweaked them, pulling them out and onto Bill's imaginary tongue.

Nice.

The noises from the kitchen were growing frantic. Venny slid her butt down further in the bath and opened her legs. Keeping one hand busy at her tits, she slid the other down between her legs and felt the hungry twitch of sensation there as she touched herself.

She thought of Bill's body as she rubbed steadily at her clit, making the ultra-sensitive tissues there scream for even more. Dark hair and solid shoulders and cheeky blue eyes.

Wait. Blue eyes?

Bill was changing into someone else. The body-frame was lighter, taller. The eyes – yes, they were blue all right. And the hair was dark, but it was gelled up into spikes. Her ripe and ready pussy was suddenly crammed with a feeling of emptiness, and she pushed two fingers inside the entrance. Wet from the bath and from her own silky juices, she jammed her fingers frantically deeper as the face came into focus.

Oh, this wasn't Bill.

This was trouble. This was someone she'd seen, someone she vaguely knew, someone who had now elbowed Bill to one side, who had usurped her usual gang-bang line-up of fail-safe film stars, all of whom were guaranteed to make her come hot and hard.

Her questing fingers moved faster, faster. She blanked out the face, made the man back into Bill. But before long, he was back, and she was too creamy, too desperate and too filled with longing to push him back out again.

He was in her. It wasn't her fingers driving her to a frenzy, it was his cock. She jammed in another finger. He was big. Not, perhaps, as thick as Bill, but certainly big, plenty big enough for her. His teasing smile and impudent eyes were more serious now, because he was intent on her, hovering over her on his elbows, bending now and then to kiss her throat, her breasts, her lips, her shoulders.

Oh, this was good. The bedroom they inhabited in her mind was lit with bronze, slanting afternoon sun, and a soft breeze swept coolingly over their fever-hot bodies from an open window. As the man pushed at her, so Venny's fingers pushed too, until her fingers and his cock were one and the same, a single pleasure-giving unit.

Venny's legs flopped wide open. Her eyes closed, and her breath came in shallow pants. She was no longer aware of the sounds from the next room; there was only this, this man whose hips seemed to be boring her into the mattress, hammering her into it like a nail into a wall.

Every time he thrust up into her, her buttocks lifted to meet the thrust, arching her up against him. He murmured filthy words of encouragement in her ear, saying what a greedy little whore she was, how she loved taking his cock inside her, didn't she? And oh, yes, she did. She had to agree, because if she didn't he would just keep on fucking her like this forever, however exhausted she became. He would just go on and on humping her.

The thought of that was too much. Venny's orgasm crashed over her, smashed her back onto the bath – not the bed. Her fingers were crushed by spasms so intense that she let out a brief scream of delight.

Dry-mouthed, and with her heart pounding hard enough to bust straight out of her chest, Venny sank back in the bath and felt the glorious feelings ebb away into faint disappointment. There was nothing better than coming like a train, and nothing worse than the let-down afterwards. Now she was coming down from it, she could hear Dani again, wailing away in there while Jamie pumped. To add to the chorus, she could hear her mobile too, perched on the edge of the sink where she could get to it if she needed to.

Her arm felt weak as wet string, just like the rest of her body, when she stretched out and picked it up. 'Yes?'

'Venny?'

Venny started to sit up, slipped, and was momentarily submerged by tangerine foam. She hauled herself up again. Spluttered and coughed. Bill bloody Thompson.

'What the hell do you want?' she asked.

'To give it one more try,' said Bill, sounding annoyingly humble. 'Look, a partnership between us would be great, and you know it.'

'No partnerships,' said Venny. Jesus! Hadn't they discussed all this already?

'What's that noise?' asked Bill.

'I can't hear anything.'

'It's a sort of bumping noise.'

'Nope.'

'And someone just screamed.'

'Must be something wrong your end.'

'There's nothing wrong my end, Venny. But there's definitely someone being shagged to death at yours.'

'My flatmate,' said Venny coldly. She was not letting this conversation be railroaded into a phone-wank. Her cunt gave a brief pulse of sensation and she squirmed in irritation. Not with Bill, that was for sure.

'Sounds good,' said Bill.

'Well, I expect he's better than you,' said Venny cuttingly.

There was a brief, hurt silence. 'Look, I won't ask again, Venny,' said Bill.

'Look, Bill.' Venny took a deep breath. 'I know this is hard to take, but will you do one thing for me?'

'What?' Now he sounded hopeful.

'Piss off.'

'You know, you really are a bitch,' he said in a rush. 'I can't imagine you peeling vegetables and taking orders and washing up and—'

Venny squinted at the phone. 'What?'

Of course she was useless at all that. She ran businesses. In fact, the best advice she'd ever been given was from a property developer. He'd told her that it didn't matter if he couldn't lay foundations or bricks or put on a ridge tile straight; his job was to hire people who could, pay them, and get paid for organising the whole bang shoot.

It was damned good advice, and she'd followed it.

She intended to go on following it, too.

'What does that mean?' she asked Bill.

'It means I've spoken to the rest of your staff, and they're not.'

'What?'

'Your staff.'

'What?'

'They're not your staff anymore. They're mine. I'm taking them with me.'

'You childish bastard,' shouted Venny. In her rage she slipped again and went down like the Titanic.

Chapter Three

On Monday Venny hustled her way across town to get to the bank on time. By some miracle she'd swung an appointment, and lateness was not an option. As she drove, she reviewed the situation. Well, she'd been warned.

Friends in the city had told her that the restaurant business was crazy, that she'd be better off putting her money into stocks and shares. Or stripping redundant manufacturing businesses of their assets. Or running a cathouse. Anything other than what she had done.

She had bought the restaurant. Redecorated it, staffed it, publicised it. Sometime soon she had expected the damned place to start showing a profit so that her current cash flow difficulty would not get out of hand.

But now her problems had got worse, not better.

Bill leaving, and the rest of the staff – the very good staff – with him.

And that might mean that he was going to set up somewhere else, in competition.

She hoped not too close.

Bill wasn't anyone's idea of hot competition, but sadly there was such a thing as a flooded market, however impressive – or unimpressive, in Bill's case – the competition might be. When a flooded market occurred, you soon discovered there was only so much trade to go around. Even if you were selling a quality product and advertising it to the hilt, there would be a limited number of takers because of all those other restaurants nibbling away at the cake.

Anyway, to hell with Bill.

There were other chefs, other waiters, waitresses, kitchen staff.

At the lights she dipped a hand into the glove compartment and stuffed a fistful of M&M's into her mouth. Was she comfort eating?

No, she wasn't.

The loss of Bill Thompson need not impede her ambition to win this year's Blue Ribbon award. She wouldn't let it. She ate some more M&M's and squeezed her nippy little car through the log-jammed traffic in the pouring summer rain. Lots of taxis, buses, four-wheel drives. Chelsea tractors, Dani's Scots friend Jamie called them. Offroaders stuck in gridlock, not a hill or a farm track in sight. Ridiculous, when you thought about it.

This morning's meeting would start to put things right.

She had come prepared.

She had all her business projections in her briefcase on the seat beside her.

She had her laptop there too, so that she could discuss her files with the bank manager.

She had put her crinkly blonde hair up so that it looked businesslike. It was already frizzing in the damp air, but was she downhearted? She was wearing a short belted pastel-blue raincoat, with blue velvet gloves and inappropriate but leg-enhancing fuck-me high-heeled strappy sandals in a matching shade of blue.

And nothing else.

Beneath the raincoat, she was naked.

Which felt good.

The raincoat was silk-lined and slipped lightly over her skin as she steered the car, changed gear, applied the brake, the clutch, the accelerator. It slid over her as intimately as a lover's hand, so that by the time she reached the bank and parked the car she was in a simmering state of sexual readiness.

Enhancing the feeling was the linked set of two squashy loveballs, studded with stimulating little protrusions, which she had inserted into herself before leaving home. As she walked into the bank, the love-balls wobbled inside her, rubbing her G-spot so that she felt wild stabs of desire. The urge to press her thighs together was strong. She suppressed it. The denial was a pleasure in itself.

After announcing her arrival to one of the female tellers, she sat down upon a low couch, as requested. The cool silk cord from the loveballs caught between her thighs, tugging hard inside her. She felt the soft lining of her raincoat rubbing her nipples into aroused peaks.

Venny also felt the eyes of several of the young male bank-tellers upon her in a speculative fashion; two of them were good-looking. She smiled at them, and slowly crossed her legs.

Their eyes widened, their pupils dilating sharply, and Venny almost laughed aloud in amusement at their surprise.

She could imagine the view they'd been treated to as she'd moved; the whole long nude length of her leg, then the tops of her thighs, and then – shock, horror! – the fuller curve of her buttock as she lifted her leg, the full and totally naked curve, and in that instant a glimpse, a mere tantalising glimpse, of her neatly trimmed bush and, beneath it, the moist slit into which vanished the thin ribbon of silk holding the loveballs in place.

Sadly she could not see their erections because of the security-glassed counter behind which they sat; but then one of them stood up and, by craning a little past the bodies of customers passing through the bank, Venny was able to see the huge bulge at the front of his trousers a moment before he concealed his excitement behind the file he carried.

Hm, she thought, assessing the dark-haired young man.

Perhaps that was her file.

She watched as he came to a door at the end of the

line of booths. He unlocked it and stepped through and looked at her with dark-brown eyes.

He was flushed.

She was amused to see that he still clutched the file in front of his embarrassingly aroused genitals.

'Miss Halliday?' he asked.

Venny rose slowly to her feet, gathering up her things. The other young man was watching this one with envy. 'Yes, I'm Venny Halliday,' she said.

'I'm David Thelwell, the manager,' he said, and it was Venny's turn to be surprised.

'I thought the manager was Mr Mustek,' she said, remembering a very handsome and vigorous Asian guy in his forties who had often listened to her business ideas, backed them wholeheartedly, and then, when business was concluded, fucked her with magnificent abandon.

Dear, kind, wonderfully endowed Mr Mustek.

'Mr Mustek has taken early retirement.' David Thelwell held out his hand. His other hand still held the file in front of the unruly bulge of his penis.

She shook hands with him. His hands were large and firm – hopefully like his cock.

And if Mr Mustek had disported himself with other female clients as he had with her, then he had earned his retirement. But the news of his going was a blow to her confidence. Mr Mustek never failed to be charmed by her ideas or her body, but who knew whether this new man was going to be even half so easy to impress?

'That's a shame,' she said, following him over to the

door he indicated. She suppressed the gnawing worry that his statement had caused her. She would just have to give it her very best shot, and hope things worked out well. 'He was a great asset to the bank.'

'He was,' said David, holding the door into his office open for her. 'The female clients in particular liked him very much.'

I bet they did, thought Venny.

She moved past him into the neat little room.

She deliberately allowed the front of her body to come close to his as she passed him – although the file got in the way somewhat. Gratifyingly she heard the sharp intake of his breath.

She looked around the office as he closed the door and walked around the keyhole desk, showing her to a chair.

Nothing, she was pleased to see, had changed in this office. It was still redolent of Mr Mustek and his ripe Kama Sutra sensuality.

'I like this office,' she said as he placed the file on the desk.

It *was* her file, she now saw. And, even better, she could now get an unhindered view of his only lightly concealed erection. She stared openly until he sat down, shifting uncomfortably, behind the desk.

Venny opened her briefcase. She took out her papers and started to explain to him why she wanted to extend and enlarge her loan. David Thelwell listened attentively, although he did seem to be loosening his collar a lot, and fidgeting. She paused, smiling at him.

'It is a bit hot in here, isn't it?' she said.

'Slightly,' he agreed. 'Shall I take your coat?'

'Yes, perhaps you'd better,' said Venny.

She stood up as he did and unbelted the pastel-blue raincoat. Unhurriedly she let the belt fall onto its retaining loops, then she opened it so that the two sides fell away from the front of her body.

David's mouth opened but no sound came out. He stared at her naked breasts, her belly, her pubes with the sleek little runway of dark blonde hair, and her shapely legs.

'That feels better,' said Venny, enjoying his eyes on her. With a little jiggling motion that set her breasts swinging, she slid the coatsleeves down over her arms and held it out to him as she stood there wearing nothing but a pair of blue velvet gloves and matching sandals.

David Thelwell numbly took the raincoat and hung it on the coat-hook behind the door.

Venny sat down again, feeling the nubby material of the seat rubbing at her naked flesh in a very enjoyable way. She wriggled slightly in the seat, agitating the loveballs that were still lodged inside her, and shivered. Her clitoris was stiff, ready to be caressed and enjoyed. The little ribbon that was attached to the balls was becoming moist with her juices.

'So, as you can see, I would like to enlarge the loan,' said Venny, placing her folded, blue-gloved hands on her thighs. Her eyes held his as he walked around the desk and sat down again.

Blast, she thought. Mr Mustek would have jumped

her by now. But this one was obviously shyer than Mr Mustek, more hesitant. Maybe he was intimidated by in-your-face girls: who knew?

'I . . . see,' said Mr Thelwell, his eyes glued to her perky coral-tipped breasts.

Having come this far, what else could she do but vamp him?

Venny reached up and unfastened the clips that were holding up her hair. Her naked breasts moved heavily as she pulled the clips free. She shook out her hair, and it fell onto her shoulders. She sat back in her chair and casually crossed her legs. The sensation was so sharp, so delicious that she had to bite her lip.

'Are you a breast man or a leg man, Mr Thelwell?' asked Venny, trying not to pant.

He was loosening his collar again.

He didn't answer the question; he just stared.

'I think you like breasts,' said Venny, and gave a little shimmy that set hers swinging. Then she cupped her gloved hands up under them, lifting them, enhancing their curves. 'Don't you?' she said.

'They're terrific,' said David Thelwell, as if hypnotised.

'I like cocks,' said Venny. 'Big, aroused cocks. Like yours.'

'Miss Halliday . . .' he began desperately.

'Are you trying to tell me it's not aroused?' Venny smiled. 'Last time I looked, it was trying to beat its way out of your trousers.'

Venny pushed back her chair and slipped through

the keyhole opening under his desk. As she passed by the wastebin that was hidden to one side under there, she grasped the silky string of the loveballs and tugged them gently out of her. Then she dropped them into the bin.

After all, if he wanted to get inside her, best not to hold him up. He was clearly shy, and needed encouragement, and she intended to give him plenty of that.

Venny's head emerged from the other side of the desk, coming up between his legs. His high-backed leather chair was on castors, so she eased it back a little from the desk to give herself more room.

She unfastened his belt with her blue-velvet-gloved hands. He drew in a sharp breath, but made no move to stop her. She could see the huge bulge of his penis pushing against the crotch of his trousers.

She slid his fly down. She could see nothing yet – just the tails of his shirt, and a pair of dark green silk boxers. She eased her hands up underneath his shirt to caress his hard, flat stomach. David sighed and leaned back.

Venny pushed her hands up further, letting the velvet smooth over his hard little nipples. She tweaked them.

He liked that.

He writhed a little in his seat and so she did it again, harder. This time he groaned.

Encouraged, Venny eased her hands back down until they were at the waistband of his boxer shorts.

His skin was lightly tanned and the muscles beneath it were very firm, she noted. He worked out; he was fit.

She liked that in a man. She eased the tails of his shirt back out of the way.

'Lift up,' she instructed. He lifted his buttocks and, as he did so, Venny pulled his trousers down to his knees. Now her only obstacle was the dark-green boxers. Through the silk she could now see the whole outline of his stiff penis. She stroked her velvet-covered hands up over his thighs, which were well muscled and covered in dark hairs, and the legs of the boxers were loose enough for her to insert the gloves into them.

David Thelwell let out a moan of pleasure as the velvet touched his balls. Venny's hands squeezed them, caressed them, while David Thelwell leaned back in his chair and moaned aloud.

Now she saw that his shyness was leaving him.

His eyes were open, fixed to her breasts as she knelt before him. He reached out and cupped them hungrily now, his thumbs pushing against her nipples.

'Oh, that's nice.' She removed her hands from the legs of his boxer shorts. 'Lift up,' she said once again.

Venny slid the boxer shorts down to his knees and he settled his naked buttocks back into his chair. His cock was very big and white, like the strip of skin around his hips. The cautious Mr Thelwell didn't sunbathe nude, although she smelled a holiday whiff of coconut oil on him. The luscious organ was bedded in a thick thatch of reddish pubic hair, and his balls were magnificent.

Gently pushing his hands aside, Venny eased forwards and enfolded his penis in her velvet-covered hands, stroking deftly up and down his shaft. With the shaft enclosed by velvet, she lowered her head to the very tip of his cock and nibbled upon it as if it were a lollipop.

Venny heard a moan from above her and his hands tangled into her mane of blonde hair. She smiled and then tongued his tip, relishing the feeling of total control she had over the situation now. He was hers. Utterly and completely in her power.

She proceeded to insert her tongue into the tiny open slit at the top of his cock, encouraging his juices to flow – and then someone knocked at the door.

David Thelwell gasped.

Venny froze.

The door opened and a female voice said: 'Your eleven-thirty appointment's arrived, David.'

Hidden and stifling laughter beneath his desk, Venny admired the calm way he replied, despite the fact that one of his customers was under his desk, fellating him.

'Thanks, Carol,' he said.

The door closed, and Venny's mouth closed hotly upon David Thelwell's still fiercely erect cock. Her velvet-gloved hands smoothed and stroked and inflamed him, and then she pushed his chair back and rose up in front of him, naked and hot and ready.

Quickly Venny straddled her bank manager and, in fumbling urgency, somehow between the two of them, panting and gasping and whispering obscenities, they got his cock into her, Venny pushing madly down, David thrusting madly up.

With true bank manager-like presence of mind he

kept his hand on her clit, stimulating her as she rode him like a bucking bronco, biting his neck, nibbling his ears, while he caressed her buttocks, her breasts, the point where they were joined, working it in and out all sticky and slippery and good. Thrusting and heaving, together.

Their climax came at the same moment, David crying out and pushing up harder, Venny bearing down like crazy, groaning, 'Yes, oh, *yes.*'

And then it was over, and they came back down to earth, and it was a hot wet London Monday morning, and this was a bank, and she had asked him to extend and enlarge her loan just before she had begun extending and enlarging his penis.

They both remembered, abruptly, why they were here.

Venny said: 'That was good,' and meant it.

David said: 'It was. But I have to say no to extending the loan. Or enlarging it. Sorry.'

And he meant that, too.

Venny left the bank and went back to her car. Her hair had frizzed in the damp air and lay lank on her shoulders. She was sore between the legs, sticky with sweat and sick to her stomach, so she sat in the car stuffing in M&M's, and now she knew that yes, she was comfort eating with a vengeance.

In short, she was losing it.

Maybe the time had come to talk to her rich pal Dani. After that, she would ring the agency. And she decided to dig out the file containing the names and addresses of the people she had interviewed two months ago for the chef's job. She had in mind those blue eyes and that spiked hairdo, and she knew she was just asking for trouble even entertaining the idea – but the truth was, she was desperate.

She started the engine, belted up and began to pull out. The windows had steamed like a sauna so she wound hers down. Behind her hovered a four-wheel-drive, waiting to fill the space she was vacating and blocking her view of the cars coming up from behind. Waiting quite impatiently, too; the driver honked a horn that blasted her nerve-endings like the QE2's coming into dock.

'All right, all right,' she muttered irritably, and eased out. A Merc shot past, honking viciously as she careered out of her space, and she slammed on the brakes to avoid a collision. At the same instant she felt an impact, a crunch, and thought she'd hit the Merc, or the car parked in front of her. She checked both out and quickly found she hadn't. Then she glanced back and realised that the four-wheel-drive had been so keen to get into her space that he'd come in way too fast. When she'd braked, he'd gone slap up her arse.

Oh, *perfect.*

She unbelted, switched off the engine, got out of the car and went and looked at her rear fender. Actually, she couldn't even see her rear fender; the four-wheel's front was hitched up over it. The cars appeared to be mating.

The shadowy figure behind the wheel of the bigger

car reversed perilously out into the traffic flow again. A multitudinous wail of horns greeted this action. Venny watched dismally as the four-wheel detached itself from her little car. The four-wheel was barely scratched, but one of her rear lights was in bits. Its remains tinkled onto the road.

'Why does no one have any patience?' Venny wondered aloud in fury. 'I mean, couldn't the prick have waited thirty seconds while I got out of the space, instead of barging in?'

'Hi,' said a voice by her shoulder as she stood glaring at the damage.

'And don't "hi" me, pal,' she went on. 'Look at that. What, seventy, eighty quid's worth of damage?'

'You braked.'

'I had to brake.'

'If you hadn't hesitated—'

'If I hadn't hesitated, that Merc would have squashed me flat.'

'You'd have been out in front of him.'

'No, I wouldn't.'

'Yes, you would.'

Venny looked at him. Properly looked. He was tall and angular. He was wearing a slouch-cut suit, a shirt and tie, and his blue eyes were watching her with impudent amusement. His mouth was tilted up in a half-smile. His dark hair, cut razor-short at the sides, was longer on top and gelled up into spikes.

Her heart did a little impromptu pitty-pat dance routine in her chest.

Didn't this guy look familiar?

Nah, she thought, turning her head away. Couldn't be. He just looked like the man who'd been hogging her dreams and her fantasies for a while now, that was all. It wasn't him.

'I'm Micky Quinn,' he said, and a large well-shaped hand entered her line of vision. 'I'm very sorry,' he offered like an olive branch.

Quinn, thought Venny. What had that dangerous-looking chef's name been? Finn? Or had it been Quinn? She looked at the hand until he withdrew it.

'Um . . . don't I know you?' he asked. 'You look sort of familiar.'

'I doubt it,' said Venny chillingly. 'Look, who's going to pay for all this damage?'

God, she was prickly, thought Micky. But she was also cute as hell. He found himself watching this fractious little frizzy-headed blonde with fascination, taking in all the details. Her legs were gorgeous. She was going to break her neck prancing around in those spike-heeled shoes. And what the hell was she wearing? The sun was now beating down like a hammer, and she had on a PVC raincoat-type thing – a person could sweat to death in that – and gloves. She smelled faintly of Chanel No. 5, and strongly of sex. There was a ring of chocolate all around her pout-lipped mouth, and he wanted to kiss it off her with an urgency that surprised him.

'I'll pay for the damage,' he said, surprising himself again. He didn't need more bills at the moment. But he didn't want to break off contact with her, either.

She did look familiar. She looked rather like that besuited uptight woman who'd interviewed him two months ago over Camden way for a job. He hadn't got it. But he'd remembered her in lust-filled dreams for weeks afterwards, indulged in fantasies about breaking down that icy reserve she had, making her pant and scream in his arms.

'Give me your address, I'll post a cheque on. Would a hundred cover it?' he asked.

'Probably,' admitted Venny grudgingly. 'You'd better give me your address too, though.'

'In case the cheque bounces?' he grinned.

'It might.'

'It won't.' He was sure of that, at least. Sure of very little else, just at the moment, and that was why he was off to the bank right now.

Venny fished pen and paper out of her briefcase on the front seat, and they got down to details. When they had each written down their name and address, they exchanged scraps of paper. Micky looked at hers.

It was her. He'd gone to this same address for the interview – not to the restaurant because there had been refurbishments going on. That was what she'd told him. Venetia Halliday. She'd been sleek and perfect that day, very much in control. Right now, she looked shattered. He wondered why. Maybe just the shock of the shunt, but he didn't think so.

'Look,' he began hurriedly, about to ask her to lunch, dinner, bed, or possibly all three.

'Gotta go,' she said, and turned away and got into her car.

'Right,' he said faintly as she pulled out into the traffic and roared off into the distance. 'Nice meeting you,' he said to the empty air. But then he looked down at the scrap of paper, looked at the address, and started to smile.

Chapter Four

'I'm not at all sure about this,' said Venny dubiously on Tuesday night as she eyed her reflection in the dressing-table mirror in Dani's bedroom. What stared back at her was a *houri*, a slave of Dracula whose function it was to drain his victims just to the point where they were too weak to escape his clutches.

Venny thought that, looking like this, no man with a single red blood cell in his veins would even want to escape her. Dani had laboured long and hard to get them both looking good for tonight's flatwarming next door, and it seemed to Venny that her friend had completely overdone it.

'I mean,' she said, and bit her crimson-painted lower lip, 'bare breasts? Dani, I look like something from a slave market. We both do.'

'Look, the breasts have to be bare,' said Dani patiently, and her reflection came to join Venny's own in the mirror. 'That's the whole point of being a *houri*, being irresistible to men.'

Venny shook her head, although her eyes stayed glued to the mirror. Dani had raided her wardrobe and used gold belts to cross over the edges of each of their breasts; the effect was that of an old-fashioned cross-your-heart bra – without the fabric. The breasts were pushed up and out. Venny found it hard to look anywhere but at her own naked, jutting tits, but she managed to drag her eyes lower to look at the fake purple amethyst stuck in her navel, then her bare hips, then the briefest of lilac thongs covered by harem pants of transparent purple chiffon. Her toenails were painted gold to match her fingernails, and flat skimpy gold sandals encased her feet. She looked up. Her eyes were heavily made up so that they looked darker than usual and positively smouldered back at her. Her hair had been piled up on top of her head, and was coiled with gold chains, dripping with pearls, studded with jewels. Dani's costume was predominantly red in colour rather than purple but, apart from that, the effect was identical.

'Well, from that point of view these costumes should be a success,' said Venny a touch sourly. 'There won't be a man in the room without an erection when we stroll in there.'

'Precisely,' said Dani with satisfaction, her eyes narrowing to catlike slits as she smiled at Venny in the mirror. 'I don't know about you, but I want to get seriously laid tonight. And just thinking of all those stiff cocks is getting me horny.'

'Well, you've got Jamie. He's coming too, isn't he?'

'Did I say I wanted to get laid by Jamie tonight?'

'Look, Dani, when he sees you in that costume he's going to hump you on the spot, I promise you.' Venny sighed and tried to look seductively back at herself. She lifted her arms up over her head and wiggled her hips in a suggestive manner. She still looked dubious, but she felt quite excited. She was thinking of walking into a crowded room and all the men turning to look at her swaying naked tits. For once she was glad she was quite substantial in that department. And the belts made her lush feminine curves look lusher still.

'You've got such stupendous titties,' said Dani enviously, staring at them. 'They're heavy, but perky. And I like your nipples, that lovely coral colour and they're big, aren't they? Mine are like little cherries on a white fairy cake. Here, let me.'

Dani took up a toffee-coloured lip pencil from the dressing table and applied a line around Venny's left nipple. Biting her tongue between her teeth in concentration, she then did the right-hand one. Then she filled them in lightly, taking care over it.

'There,' she said, drawing back to admire her handiwork. 'That makes them show up even better. Oh, look, they've stood up. Did I excite you then, Venny?' Smiling, Dani put the pencil down. 'I know a trick that'll make them pucker up even better than that,' she said, and leaned forwards and, to Venny's surprise, kissed one erect nipple. Then her lips lingered on the nub, and her little tongue darted out to stroke it.

'Oh,' said Venny in pleasure and surprise. Dani's tongue was hot, wet, and remarkably stimulating, sending a luscious message of arousal straight down from Venny's breasts to her cunt. Watching their reflection, Venny puzzled over this sudden and unexpected development. Was Dani coming on to her? Dani had never appeared to be anything other than totally hetero, but Venny supposed that in these enlightened times anything was possible. And there was no denying that her natural reserve was a little diminished by this surprise treat. She watched Dani's dark jewelled head moving against her pale skin, pushing at the heavy globes of her tits, and felt that adventurous tongue probing at her most sensitive parts.

If Dani was coming on to her, Venny suddenly knew that she would welcome it. But then, all too soon, Dani drew back.

'There. They look better now.' Dani gazed admiringly at Venny's heaving chest. Venny glanced down. Her nipples were completely erect now, swollen and grown darker from Dani's ministrations. They felt moist from Dani's enthusiastic tonguing, and doubly sensitised because of it.

'They feel better too,' said Venny, trying to keep her voice as level and casual as Dani's was. The thong between her legs felt damp. She wanted Dani's mouth back at her breast, right now. But there was something else to consider. If Dani was trying to move their relationship onto a more sexual plane, maybe – and she hated herself for thinking this at such a time, but she was a businesswoman first and foremost – she could make use of that.

'Dani,' she said.

'Hm?' Dani was still admiring her breasts, dark head cocked on one side.

'I need a loan. Quite a big one actually. Is there any chance?'

Dani looked momentarily surprised, then she drew back, clicking her tongue and shaking her head. 'Good old Venny, always the cool one. No, babe. Sorry and all that, but I'm stretched myself at the moment. And even if I weren't, face it. It would be a disaster. Trust me on this. I've loaned money to friends in the past, and it's always finished the friendship, killed it stone dead.'

Venny nodded, swallowing her disappointment. Of course Dani was right. She knew that. But the situation was a little desperate. She'd managed to get some kitchen staff organised at least, but money was awfully tight, and she still had no chef.

The doorbell rang.

'Saved by the bell,' they chorused, and then laughed.

'That'll be Jamie,' said Dani. 'Come on, let's open the door to him together, give him a thrill.'

They went through to the hall, and Dani carefully positioned Venny beside her as she opened the door. Jamie stood there in full Bram Stoker regalia. Like the Dracula in Coppola's film, he wore the stylish Victorian three-piece grey suit, the grey top hat and cane, the long dark wig and teensy blue sunglasses, which were pushed down his nose.

'Wow, you look great,' said Dani, and wiggled her tits at him. She put an arm around Venny's naked waist and eyed Jamie challengingly. 'Don't you think we look great too? We're Dracula's sexual slaves, his *houris*. Your *houris*, Jamie. We'll do whatever you want. Just name it.'

Jamie managed to pull his eyes away from their exposed breasts long enough to look down at the front of his trousers, where the effect they were having on him was obvious.

'A blow job?' he suggested hopefully.

'Sorry, we haven't time right now.' Taking Venny with her, Dani stepped out into the corridor, gently pushing Jamie back at the same time. The lift was clanking up and down busily and there were other people out here now, ghouls and lawyers in straitjackets and black-caped vampires. Several of them stared with interest at the two women and their revealing costumes.

'And why do they call them blow jobs?' wondered Dani aloud, crossing the hall to ring the doorbell of the opposite flat. 'You don't ever blow down a penis, do you? You suck. They ought to be called suck jobs.'

'A suck would do,' said Jamie as his eyes lingered on Venny's nipples.

Dani gave him a teasing glance and gave his tumescent cock a friendly squeeze. 'Venny's already had one. I sucked her nipples to make them stand up. Don't they look terrific?'

'They do,' said Jamie, transfixed.

Everyone in the corridor was now staring at her naked, aroused tits. Venny felt colour flood up over her throat and into her cheeks and a little shiver of excitement went through her. Her cunt throbbed briefly and she was suddenly glad that Dani had talked her into this. Her own behaviour seemed to her outrageous, but it also felt like the hottest, sexiest thing she had ever done. Instead of hiding her female bounty as she had earlier felt inclined to do, she thrust the big globes out and let them all look. Including the tall angular man dressed all in white who had just stepped out of the lift in company with two asylum guards in square helmets. Heartbeat accelerating, Venny recognised him, his spiked dark hair, his blue, blue eyes that were burning like cold fire as they stared at her tits.

The door to the flat was thrown open at Dani's ring, and they all surged inside. The woman who opened the door had very long red hair, a face full of freckles, grey eyes. She wore a somewhat tremulous smile above a standard victim-virgin outfit – a white silk gown cut low over very large breasts. Venny felt momentarily outclassed as they all surged inside, avidly looking around, air-kissing their hostess, showering her with bottles of wine and bouquets of cut flowers.

'Wow,' whispered Dani in her ear, 'who is that?'

Without waiting for any sort of a reply, Dani shot away across the room to meet the man who was slouched upon a copy of Dali's famous red lips couch. Venny looked around eagerly at the rest of the furnishings. The flat was different from theirs in that the sitting room led straight off the front door without a hallway in between. All the colours in here were vivid and primary, and there was the whiff of new pine flooring and paint.

In this riotous mix of colours the man in black, slouched as if exhausted by sexual excess, stood out like a beacon. And Venny had to admit that Dani's interest was more than justified.

'Hello, I'm Flora,' said the redhead as she air-kissed Venny. She glanced over her shoulder and her mouth twisted in a mixture of amusement and irritation. 'And that's Caspar, my husband. Busy doing nothing, as usual. Do help yourself to a drink.'

Venny thought that Caspar didn't have to do a thing to justify his existence. Caspar was simply the most elegant and languid man she had ever seen. His dark curls fell to his shoulders in a lush tangle. His face was beautifully defined and faintly familiar, the face of a tortured angel. His dark eyes were set very deep beneath lowering black brows, his mouth was a perfect kissable bow. His skin was pale, and not from makeup. Caspar looked drained and poetic. Caspar was dynamite.

'Spotted my brother, I see,' said the man in white with the spiked hairdo and the impish blue eyes.

'Hm?' Venny half-turned in surprise to find that the crowd upon which she was being swept towards the drinks table included him. He was standing very close, and his eyes were gazing as if mesmerised at her naked breasts. Venny felt her heartbeat pick up alarmingly. 'Oh, it's you,' she said, deliberately cool. 'Wrecked any good cars lately?'

He smiled. He had the most wonderful smile. Irritated by the observation, Venny looked back at Caspar, who seemed to be reviving slightly now that he had a luscious dark-haired *houri* leaning over him so solicitously.

'Only yours,' said the guy in white. 'My name's Micky Quinn, do you remember? And you're Venetia Halliday.'

Venny winced. 'Venny,' she corrected, her eyes avoiding his as she secured a glass of bubbly. 'So Caspar . . .' she pondered.

'He's my brother. Caspar Quinn. Younger than me by two years.' He nodded to the redhead, who was circulating among the sudden throng of guests with an almost manic gaiety. 'That's my sister-in-law, Flora.'

'They don't look very happy,' observed Venny. She turned and looked at Micky, and although he was drinking champagne he was *still* looking at her breasts. She turned away again, feeling hot colour engulf her cheeks. Damn Dani and her wild ideas. She should at least have worn a shrug or slung her cosy old pashmina around her shoulders. She felt so exposed.

'They lived together for four years in perfect happiness,' said Micky with more than a trace of irony. 'Then one mad New Year's they decided to get spliced, and they've been miserable ever since. And incidentally, that bloke in the pale grey suit and the dark wig is looking very hacked off at your friend.'

'Oh, that's Dani,' supplied Venny, draining her glass and anxiously reaching for another before draining that too. 'And the man in grey's Jamie, who has it rather fixed in his narrow Glaswegian brain that Dani's his own personal property.'

'She's obviously not,' said Micky.

'Tell him that,' suggested Venny truculently.

'I saw you come out of the bank yesterday,' said Micky. 'Hope you're not having problems.'

Venny turned on him with a look that could have shattered stone. 'I certainly am not,' she lied.

'Good,' he said, and watched her reach for another drink and swill it back. 'You really ought to eat something with that,' he said. 'Or you're going to be totally pissed in an hour's time, I promise you.'

Giving him a withering glance, Venny snatched up another glass and drained the contents. 'And what the hell have you come as?' she demanded. 'I think I ought to point out that Dracula never wore white in any of the movies.'

Micky shook his head and stretched out an arm to the buffet table. 'I haven't come as a vampire. I'm a virgin.'

Venny almost swallowed her tongue in shock as she stared at the roguish blue eyes twinkling away at her frontage. 'I hate to break it to you, but you're not convincing anybody.'

'Well, it's just a costume,' said Micky, her sarcasm zinging off his hide like grapeshot off a rhino. 'I thought it was a neat twist.'

It was, but Venny was not about to say so.

'And you're supposed to be what?' he prompted curiously, eyeing her up and down.

'A *houri*,' said Venny frostily, not feeling very *houri*-like right at that moment. In fact she felt most unusually temperamental, for her. Spitting mad, in fact. It seemed to be the effect he had on her.

Micky managed to grab a paper plate and get several bite-sized morsels onto it. He eyed them dubiously. 'A what? Did you say a whore?' he asked absently, prodding at the food.

'I said a *houri*,' spat Venny. 'Dracula's slaves, you know. Who kept his victims drained just to the point where they couldn't escape.'

'Drained?' Micky's attention was suddenly fully on her. 'In what way drained, exactly?'

'Of blood,' said Venny.

'Ah. Shame.' And the laughing challenge in his eyes as they sparred with hers was blatantly obvious. He bit into one of the mini pizzas, chewed and said: 'Holy shit, they're trying to poison the lot of us.'

Venny smirked as she watched him swallow the offending article with a grimace.

'Something of a foodie, are we?' she goaded. 'Bit of a gob snob?'

Micky put the plate down hurriedly. 'I do know a bit about food,' he shrugged.

'Like what?'

Micky told her.

Several minutes later Venny said: 'OK, stop.'

'Sorry.' Micky smiled. 'I'm a chef.'

'Oh. Right.' Venny's green eyes narrowed. Hadn't she interviewed someone who looked rather like this for the job at the restaurant? The name was certainly familiar, and the looks too. In fact she had fantasised about those looks more than once over the past few weeks.

'Excuse me,' she said finally. 'Didn't I interview you for a job?'

'You remembered!' Micky gave a delighted smile. 'At last,' he added, snidely. 'And you gave it to someone else.'

Yeah, she thought. Bloody Bill Thompson. But while Bill had been a pain, she looked at this laughing-eyed hunk in front of her and acknowledged that life with this man working for her would make the time spent with Bill seem like a family outing. She had correctly identified him as trouble at the interview, and so far she had seen nothing to make her change her mind. No, she wanted a quiet life.

But she needed a chef.

'I'm still available, you know,' Micky said, watching her face instead of her chest, for a change.

She looked at him, half-opened her mouth to say something irreversibly stupid, recovered herself and managed to say instead: 'Well, I hope you find something soon. Hey, it's been nice, but I'd better mingle.'

And she dashed off into the crowd.

She managed to avoid him after that, busied herself eating and drinking and dancing. She had to admit she felt slightly slewed, but that was good. It gave her the nerve to carry on with this outrageous costume without resorting to borrowing a bra off Flora – which wouldn't fit her anyway, she had to admit. During that sexy old

Dean Martin marimba track she got locked in a clinch with Jamie but, despite her rivetingly bouncing tits, she felt that his attention was elsewhere – even though his erection was pressing against her belly. Later, she met up with Dani, even managing to prise her away from Caspar for a bit of a chat.

'What do you make of them, our host and hostess?' Venny asked as Dani sipped seawater-blue absinthe and continued to sway to the hard Latin beat. Her pert little cherry-nippled breasts swayed too, and Venny found her eyes tracking them back and forth. It was like watching Wimbledon, only more fun.

'What do you make of them?' countered Dani.

Venny told Dani what Micky had told her. That they were miserable together because they'd got married rather than continue living in flexible sin.

'That's precisely the impression I got,' said Dani, jiggling away now that the tempo had quickened. Their hostess passed by, smiling briefly. The grey eyes dipped reflectively to Dani's front, and then up to Dani's face. Dani smiled back at Flora. 'Her tits are enormous,' Dani hissed to Venny. 'Every man in the room's wishing she had them out on display like ours. What was I saying? Yes, her and Caspar. Well, that's marriage for you. You know how you can tell if a marriage is heading for the rocks?'

'Nope,' said Venny, seeing Micky pass by arm-in-arm with a dinky little blonde vampette. They were dancing so close together that you'd need a machete to get them apart. She watched Micky's hips rubbing against the blonde, and noted the rapt, dazzled expression on the blonde's face. God, she was almost at the point of orgasm, thought Venny, turning away.

'They move, they build an extension, or they have a baby. They've moved, right? You just watch. Next comes the extension, then the baby. Then it's off to the divorce courts and change partners.'

'You're such a cynic,' said Venny.

'I'm never wrong.'

'And you'd be waiting to comfort Caspar, I suppose?'

'Isn't he gorgeous?' Dani crowed with delight. 'He looks so wrung out, poor sweetheart. Do you think they still fuck? Do you think she climbs on board him every night, slips his cock up her and puts those stupendous great tits of hers to his mouth so he can suck her nipples? I bet she does. No wonder he looks shattered. She must take a lot of keeping up with.'

'His brother's here, too,' said Venny, pondering interestedly over the vision of Flora and Caspar in a fucking frenzy.

'Caspar told me he was. The tall gorgeous bloke with the spiky hairdo. Nice eyes, too. Micky.'

'He's a chef,' said Venny.

'Is he?' Dani's eyes widened. 'Well, that's just great. You're looking for a chef.'

'Yes, but not him,' said Venny.

'Why not him?'

'Because he's trouble.'

Dani tutted and leaned confidingly towards Venny. One of her nipples brushed tinglingly against one of

Venny's, and Venny experienced an almost unbearable flash of heat. God, I'm drunk, she thought. Being drunk always got her incredibly randy.

'Honey,' said Dani with a smile, 'you need that sort of trouble. Desperately. Take it from me, you do.'

'What I need is to lie down,' Venny informed her stiffly. She had to speak stiffly, because she was afraid that if she didn't keep rigid control over her speech, she would start slurring her words. 'Next door. Right now.'

'What, already?' Dani looked around at the heaving merry-making crowds. 'The evening's young, babe.'

'I am going next door,' said Venny carefully. 'To bed.'

'Well . . . OK,' said Dani with a regretful shrug.

Venny started to weave her way – stepping carefully, because she was drunk, and when she was drunk her knees seemed to go in the most alarming fashion – across the room to the door. She cordially and carefully thanked Flora and Caspar, and nodded and smiled her way towards the exit. Basking in a rare sense of achievement, she opened the door. She'd made it, drunk though she was, without falling over or embarrassing herself in any other way. And then she realised that someone had followed her out into the cool, airy corridor. It was Micky Quinn.

'Glad I caught you,' said Micky, closing the door on the party noise. Still the Latin beat thrummed through the walls. Suddenly the corridor outside the flat seemed cold and empty to Venny. 'Look, my cheque book's in the car. Walk me down and we'll settle up now, OK? Save me posting the cheque on to you.'

'No, I—' started Venny, but he had taken hold of her elbow and was guiding her towards the ratchety old steel-cage lift. Micky stepped inside, taking Venny with him. She propped herself against the wall of the lift and watched as he closed them into the steel cage and pressed the button for the ground floor. The lift lurched after a stuttering moment or two and started edging its way downwards. This was not high technology or high speed, this lift. In fact, all the residents had complained to the builders who had refurbished the warehouse block about the lift being so slow; but the builders had insisted that the character of the building called for such a lift. And maybe they were right, thought Venny foggily. It was charming. You could see the corridor and the stairwell through the meshed steel bars as the lift ponderously descended. It was a nice lift.

'Don't nod off on me,' said Micky.

Venny opened her eyes with a jolt. She had been going to sleep, right here against the cold lift wall. She shook her head a little to clear it. Micky was standing very close to her.

'So *houris* drain their victims, do they?' he asked, his eyes twinkling blue as neon.

'They do,' said Venny positively. Ten out of ten, full marks. She wasn't slurring her words at all.

'So.' He leaned both hands on the wall, one on either side of her head. Venny glanced at the hands. Long and thin, dextrous. She liked his hands. She looked up into the laughing blue eyes. 'Drain me, Venny. Drain me to the dregs,' he said, and his head came down and his mouth covered hers in a hot, enveloping kiss.

Wow, she thought. Oh, holy wow.

Either this man was a great kisser or she was even drunker than she'd thought. She swayed into the kiss, into his arms. She felt how hard his body was, how stiff his cock against her belly. The suit he wore was soft, summer-weight, silky. Such thin material. And with her belly naked as it was, with only the tiny thong and the purple chiffon covering her crotch and her legs, she could feel the whole length of his cock. As his tongue entered her mouth and teased her own, her hands dropped irresistibly between their bodies to feel him.

She outlined the big rearing organ with her hands, smoothing the fabric that covered it, marvelling at its concealed strength. Her touch had the desired effect. Micky's mouth left hers suddenly and his head went down with a moan of pleasure. He stretched out a hand and the lift juddered to a halt beside the stairs. Anyone using those stairs could see them in here, Venny thought. And she found that she didn't care. As Micky's mouth sucked on one rock-hard nipple, she clutched his head with her hands and sighed with complete delight, throwing her head back in abandon.

'I haven't been able to take my eyes off these all night,' muttered Micky, changing over to the other breast in case it should feel it was being neglected. Then his mouth was too busy for speech.

Venny leaned back and let him take her tits into his mouth with long, greedy sucks and kisses. Her cunt felt like liquid fire, wide open and flowing like honey. Her clitoris twitched and rose so that she pressed her hips against his, seeking release from this crazily mounting inner pressure.

Micky's mouth left her nipples and trailed downwards. His hands clutched at the narrower indentation of her waist and his lips anointed the skin of her belly until the skin fluttered and she moaned louder. Then his hands slipped down, and were suddenly under the sides of the thong and beneath the flimsy chiffon of her harem pants, and he pushed both down around her ankles so that she was totally naked for him now – or at least only wearing the crossed gold belts at her breast, and her jewellery.

With a long gasp of pleasure Micky ran a hand down over her neat little toffee-coloured bush and, with one deft movement, his outspread fingers pushed her legs apart so that he could see how wet and ready for him she was. Venny was panting helplessly now, almost lying against the lift wall for support. Micky went down onto his knees and stuck his tongue out to tickle her clitoris. Then he moved in closer to suck at the tender little nub while his hand moved back and found her opening. His thumb slid easily into her. Venny cried out and ground her hips mindlessly against his probing mouth, begging him for more.

And Micky gave it. Through half-open eyes Venny was aware of someone – a girl – passing the lift as she went downstairs, and pausing for a moment to look at the enticing scene inside it; the man on his knees, his head buried between the wide-spread legs of the naked, gasping woman.

This is crazy, thought Venny, but she could feel the mad pleasure building and building as he lapped at her, eagerly cramming his fingers now into her wide-open and willing cunt, pumping wildly at her as if he was using his penis, his lovely stiff penis, and not just his hand.

A couple passed by on the stairs, pausing to smile and point at the lovers in the lift. Venny saw them, was scandalised at her own reckless behaviour, but she didn't care. She couldn't, not when these glorious feelings were overtaking her, changing her into the *houri*, the man-eater, the wildcat she only ever was in her darkest dreams. Now, with Micky giving her cunnilingus, right now she enjoyed their startled, eager eyes upon her naked, heaving breasts, enjoyed the fact that she could see the watching man had come erect, that the woman's eyes were avid with arousal. The couple passed on and were gone, and at that instant she came in hot, crashing waves of release, shrieking with pleasure. Micky's hand squeezed her thinly concealed mound and she came again, instantly, and kept coming until the unreal feelings of sublime ecstasy were gone and she was left there panting in the lift, with this laughing-eyed stranger who was now standing up and kissing her lips so that she tasted herself on his tongue.

'Oh God,' said Venny weakly when they finally broke apart. Coming back down to earth, she realised that she felt a little cold; quickly she bent and tugged up the thong and the transparent purple harem pants, aware of him lustfully watching the heavy swing of her breasts as she moved.

'Your nipples are still sticking out,' Micky observed in a voice roughened by passion.

'I'm cold,' Venny excused herself.

'I could warm you up.' He kissed her hotly, stirring her again in a way that she could not quite believe possible. 'And why did you pull your pants up? What makes you think I've finished with you? I haven't come inside you yet.'

Venny glanced down the front of his body and saw the hard jut of his cock under his trousers. She had a momentary vision of her hands unzipping him, letting his cock spring naked and hot into her hands. He wasn't, she thought, wearing underpants. His penis would be bare. And what colour would it be? Brown or white or red or even purple in its passion? Venny groaned lightly, unable to stifle it, and looked up to see that he had read her thoughts.

'You want it,' he murmured, coming closer. 'Come on, Venny,' he whispered coaxingly. 'Push your pants down. Let me in. Let me fuck you now.' His lips were leaving a trail of kisses upon her shoulders and on her throat. She shivered with arousal. 'I'll fuck you hard, Venny. I'll fuck you until you can hardly stand, and then I'll lay you on the floor right here and bring you off so hard you'll think World War Three's started. What do you say?'

Chapter Five

What Venetia Halliday said, to Micky Quinn's absolute shock, was no. Even when he woke up the next morning in his little Whitstable base, yanking back the curtains to stare accusingly at the grey ocean as it churned up onto the pebbled beach not twenty yards away, he could still not quite believe it. He wasn't the type of guy to think he was God's gift to womankind, but even so his pride was hurt. He was, after all, an excellent cocksman, and she'd certainly enjoyed herself in the lift, and so, not surprisingly, he had thought that her answer would be yes. Or even yes, please.

But she had said no.

Damn.

He glared at the gulls, dipping and spinning in the hot shrieking blue of the summer sky. He glared at the fishermen's boats, which were hauled up along the beach. Some of the men were mending nets. Others sat and smoked and talked. He exhaled, releasing his pent-up irritability as he always could when he was here. He loved this place; it had always felt like home to him. All right, it was little more than a shack that had been passed down through the mostly impoverished Quinn family for years. The hut had been changing hands within the Quinn clan long before Whitstable had become the chic weekend retreat it now was for Londoners – long before he had even been born, much less dreamed of being a chef, of owning his own restaurant. Or chain of restaurants, better yet.

He wasn't normally the type of guy to brood, either. That was brother Caspar's bag, not his. He was happy-go-lucky, cheery, the life and soul of every party. But as he stood there naked and looked out at the pounding surf and the sky and the birds and the fishermen, he felt far from his usual happy bunny state.

She'd said no.

And dammit, he had really wanted her to say yes, because, OK, he fancied her like crazy. But he did have another angle. Her pal had filled him in on the dirt about the restaurant she owned. The bank had turned her down on Monday for a loan, and her chef had walked, taking her staff with him.

Well, snap, he thought. The bank had turned him down on Monday too. That had really pissed him off. He had sussed out a good little place in the West End that he could convert and get up and running. He had worked out a business plan, and he hated working out business plans. He had even forced himself to be appropriately obsequious to that pain-in-the-arse bank manager, and he loathed having to kiss arse.

So here he was, standing in his one single asset, this hut on the seafront, without a business of his own or a job working for someone else. He would have to settle – he knew this and accepted it as a thoroughly bitter pill – for working for someone else. But there was Venny, and where was the harm in combining a little business with a whole lot of pleasure? It could all work out so well. He was a chef; she needed a chef. Perfect.

But when he'd hinted pretty heavily that he was free, she had blanked him. And then, after he'd pleasured her in the lift, she had cut him dead again.

Incredible.

But hey, are we downhearted? he asked himself briskly.

He thought about that.

Well, yes, actually we are, he admitted. In fact, we are very pissed off indeed with that uptight hyper-controlled bitch Venetia Halliday, OK? She'd told him to post the cheque on, and then she'd punched the button to take them back up to her floor, and she'd stepped out, leaving him cold.

Amazing.

And for now he had absolutely no idea what he was going to do about it. None whatsoever.

'Hey, lover?' said a soft female voice from the bed. 'What's so interesting out there, hm?'

Shaking Venny Halliday from his mind – if only temporarily – Micky turned back to the bed. There, dishevelled from sleep, lay the blonde vampette from Flora and Caspar's flatwarming party. She smiled seductively up at him, and her eyes strayed down his body with every sign of appreciation.

'I like the flame,' she said huskily.

'What? Oh.' Micky caught up suddenly. 'Oh, this.' He swivelled and glanced down at the inch-long flame tattoo on his left buttock. Then he straightened and grinned at her. 'I was seventeen when I had that done in Soho. I was a bit drunk too. In fact, it pretty much came as a surprise when I woke up with it the next morning.'

'I bet all the women love it,' said the vampette, sitting up without bothering to pull the sheets up with her.

Micky smiled at her. She was extremely pretty and petite everywhere except in the tits department. Now those had definitely come off the peg, he thought. No way were they for real. He'd noticed last night when he was busy mounting her that they didn't move by a centimetre while he pumped away, and that was a sure sign of plastic pulchritude. Micky held very liberal views on breasts, as he did on most things. He liked them in all shapes and sizes and colours, and if they were plastic – well, that was OK. The only thing he really hated was those cheaty little bra inserts that made everything look more promising than it really was. By the end of the evening, when the bra came off, a guy couldn't help but feel disappointed.

His little vampette was also a dyed blonde, but he didn't mind at all that the hair on her head didn't match that between her short but shapely legs. It was kind of sexy. She'd been hanging around outside the flats getting some air when he'd come out like thunder after being blown out by Venny. And somehow she'd ended up in his four-wheeler, and he'd driven down to the coast, as he always did when he was pissed off.

When he needed to stay over in London, he usually crashed out on Caspar and Flora's couch, but last night he had felt the need for space, for distance, for freedom in which to think things through. And now here he was, him and his little vampette, and they'd had an enjoyable night – a very enjoyable night, in fact. And he didn't even know what her name was. Nor, he realised, did he want to.

'Come on.' He held out a hand. 'Let's get cleaned up.'

The vampette scampered out of the bed like a child after a treat, and they ran naked into the bathroom and into the shower stall. Micky switched on the hot water and found the vampette already stroking his erect cock as he reached for sponge and shower gel. It was one of those citrus-scented gels, the sort he loved, reminding him of sherbet lemon sweets from his childhood. He tipped a thick splodge of it onto the big natural sponge and started to soap the girl's breasts. Enhanced or not, they were certainly eye-catching. He concentrated on her coffee-coloured nipples, giving them plenty of rubbing in varying degrees of pressure, from tiny tickles to hard presses. The vampette groaned and leaned back against the sea-green tiles of the stall, her hands still clamped upon his rigid penis, stroking and pushing in a way that promised a rapid descent into orgasm and sexual oblivion if he wasn't very careful.

He drew back a little to free his cock, which was already oozing a little drop of come from the slit at its tinglingly sensitive tip. Reluctantly she let him go, only to make a lunge for his balls with a roguish giggle. He liked a girl who could laugh during sex, although preferably not at too crucial a moment. He took deep calming breaths and thought of light bulbs while she kneaded the old love dumplings, cooing over them and whispering flattering little things about them.

'They're big,' she whispered, and that was always a winner as far as he was concerned. Didn't all men like women to comment on the huge dimensions of their sexual equipment? Of course they did.

'Oh, they're getting hard,' she cooed.

Hard was good. He liked hard, too – almost as much as big. It was getting difficult to concentrate on the light bulbs, though. He tried fluorescent tubes instead, but the tubes made him think about upright cocks, and then he looked at her beautifully enhanced breasts and felt her fingers lifting and fondling his balls, and he was done for.

With a growl of releasing passion he lifted her up against the tiles and pushed her legs open with his hips. She wriggled a bit further up between him and the wall of the shower stall, eagerly angling herself to get the head of his penis aligned with her cunt.

'Come on, lover, do me – do me now,' she whispered excitedly, and Micky put the sponge aside and used his mouth instead on her delightful tits with their dark erect nipples while he used one hand to guide himself to her. Oh, and she was so wet! So deliciously, wonderfully wet and welcoming again, soothing him like a balm and inflaming him too. This was better than eating oysters, better than caramel sauce on chocolate pudding. Now he realised he was thinking about food. And food wouldn't help him hold back. It would only turn him on even more; it always did. Food and sex were inextricably linked, for him. Food and sex were all that mattered, when you got right down to fundamentals.

'You like seafood?' he panted against her ear, grabbing the lobe gently, so gently, in his teeth and nibbling at it.

'Mm,' she murmured. 'Do that harder,' she gasped.

'We'll get seafood for breakfast,' said Micky, happy to oblige. He bit her lobe quite hard as he pushed the first crucial half-inch of his full penis up into her wide-open vagina.

The vampette whimpered with pleasure.

'Oysters,' breathed Micky in her ear, pushing his cock up just a tiny bit further. Her cunt clasped him like a silken glove.

'Lovely,' she groaned.

'Shrimp,' he said, pushing deeper, but not too deep. Too late to hope for restraint now; still, he was doing his best.

'Crab in butter sauce.' Push. 'Lobster tails with fennel and mustard.' He pushed up, up, *up*. Suddenly he was lodged in her as deep as he could go. 'Sea bass poached in cream and Cassis – oh, you're like cream too, aren't you? All creamy and wet.'

He pushed his hands up over her water-slick belly

and up to those humongous naked breasts so that he could caress them. Her legs, up around his waist, clutched at him harder as he pinched a nipple in perfect time with each thrust of his cock.

'Oh,' she moaned, her head back, her chest thrust out in invitation. He slipped his free hand lower to find the little button beneath her mound and pinched that, too, very gently.

Now he started thrusting in earnest, and each thrust was accompanied, like a perfect meal, with a thrilling assortment of added sensations. Her nipple was pinched and kissed and bitten, not to the point of pain but very much to the point of pleasure. Her clit was tantalisingly tugged with each urgent thrust of his penis into her. Micky thrust very deep, luxuriating in her moistness, her heat. To hell with slowing down now. He was relishing her like a feast.

And like all feasts, sadly, this one had to end. It ended when the vampette climaxed with furious gasps of ecstasy, clutching at him and madly writhing against him. Suddenly it was too much and he came in hot jolting spurts, groaning with the pleasure of it, pumping crazily at her until every last drop of his passion was spent.

'Oh, you're something special,' murmured his little blonde vampette luxuriously, kissing and biting his ear as they descended gently from among the clouds. 'I've never met a man who's kinky about food before. It's an amazing turn-on, hearing you talk while we're doing it.'

Well, Micky thought, now they'd done it. And as they

got washed off and dressed, and the vampette dried her hair while he grabbed a shave, he started thinking about this new day and the possibilities it offered. Buoyed up by good sex, he felt fairly invincible and happy to say yes when she asked for a lift back up to London after breakfast at Wheelers' Oyster Bar. He realised that he had been planning on going back there today anyway; he might have been blown out by the dragon lady last night, but this was another day, and he was not about to give up on her quite yet. After all, she had been pretty drunk last night. He smiled to himself about that. Drunk as a skunk, in fact. And who could say how much she could remember about it?

Despite the most raging hangover she had ever had in her entire life, Venny was dressed and ready to leave for work at her usual time on the morning after the party. She had new staff arriving at ten, and she had to be there to greet them, point out their assorted duties, reassure them that they could all muck in together for a couple of days and get through a pretty heavy workload until she sorted out this chef problem.

Hell, she was even prepared to roll up her own sleeves and peel the veg, if need be. One way or another, she was keeping the all-singing, all-dancing show that was Box of Delights on the road, even if she had to push the damned thing along single-handed. She hadn't cancelled any bookings. She could handle the bookings, with some semi-skilled staff and a fair wind behind her. Even with a headache, even with blurred vision, even with a ghastly white-coated tongue, and even without a professional chef.

She poured out tea in the kitchen and trod carefully along the hall with Dani's cup and saucer. She tapped on the door, winced at the noise, and went in, placing the tea on the side-table in the half-dark, able to do this because this was what she always did, part of their comfortable routine as friends and flatmates. Venny walked straight across to the window and pulled back the curtains. The summer sun blared in, almost batting her over with its intensity. Oh God. Oh, she had to wear shades today. Another bright, hot day coming. She turned back to the bed, and started to say – very quietly – that she was going now, see you later, Dani, don't oversleep, because Venny was the practical one, the boring one, the one who, she freely admitted, had totally chickened out last night when confronted with Micky Quinn. Chickened out twice, actually.

'I'm going—' she started, and stopped dead.

There were two people in the bed, lying naked and tangled together on top of the thin summer sheets, and they were both staring at this intruder. Venny thought that she shouldn't be so surprised. But she was. She was shocked. Because the other person in Dani's bed wasn't Jamie, whom she had expected. Or even Caspar, whom Dani had spent last evening drooling over and flagrantly pursuing. It was red-haired Flora, Caspar's alarmingly full-breasted wife.

'Oh,' said Venny when she'd recovered the power of speech. 'Sorry.'

'Oh, it's OK,' said Dani, sitting up and yawning hugely. She smiled at Flora. 'You know Venny, my flatmate, don't you, Flora? You met her last night at the party. Venny, you know Flora.'

'Yes, thank you for the introduction,' said Venny tartly. 'But what happened to Jamie? I thought—'

'What, that I'd be spending the night with him?' Dani gave a disapproving pout. 'God, that boy is so moody. Just because I was chatting to Caspar last night, he stormed off.'

Venny nodded, thinking that Dani's definition of chatting was a bit loose in this case. She had distinctly seen Dani fondling Caspar's crotch at the party, and she had seen Caspar handling Dani's breasts pretty freely. What she had missed, apparently, had been Dani and Flora pairing off at some stage.

Well, so what? she pondered. It was clear that Flora and Caspar's marriage was rocky; if either of them wanted to grab a little extramarital fun along the way, good luck to them. Venny had seen enough bad marriages to know that when the going got grim it got very grim indeed, and any sexual time out was a relief for the protagonists.

Venny smiled at Flora. She was very pretty, with that long straight red hair and those grave grey eyes. And those breasts! Flora was made upon statuesque lines, with generously curving hips to match the bounty set above them. Dani had been right, thought Venny. They were absolutely huge, and they looked natural too. They were heavy enough to hang a little, but still pert enough to have upright and exceedingly large nipples of a delicate shell-pink. When Flora propped herself up on an elbow, they dangled and swung most invitingly. Venny had never considered her sexual proclivities to be anything other than straight, but she suddenly found herself wondering what Flora's breasts would feel like under her hands. Seeing the direction of her eyes, Flora smiled sleepily and stretched in a deliberately inviting manner, lifting her arms and accentuating those gob-smackingly beautiful breasts, the smooth indentation of her waist, the curves of her long and splendid legs, and almost accidentally flaunting the fire-red thatch of thick pubic hair between her milky-white thighs.

'Perhaps you'd like to join us for some fun?' asked Flora hopefully, eyeing up Venny with interest.

Dani leaned over and ran a hand over Flora's lolling right tit, then she glanced up at Venny with an almost proprietorial smile. 'How about it, Venny?' she asked.

Venny almost weakened sufficiently to say yes; a morning lovefest with these two glorious women could only do her hangover good, she thought. But then her sense of duty got the better of her.

'No can do,' she sighed, slipping on her shades. 'New staff coming. I've got to be there to sort them out.'

As she shut the door on the embracing couple, Venny distinctly heard Dani say: 'You see what I mean? It's always business before pleasure with Venny. That girl is *so* straight.'

She was only in the nick of time. Outside the restaurant

her new staff waited: two handsome young men, two attractive young girls, all eager to please and ready to get started. Cynically Venny acknowledged that this 'honeymoon' stage would only last a couple of weeks. Before very long she knew that these go-ahead youngsters would be like all the other staff that had gone before, and had left so summarily with Bill Thompson – lazy, truculent and light-fingered. Still, for now they were keen; and in her delicate hungover state she was glad of that. They shopped in the market and then got on with the vegetables and the cleaning and even the menu planning without having to be watched every step of the way.

At about eleven she took the opportunity to creep upstairs to her office. She put the coffee on to percolate and fished out a couple of paracetamol from her bag. After checking that the blinds were safely down, she removed her shades and sat down in her big leather chair with a huge sigh of relief. She leaned her elbows on the desk and rubbed her temples slowly, vowing never ever to drink again. Even her skin, confined beneath her navy business suit, felt itchy and sore. And her mouth. She didn't even want to think about her mouth.

She shuddered and poured herself a cup of coffee. She sipped it cautiously, wincing because it was still very hot, grimacing because everything tasted awful today, and it was nobody's fault but her own. She swallowed the two vile-tasting pills along with the vile-tasting coffee.

'Oh, God,' she moaned, closing her eyes in anguish.

'You called?'

Venny's eyes flew open. There was a man's shape in the doorway. The light from downstairs was backlighting a tall, angular body with a hedgehog shock of dark hair. The shape looked horribly familiar. The hair looked familiar, too. He was carrying, incongruously, a steel briefcase. Micky stepped forwards into Venny's office.

Venny stood up and quickly opened the blinds. She almost staggered back into her chair as light zapped in and connected with her optic nerves, frazzling them like lasers. She clutched a hand to her head, half-suspecting that it was about to fall off of her shoulders and roll across the floor.

'What do you want?' She squinted worriedly at him. This might be the DTs. After all, Micky Quinn wasn't very likely to be standing here in her office, was he? He was wearing a grey slouch suit and a cream polo shirt. He looked fresh, neat, stylish. His blue eyes twinkled. He didn't look as if he'd got totally wasted last night and was now paying the price, as she was. He looked perfectly in control. It was maddening.

'What do I want?' He stared at her as if she must be joking. 'I want to start work, what else?'

'Work?' Venny decided to risk it. She took her hand away. Her head stayed on.

He came forwards and sat down in the seat opposite, expansively crossing one leg over the other and dumping the case on the floor. He looked at her with concern.

'Wow, you really did get plastered last night, didn't you?' He smiled and the blue eyes glittered with good humour. 'You mean you don't remember that you offered me a month's trial last night?'

Venny blinked in disbelief. 'What?' she asked, dry-mouthed.

'A month's trial,' said Micky patiently. 'Last night. You offered it to me. And I said yes.'

'I couldn't have!' Venny burst out.

'But you did.' Micky looked at her sympathetically. 'Really, Venny, you ought to take it a bit easier on the sauce. Blank spaces are a bad sign. Flora's a big drinker, and she tends to think that everyone else can take as much as she can. Was she forcing it on you?'

'No. Not at all.' Venny was back to clutching at her head again. This could not be happening. She couldn't have offered the chef's job to this bolshy, overconfident, brash male person who had – oh, God, she didn't want to think about it, but it was true, it had happened – who had done such rude things to her in the lift. And people had passed by while he was doing it to her; people had seen her with his head between her legs and her body totally exposed. And it had been wonderful. So wonderful, in fact, that she had beaten a very hasty retreat right after he'd brought her to orgasm.

Yes, she had bottled out. And she had been terribly drunk, that was true. It was entirely possible that she had offered him a month's trial. Perhaps she had. She looked at him, blinking through bleary eyes. He was looking back at her with calm expectancy. I must have, she thought in amazement. I really must have offered him a month's trial.

'Look, whatever I said—' Venny started uncertainly.

'You said I could have a month's trial,' said Micky positively. 'And I wouldn't be so boorish as to get difficult with you or anything but, well, there is such a thing as a verbal contract, you know. I think you'd find the law's on my side. Not that I would ever consider reverting to law.'

Like hell you wouldn't, thought Venny painfully. Whether she'd said it or not, he had her as neatly stitched up as a kipper.

'Look,' she said, trying to get her scattered thoughts in order. 'If I said that—'

'You did.'

'If I did, then I'll honour it, of course.'

'Well, of course you will,' said Micky cheerfully, as if that went without saying.

'Yes, I will.' Venny took a deep, steadying breath. 'But if at the end of the month I'm not happy with your work, then I want it understood between us that I will then dispense with your services without any further notice.'

'Understood,' said Micky, nodding.

Venny stood up. Pride made her manage it without clutching her head in agony. She stared down at him. 'And that's a verbal agreement,' she said smartly. 'Understood?'

'Absolutely.' Micky stood up too. He was tall. She liked his shoulders, wide and strong. She remembered in a brief humiliating flash that she had clutched at them last night while he was lapping at her. She felt herself start to blush.

'What's in the case,' Venny asked, adding with sarcasm, 'your sandwiches?'

'No.' Micky grinned, apparently unoffended. He put the case on the desk and popped the catches open. There were a dozen knives of various sizes and types cushioned inside on a bed of dark blue velvet. 'My knives. Every chef worth his salt has his own knives.'

Bill hadn't, thought Venny.

'OK.' She turned her back on him in a deliberately dismissive gesture. 'You'd better get on with it, then.'

When she peeked over her shoulder a few seconds later, he'd gone downstairs. She felt a little lurch of what felt like disappointment. With angry movements she switched on her computer. He might have wheedled a month's trial out of her, she thought, but he needn't forget who was the boss around here. She'd keep reminding him, just in case he ever did.

Chapter Six

For the remainder of the week Venny concentrated on keeping out of Micky Quinn's way. But, irritatingly, news of him nevertheless reached her from every quarter. The new waitresses each told her, on separate occasions, how much they fancied Micky. Then on Saturday one of the new waiters came up to her office and said in outraged tones: 'All that stuff we got from the market, he's saying it's rubbish, unusable.'

Venny had to admit he had cause to be outraged. She thought he'd done a good job and had told him so. He had bought carefully, choosing only top-quality goods and haggling for the best prices.

'But what's wrong with it?' she asked, puzzled.

'It's not organic,' said the waiter, whose name was Neil. 'He says that no client of his is going to eat lettuce that has been sprayed with pesticides up to forty times before it gets to the table, and he says it's ridiculous to pay the mark-up on cherry tomatoes on the vine when there's a sunny backyard here where we could grow our own – organically, of course. Venny, the man's a pain.'

Venny returned her attention to her computer. 'The man's the chef,' she said flatly. 'In the kitchen, what he says, goes. OK?'

Neil retreated sullenly. Venny hoped to hear no more about Micky, but then Dani phoned in a panic and told her that Jamie had not shown up, and tonight was the night of the hen party she'd made the fake cake for. He was supposed to be there at the flat but he was sulking again, as usual, and she couldn't find him anywhere.

'So what do you want me to do about it?' asked Venny, sighing heavily. 'Offer to jump out of it myself? Lend you a waiter or something?'

'Lend me Micky,' said Dani.

'Micky?' Venny stared at the phone, then said: 'Micky's busy getting ready for tonight's trade, as you well know.'

'Flora says he'll do it,' said Dani.

'And that's another thing,' said Venny. 'This thing with Flora. How does Caspar feel about it?'

'Pig-sick,' said Dani, and laughed. 'That's why Flora's doing it, you berk. She says the spark's gone from their marriage, and she's trying to put it back.'

'That's a neat analogy, Dani, because sparks are definitely involved; she is in fact playing with fire and she might get burnt to a crisp if she isn't careful.'

'You sound like bloody Queen Victoria,' complained Dani. 'Oh, come on,' she wheedled sweetly. 'Lend me Micky. A couple of hours, and you can have him back.'

'What about Caspar?'

'Caspar wouldn't do it. I asked him. He looked at me as if I'd suggested he take up cannibalism as a hobby. And then he suggested Micky – who's always up for a laugh, apparently – and Flora said what a good idea, and thank God someone in the Quinn family had a sense of humour.'

Venny closed her eyes and said: 'Can you hold?'

'Sure can,' said Dani.

Venny buzzed Micky's extension in the kitchen. Carol, the new waitress, answered, then put him on the line.

'Speaking to me at last, then?' said Micky, and she could just picture the teasing grin on his face.

'I have Dani on the line for you,' said Venny coolly, and replaced the handset. She was aware that her heart was thumping hard. How did he do that to her? And Dani was right. She did sound like Queen Victoria. She tried to get back to her figures again, but her concentration was shot. Irritably she caught herself glancing at the red light on the telephone. When it blinked off, she snatched the phone up and buzzed Micky again.

'This is the funny farm,' said Micky's voice briskly. 'Who's that?'

'Come up here a moment, will you?' Venny slapped the receiver back down onto the cradle.

About ten minutes later, Micky showed up, carrying a tiny heavy-duty pan and a wooden spoon. His spiked hair still pointed resolutely upward, but his sharp-boned face shone with sweat and his chef's whites were grubby at the front. He placed the pan and spoon on the desk then flopped into a chair and gave her a challenging stare from those glittering blue eyes.

'Well?' he said. 'I hope this is really important, because we're terribly busy down there tonight.'

There he went, Venny thought angrily. Wasn't that the whole nub of the trouble, right there? She'd expected him to start pushing his luck at the first opportunity, and he was talking as if she had a cheek interrupting him, proving she'd been right.

'Look, is this thing you're doing for Dani going to interfere with our cover for the evening?' said Venny, very businesslike. She sniffed. She could smell something like toffee, and it was mingling with his cologne and with a whiff of fresh male sweat. The combination was extraordinarily potent. Despite herself, she felt her pussy give a little twitch of hunger.

'No, we're covered,' said Micky confidently, lounging back in the chair and looking at her in an unnervingly sexual way. 'I'm prepreparing most things, and I'll be back by ten; everything's cool.'

'Right.' Well, she'd wanted to be sure about that. But still, she was annoyed that his easy assurance had somewhat taken the wind out of her sails. She realised that she'd wanted to berate him, to reclaim the authoritarian ground she felt she'd somehow lost over the manner of his starting work here. True to form, he hadn't given her a chance. 'So what's this?' she asked, pointing with her pen to the small pot on her desk.

'Oh, yeah.' Micky stood up and came around to her side of the desk. 'I wanted your opinion on this.

It's caramel sauce, which I'm thinking of putting with home-made vanilla ice cream and a summer fruit sorbet. Taste.'

Micky dipped a finger into the thick buttery mixture and held it to her mouth.

'Um . . .' said Venny, leaning sharply back in her chair.

'Come on, Venny. Just a little taste.'

Oh God. Her nose for trouble was telling her in no uncertain terms that things were beginning to spiral out of her control again. But she'd look like the world's worst-ever prude if she refused to lick the sweet-smelling goo off his index finger, so she leaned forwards and cautiously took a small lick at it.

'Good?' he asked, leaning against her desk and grinning down at her.

'Yes,' said Venny honestly. It was completely yummy. She wanted another taste, but was afraid he would misinterpret that if she confessed to it.

'Let me have a taste,' said Micky, smiling into her eyes with maddening composure. Before her disbelieving eyes he took the spoon and smoothed a three-inch wodge of the sauce up her bare forearm. Dropping the spoon back into the pot, he took her hand in his and drew her arm up to his mouth, then licked the sauce from her arm in a series of long, thoughtful strokes.

Venny felt her nipples rise against the scratchy cotton of her new sleeveless lemon-coloured top, in response to the touch of his tongue. She wanted to protest, to say stop, what the hell are you doing? But she stayed there, unable to utter a word, watching that dark head bend over her arm, feeling the hot moistness of his tongue at work on her skin. His vivid blue eyes, usually so full of laughter, had taken on an intensely concentrated expression.

'Oh, that's good,' he murmured, and licked again, closing his eyes and inhaling deeply. Venny shivered. Close up like this she could see that Micky had thick sweeping black lashes, the sort that any woman would kill for. His tongue on her arm felt very strange – weird, almost, as if he were about to open his mouth and fasten his teeth onto the tender flesh of her arm, about to tear and savage her flesh, eat her whole. But his touch was so gentle.

'The caramel's very creamy,' he said consideringly, and his head lifted a little so that his eyes could meet hers. 'But there's the undertone of your skin too, like milk and strawberries.' Venny could only stare. Slowly, so slowly, Micky's head lowered and his lips, tasting of caramel, of toffee and childhood tuck shops, touched hers. His tongue stroked along her lower lip, then his teeth caught at her top lip, and this had the desired effect. Her mouth opened and he leaned forwards, leaned into the kiss, tasting her as he had tasted the sauce and her fragrant skin.

'You taste good all over,' he growled against her hot cheek. 'Your mouth tastes like wine, your skin like fresh fruit, your cunt like oysters.'

His lips found her ear and tugged at the lobe. Venny arched her neck mindlessly, allowing him free access. Intent on the course his mouth was taking, she was surprised to feel his hand freeing the tiny buttons at the back of her blouse. For a moment she thought about protest, but he moved so quickly, freeing the last button before she'd had a chance to gather her thoughts. He pulled the flimsy material down over her arms, laying the blouse across her skirted lap. Then he sat back on her desk and looked hungrily at her naked, aroused breasts before reaching out and tweaking the hard, hungry nipples with his fingers.

'We can't do this,' said Venny urgently, her voice wavering. 'The door's open.'

'Mm, so it is. Don't you find that exciting, the thought that at any moment someone could walk in and find us like this? Venny, we can do it. We are doing it.' Micky was rubbing his thumb luxuriously over the erect points of her coral-coloured nipples. 'I didn't have time to do this when we were in the lift, did I? I only had time enough to lap your deliriously creamy little slit. And you didn't have time to reciprocate.'

Venny watched dazedly as Micky pushed his apron aside and lowered the fly on his checked trousers. His erect penis was pushing madly at the fabric and seemed almost to spring into his hand when he reached into his trousers for it. He pulled his cock out. No underpants impeded its progress, and Venny could understand that. It was too hot in the restaurant kitchen for underpants. It was so hot outside today that she hadn't even worn a bra. But maybe that hadn't been the only reason she had not worn one. Maybe she had wanted Micky to see the nude outline of her breasts as she strolled through the kitchens without her jacket on this morning. She knew that he had seen a tantalising glimpse of them; she had looked down at the front of his chef's whites and had seen the hungry surge of his erection there, fierce and sudden.

Whether he annoyed her or not, she had wanted so much to see his cock, and now here it was naked in front of her, eight inches of ruddy, pulsing manhood, thicker than she would have expected – certainly longer, too. Micky, seeing her extreme interest in his organ, pushed his trousers down onto his thighs to reveal a thick dark thatch of hair. Even his balls were gorgeous, she thought lustfully, pushed up by the edge of her desk as if inviting her to touch, to weigh them in her hands. His thighs were spread open, so that she could look her fill.

'God, stop looking at me like that. You're turning me on,' moaned Micky. He grabbed the spoon from the pot. Venny, naked to the waist and staring at eye-level at his beautiful erect cock, felt her hot juices dampening her skirt where she sat. No pants today, either. She hadn't worn pants or a bra since he'd started work here. And she accepted now that this had been because she wanted him to have access, instant access, to her body, should he want it.

And oh, how he wanted it. His cock wavered enticingly, as if it could smell her arousal, and be guided to her portal by scent alone. And as it quivered and oozed a droplet of come from its engorged tip, Micky drizzled a little of the caramel sauce from the wooden spoon onto his naked penis. He groaned as he did so, as if the sensation of warm liquid coating his glans assaulted his senses, and almost before he had put the spoon back in the pot, Venny knew what he was going to say.

'Come taste me,' he whispered, putting a hand to her tangled curls to guide her head to his cock.

By now Venny needed no encouragement. She dipped her head to his glans and opened her mouth to suck in the sauce. The taste was one of mingled sweetness and saltiness as she encased the pulsing tip of his caramel-covered cock within her wide-spread lips. She grasped the throbbing stem in her hands, massaging lightly as she tasted the sauce and tasted him too. Micky was groaning soft curses and clutching at her hair when they both heard a slow tread on the stairs.

'Jesus!' hissed Venny, pulling back and hurriedly shrugging into her blouse. Micky reacted equally fast, popping his stiff toffee-coated cock back into his trousers and dropping the apron in place over it to cover the embarrassing extent of its arousal.

'Turn,' he said quickly while Venny fiddled desperately with her buttons and the footsteps kept coming closer. Venny turned around, and Micky adeptly refastened her buttons.

'You've done this before,' accused Venny.

'Would you rather I hadn't?' Micky hissed in her ear, giving it a quick kiss before bolting around the desk and sitting down. When Neil appeared in the doorway they were sitting there, perfectly decorous, having a conversation about whether or not the caramel sauce was a good thing with the ice cream. Too heavy, perhaps? Maybe better for the winter menu?

'You could be right,' said Micky smoothly, as Venny looked up questioningly at Neil. Thank God he couldn't tell how hard her heart was pounding. She might look a bit flushed, but that could be put down to the heat.

'I've got all the vegetables and the sea bass and the sauces ready, Micky. You said you wanted to build the plates for the starters, didn't you?'

'Oh, right.' Micky jumped to his feet and snatched up the little pot and the spoon. 'See you later, boss,' he said casually to Venny, and then he was gone.

'Bastard,' said Venny to the empty office. Every pulse in her body was thrumming away like a tightly drawn clutch of strings. She felt that if she didn't get some relief, she might explode and spatter the walls with sexual juices. She thought of his hot, sweet cock and felt the trickle of her moist sex dampening her skirt.

'Oh, hell,' she moaned, dropping her head into her hands and closing her eyes tight shut. Think of something else, she told herself. Think of shopping. Suits. Tops. Sexy underwear. Crotchless knickers so that he could get at her so easily.

No.

Think of something else. Sanders. Drills. Hammer drills, big pounding machines.

No.

She thought of food. Another mistake: it took her reeling brain straight back to that delicious caramel sauce – and to his penis twitching in her mouth. Cakes, then. That only called to her mind Dani's huge fake cake, out of which Micky was going to jump tonight. Naked and erect. She'd seen him erect, but she hadn't yet seen him completely naked, and she wanted to. Suddenly she wanted to with a determination that astonished her. Well, she could. If she really wanted to.

Oh, and she did, she did.

Venny snatched up her bag and stood up. She grabbed her oatmeal linen jacket, which was draped over the back of her chair. Then she left the room and went downstairs and through the studded burgundy door to the kitchens.

It was like a scene from hell in there. Heat hit her like a brick wall met at high speed. Steam billowed, flames flared, and in the midst of it all like some mad magician was Micky, issuing orders and sending his troops scuttling hither and yon to do his bidding as he worked, sweating, over plates of food – adding a little of this, a little of that, in some bewilderingly powerful alchemy that she had never seen Bill Thompson perform. The kitchens were buzzing with enthusiasm. And she hadn't seen much of that under Bill's rule, either.

She swallowed, composed herself, and walked over to where Micky toiled, totally absorbed in the job.

'I'm going to be out for the rest of the evening,' she said to his back. He was crouching over a plate, spooning a little savoury *jus* around a sliver of jewel-coloured vegetable terrine. He added a small sprig of fresh basil from one of the new terracotta pots bulging with assorted herbs that he had asked Neil to buy, and paused to admire the finished effect.

'Fine. We'll cope,' he said offhandedly, then turned and to her shock kissed her lingeringly on the lips. 'See you, then,' he said huskily, his eyes glowing warmly into hers.

Venny was uncomfortably aware that the rest of the staff were watching them and grinning hugely. Again, he was undermining her authority. Again, he was trying to gain the upper hand. Well, two could play at that game. 'Fine,' she said coolly, and stalked outside.

What am I doing? wondered Venny as she sat in her car not far from the Pig and Plume, the East End public house where the hen night was being held. What am I *doing?* Passers-by gave her the occasional look as dusk gathered about the city streets, but she pretended to be checking her road map when they did so.

She had been sitting there for almost an hour, watching the women going into the pub, seeing their excited faces, hearing their raucous laughter. The bride had been instantly identifiable – the poor sap was dressed up in veil and L-plates. On a fluorescent pink poster pasted to the outside wall of the pub was the announcement that a private party was in progress and so the bar would be closed for normal custom.

Normal custom, thought Venny. She was beginning to feel distinctly uncomfortable with this whole idea. It was something she would never admit to a living soul, but she had never been to this type of thing before. She hadn't ever seen a male stripper on stage. She hadn't even seen the Chippendales perform. And hen nights, where unclad males might – and probably did – stroll among the female audiences inviting bawdy comments, made her squirm. But here she was, waiting for nine o'clock so she could go inside and watch Micky Quinn jump naked out of a cake. She had the nagging suspicion that what she was doing was actually stalking Micky Quinn, like some sorry old perv in a tatty raincoat.

Dani was in there, working. Dishing up food to the female troops, keeping their enthusiasm up as the evening wore on. Micky must also be in there by now, although Venny hadn't actually seen him go in. She'd been too busy keeping her head down, looking inconspicuous. But now it was ten to nine, and the cake event was happening at nine, so she had to move.

She got out of the car, careful of the traffic speeding past. Several male motorists gave her interested looks, but she kept her head down and ignored them. Still wearing her oatmeal work suit with brown kitten heels, she went over to the pub and hesitated in front of the main entrance. Music pounded out a powerful beat as someone slipped past her and went inside. Venny tried for a peek, but the door swung closed too fast, muffling the compulsive sound of the music and the almost overwhelming swell of overexcited women's voices. She was suddenly full of doubts. Suppose they had bouncers on the door? Suppose she was very publicly flung out? Suppose Micky should realise amid all the hooha and fuss and bother that she had come to gawp at him like some silly lust-struck teenager? God, how embarrassing would that be?

Cautious as ever, Venny instead walked around the side of the old building and, by looking for whirring extractor fans and wide-open windows, found the pub kitchens. She considered going straight back to the car, going back to work. What the hell was she playing at, doing an underhand thing like this? Venny steeled herself and pushed open the kitchen door, just a little. She saw Dani there with her two assistants, unpacking dainty eats onto a salver. No sign of the cake. She let her breath out in a rush and stepped inside.

'Hi,' she said casually.

Dani turned and looked at her in amazement. 'Venny! What the hell are you doing here?'

'Oh, I just thought I'd come and see how it was going,' said Venny, aware that this might not be the most convincing excuse ever invented. The roar of the voices in the public bar seemed even louder from in here. In fact, there was something primal about the sound, something a bit alarming.

'Where's the cake?' she asked, still determinedly casual.

'In the bar,' said Dani, staring at her friend in bewilderment.

'And Micky's inside?'

'Ready to jump out in precisely' – she glanced at her watch – 'three minutes.' Dani gave a rakish grin. 'Come to check him out, Venny?'

Venny felt herself colouring uncomfortably. Well,

wasn't that what she was really here for? She supposed so. But now that she was here, she was aware of other things happening. And it occurred to her now, quite forcibly, that there must be fifty or so women in the bar, and only one naked man. Maybe she was being laughably cautious, but she was beginning to feel that the situation could develop into something downright hazardous.

'Are there bouncers?' she asked.

'No. Why would they need bouncers?' Dani said, getting back to her work. 'Listen, go ahead, be my guest. They're all so slewed they won't even notice you're there.'

Venny considered. She felt suddenly nervous and wary. Then she had a thought. 'Dani, have you got your cuffs? Those little play ones?'

Dani indicated her bag, which was on the floor under the table. 'Sure. I take them everywhere with me. Never know when there might be an opportunity for a little impromptu fun.'

'Can I borrow them?'

Dani looked up at her in surprise. 'Well, sure. If you want. Why not? They're in my bag, right there; help yourself.'

Venny fished out the cuffs and, using the velcro fastening, closed one about her wrist. She tucked the loose cuff into her jacket pocket. Then she pushed through the swing door into the bar. Her first impression was one of heat, then of noise. The music was nearly drowned out by the increasingly raucous promptings of the women as they looked at the big pink cake set up near the bar and urged whoever was inside to come out right now. And he was about to. Venny looked at her watch. Thirty seconds to go. She stationed herself not six feet from the cake, elbowing herself into position against the jostling crowds. They set up a cacophonous and constant cry for satisfaction as nine o'clock drew nearer and nearer.

'OUT! OUT! OUT!'

Ten seconds.

'OUT! OUT!'

Five.

'OUT!'

The lid of the cake flew back to a tumultuous roar from the crowd of women. Micky sprang out of it and was greeted by a wall of cheers and catcalls that must have half-deafened him. Venny stared, enraptured. Her concern, her reluctance to be discovered, all her reticence, vanished as she looked and looked at Micky Quinn, standing there with arms wide-spread and that unbearably cocky grin on his handsome face, naked as the day he was born and flaunting an erection that could easily win a prize.

Something seemed to melt in Venny's stomach as she gazed at him. Oh, he was so gorgeous! He was lightly but strongly muscled; there wasn't a spare ounce of flesh on him anywhere. She stared in something approaching wonder, and puzzlement. She had seen her share of naked men. But she had never felt this way about any of them. The women were clearly impressed too; they surged towards Micky, and Venny saw a flicker of concern flash across his face as he realised he was about to be mobbed and possibly gang-raped.

Venny got a grip and pushed forwards furiously, shaking out the loose cuff. Doing a very good impression of a possessive and enraged lover as she reached the stage, she slapped him a resounding whack across the face – which wiped the smile right off it, she noticed with some satisfaction – and then clamped the other cuff onto his wrist, joining them together.

'You bastard!' she shrieked at full volume as the women floundered and looked on at this new aspect of the show. 'Come on, you're coming home!'

Venny, heart thudding in her chest, turned and dragged Micky after her towards the kitchen door. Fortunately he had the presence of mind to simply follow. She glanced back and saw him giving the watching, clapping women a sheepish wave. Jesus, he was such a ham! They got through the kitchen door in one piece, and Venny led him straight past a speechless Dani and her two grinning cohorts.

As they reached the outer door, Micky started to protest.

'Venny!' He was laughing, trying to reason with this madwoman who appeared to be forcibly abducting him. 'I'm stark naked! I can't go outside like this!'

'The car's right outside,' countered Venny determinedly. 'See you, Dani,' she called, and hauled him out the door and into the alley. It was a painful twenty yards to the car for Micky.

'Ow!' he complained, hobbling slightly. 'Cobbles damned well hurt, Venny.'

'Listen, be grateful,' advised Venny, not looking back at him as he trailed behind her. 'They were about to rip you to shreds and eat the pieces, or didn't you realise? How come they didn't have bouncers in there? How could Dani, or the publican, or someone not think of that?'

'So you thought of all this, and came to rescue me from a fate worse than death?' Micky panted as they hit the pavement. 'Now, why don't I believe that?'

'Why shouldn't you?'

'Because I'm getting to know what a hot little fox you are, Venny. You came to see me stripped. Be honest. Admit it. And you only realised I was going to be mobbed at the last minute.'

'Your ego,' said Venny frostily as they reached the car, 'is the biggest thing about you, Micky Quinn.'

She opened the passenger door first, unfastened the cuffs and shuffled him hurriedly inside.

'I thought my cock was the biggest thing about me.' Micky grinned sweetly up at her. Venny slammed his door closed and trotted round to the driver's side. She got in, closed her door, and reached into the back seat to pick up the old travelling rug she kept there. She flung it into his lap, where it sat suspended over his still rigidly upright penis like a makeshift tartan tent.

'For God's sake,' Venny complained, glancing at it as she started the engine, 'what are you taking for that thing, Spanish Fly?'

'Sorry, my little dominatrix, but I love bossy women. They turn me on something cruel. As you can see.'

Venny tutted impatiently and pulled out into the flow of traffic. At least it wasn't too heavy at this time of night. 'I'd better take you home,' she said, glancing at him in annoyance. 'Get you some clothes.'

'I had clothes right there in the pub kitchen,' Micky pointed out. 'You dragged me straight past them. And incidentally my car's parked back there, too.'

'Tough,' said Venny shortly. 'You'll just have to collect it later. Which way?'

'Um. Well, keep going,' said Micky.

After a long while and several concise directions from Micky, Venny started to get suspicious. 'Look, where is it exactly you live? Because I don't want to land up in Calais, thanks all the same. I could have dropped you off at Caspar's; you could have crashed there for the night.'

'Or your place, which is, after all, right next door to Caspar's,' suggested Micky, tongue-in-cheek. 'Only trouble is, all your flash neighbours would see me trot in there wearing nothing but a travel rug, and I think your reputation's already had more flak than it can take, don't you, after that interesting little interlude in the lift?'

'I was drunk.'

'Ha! You loved it.'

'I could stop this damned car, you know. I could dump you on the hard shoulder and leave you there.'

'Truth hurts, huh?'

'Look, just shut up, will you?'

Micky shut up. He shut up as they sped along the M2, he shut up right until they eventually hit Whitstable, and then he directed her again until they were near the seafront.

'I don't believe this,' complained Venny. 'When I said I'd drop you home, I assumed you had a place in London.'

'I know you assumed that,' said Micky calmly. 'However, I don't. If I stay in London, I crash at Caspar's.'

'Now he tells me,' she muttered, and turned where he directed. Suddenly there was shingle crunching under the tyres and Venny heard the heavy roar of the sea. Her window was half open, and through the gap she smelt a powerful whiff of ozone. There was a line of little wooden buildings here, each one not much bigger than a double-sized garden shed. They pulled up outside one of them, and Venny killed the engine. It was very dark down here, and apart from the pounding waves washing up close by, very quiet.

'Here we are, then,' said Micky, jumping out. 'Home sweet home. Coming in for coffee?'

Chapter Seven

Having told him that the place was insecure – no alarm system, and a spare key hidden under a pot near the door, for God's sake – Venny followed Micky inside.

'But they were expecting you back at the restaurant at eleven,' she fretted.

'Chill, Venny, will you? They'll manage.'

'Oh,' she said in surprise as he turned on the lights. It was a lovely little place. There were bare bleached boards on the walls and floor, and a cream-coloured couch and fluffy rug set out in front of a thin, circular wood-burning stove. Nautical ephemera dotted the place – model sailing ships and starfish and old gnarled pieces of driftwood.

'You like, huh?' He grinned. He pushed open a door. 'That's the bathroom right there,' he said, then moved across the room to push a floor-to-ceiling curtain to one side. 'Bedroom's right here,' he told her, pleased he'd changed the sheets and tidied the place up since the vampette's visit. 'And this is the kitchen,' he said, pulling back another curtain to reveal a tiny galley-shaped place for cooking.

'It's beautiful,' said Venny.

Micky shrugged. 'It's basic, but it's home,' he said. 'Look, put the kettle on, will you? I'll get some strides on.'

Venny went into the kitchen and filled the kettle with water. 'How long have you had this place?' she called out as he went into the bedroom.

'What?'

'I said, how long—' Venny started, coming out of the kitchen alcove. Either by accident or design, Micky hadn't pulled the curtain across after him. He was facing away from her, standing naked by the double bed. He'd dumped the rug. Venny stared at the broad shoulders, the narrow waist and hips, the tight, muscular globes of his buttocks as he shook out a pair of jeans. There was a birthmark – no, it was a tattoo – on his left buttock. She was staring at it curiously when he turned his head and saw her standing there. Their eyes met.

'Kettle's boiling,' said Venny suddenly, and bolted for the kitchen.

'Actually, I think I'd rather have wine,' said Micky, coming into the cramped kitchen behind her and opening the fridge to take out a bottle of white. Now he was wearing just the hip-skimming jeans and his torso was bare. Venny seemed to be able to focus on nothing but his torso, which was an embarrassment in this small space. His chest was well- but not overdeveloped, and there was a faint suggestion of a six-pack around his well-toned midriff. A tiny line of black hair ran down from his navel and disappeared beneath the waistline of his very faded and torn jeans. She wanted, insanely, to trace it with her tongue right down to the root of his penis.

'What was that you said?' Micky had pierced the cork with the opener and was turning it while watching her face.

'I wondered how long you'd had this place,' said Venny, after she'd cleared her throat.

Micky yanked out the cork and poured the wine into two glasses. 'Let's go sit down,' he suggested, and ushered her over to the couch. When she was settled, he bent over the stove, opened the little door in its front and set a match to the kindling that was already laid there. Flames started to flare. He closed the door and joined her on the couch, taking up his glass and drinking deeply.

'It's cool enough in the evenings for a fire,' he commented, and Venny stared at the flames. She loved real fires. In fact, this was the perfect romantic setting for her. The flickering flames, the cosy couch, the wine, the subdued lighting. Perfect.

'I've had it just about forever,' said Micky in answer to her question. He clinked his glass to hers. 'Cheers.'

'Cheers,' said Venny faintly. She drank slowly. 'Nice,' she said as the fruity bouquet exploded on her palate.

'It's better than nice, it's a really decent Vouvray,' said Micky mildly.

'Well, I'm no wine buff,' said Venny defensively.

'How could you have had this place forever? You're not old enough.'

Micky smiled at her. His blue eyes twinkled. 'I've had it forever because it was passed down through my family to me. My grandparents used to come down from London to Kent for the hop-picking; they liked the area so much they bought this place – struggled to get it, too, as they were pretty poor. Then it passed to my father, and when he died it passed to me.'

'Not Caspar?'

Micky shook his head. 'It's sort of a tradition. The oldest child gets the hut. That's what we've always called it, the hut. And God knows, there was sod-all else to inherit. A few sticks of utility furniture maybe. And Caspar doesn't much care, because he can use it if he wants. We just arrange it between ourselves. He likes city life better, and he's in the IT industry, going after the loot like any sensible person would do. Flora's got a stall in Camden market selling clothes she designs herself – she does pretty well out of that, and her family have always had money. No, only a crazy like me trains to be a chef.'

Venny looked at him with interest. 'But you are ambitious,' she observed.

'Sure.' He drained his glass and picked up the bottle for a refill. He held the bottle up. Venny nodded, and he refilled hers too. 'Ultimately, I'd like my own place. I make no secret of that fact.'

'Difficult to raise money for a restaurant business in London at the moment,' said Venny sympathetically.

'Is that what you were doing at the bank?' asked Micky. 'Raising cash? But you've got your place.'

'I've got a business,' said Venny frostily, 'and it has to pay its way. As for what I was doing at the bank,' she added, and a sudden vision of David Thelwell's full-to-bursting cock straining between her blue velvet gloves made her falter for a moment, 'I don't actually think that's any of your business.'

'Fair enough,' said Micky, unoffended.

'I can't understand Caspar not coveting this,' said Venny, hastily changing the subject as she looked around the cosy little room. It was getting warm now as the stove heated up. 'These little places are terribly chic now, you know. Weekenders from London adore them. And that's driven the prices sky-high, apparently.' She looked at him sharply. 'If you wanted to raise finance for your own restaurant, couldn't you put this place up as security? It's worth quite a lot, surely?'

'For God's sake!' burst out Micky suddenly. He slapped his glass down onto the low table beside the couch. The fruit in the cut-glass bowl there jumped at the impact. 'Don't you ever let up with that business brain of yours? Some things are worth more than money, Venny. I wouldn't risk losing this place for anything.'

'But you're confident in your abilities as a chef,' she pointed out.

'Of course I am.'

'So?' she prompted.

'It's too big a risk,' said Micky, shaking his head firmly. 'Far too big a risk.'

'Ha!' said Venny.

'Ha? What does that mean – ha?' asked Micky hotly.

'It means you have to risk to gain. Within reason.'

'Yeah, but what if you risk and then lose?'

'Micky Quinn!' Venny looked at him, smiling in triumph. 'You said I was the cautious one.'

'Yeah, well.' Micky sat back on the couch, looking very subdued for him. He gazed at her acutely. 'Some things are just too important to risk, Venny. Don't you know that?'

'Sorry,' she said faintly, aware that she had hit a nerve.

'Ah, it's OK. Come here,' he said, holding his arms open.

Venny moved along the couch until she was snuggled up against him. She let out a deep sigh and stared, blinking wearily, at the flames. She could hear his heart beating beneath her head; she could smell woodsmoke from the fire, the fragrant tang of his skin and of the fruit in the bowl nearby. There were strawberries there, and peaches, and mangoes. Brown-spotted bananas exuded a scent of almost overwhelming sweet, potent richness.

Micky's warm breath was soft on her brow as he bent and kissed the tip of her nose. Then he tucked a hand under her chin, raised it, and kissed her lips too, a kiss that deepened and intensified until at last they broke apart, gasping. Micky grinned and glanced down at his lap, where an impressive bulge was clearly delineated against his jeans.

'Think I'll just get rid of these,' he said huskily. He

unbuttoned the jeans unselfconsciously, lifted his hips a little and pushed them down onto his thighs.

'That's better,' he breathed as Venny stared intently at his thick, strong cock, rearing up naked from its black nest like a viper about to strike. She could smell its musky scent. She reached out a hand and touched its heat and silkiness with her fingertips. It twitched as if in answer. 'Oh, that's nice,' said Micky, bending slightly to kick the jeans aside. He looked at her. 'Come on, Venny. Time to get naked. Strip off; let me see you.'

Venny straightened and shrugged off her jacket. She turned her back to let him handle the fiddly buttons of her blouse, just as he had this afternoon. Micky happily obliged, pushing the frail garment down over her arms as soon as he had undone it, then slipping his hands under her arms to cup and caress her breasts. Venny's head went back against his shoulder and she groaned delightedly. His fingers tweaked and rubbed lubriciously. But then he drew back. Her nipples, taut with arousal, instantly missed his hands upon them.

'Come on, get your skirt off,' he encouraged her, sitting back to admire the view as she unfastened the skirt and slipped it off. Suddenly shy, Venny clutched the lightweight garment between her thighs. 'Wow,' he said softly. 'No knickers. What a naughty girl you are, Venny Halliday.' Micky ran a warm hand down over her naked flank, making the flesh there quiver with pleasure, then moved above the material of the skirt to smooth over her belly. Venny felt her cunt trickle with awakening moisture as he did that, pressing low on her belly in a warm but firm caress. She gasped. The feeling was exquisite, intense.

'That's your T-spot,' whispered Micky, running a trail of light kisses over her shoulder. 'Did you know that?'

Venny shook her head dumbly. She felt embarrassed by her lack of knowledge. She also felt that she might come immediately, just from the pressure of his hand there. It moved in a circle, exerting a steady but relentless pressure.

'Come on, put the skirt down,' ordered Micky, 'I want to see everything.'

Venny complied helplessly. Her eyes opened and Micky was still stroking her stomach, his head bent over in an attitude of intense concentration as he stared at her naked pubes. His hand slid down, parting the lips of her sex. Venny leaned back instinctively, arching herself towards him. Her clitoris twitched eagerly as his fingers found it, trapped it between them, and squeezed.

'Oh, God,' moaned Venny, falling back onto the couch. Micky moved closer, the fingers of one hand working her smoothly while the other lifted her leg over his shoulder, stretching her wide apart for him. Venny lay back and watched, panting, while Micky slid a cushion under her hips, lifting her up until she felt as exposed and vulnerable as a gynae patient in the stirrups.

The backs of her knees were resting on his shoulders, and he was still moving those fingers on either side of her trapped and tingling clit, when suddenly he pulled back, grabbed the wine bottle and leaned over her again. He manoeuvred up onto his knees between her legs, and tipped her hips back a little higher, then trickled the sparkling Vouvray into her cunt. The bubbles exploded against her flesh like tiny bombs of sensation. The chill was like ice against the fiery heat of her groin. She gasped and squirmed.

'Don't you dare come yet,' warned Micky, bending his head.

What the hell was he going to do now? wondered Venny as Vouvray trickled down between her buttocks, tickling her almost unbearably. Then Micky's head dipped down between her legs and he started lapping the wine from her slit with his tongue.

Mindlessly Venny arched her back. Her arms went back above her head in complete surrender. Oh, that felt so incredibly good! Her fingers grabbed the plush cushions above her head and dug into them like crazy. She felt like every nerve in her body had been wired up to the National Grid, hypersensitised and jolting with the power of the charge that was going through it.

Then she felt him slipping inside her – but he was cool, not hot. She opened her eyes and looked down, trying to see past his dark, busily working head. His penis was not inside her. He had slipped one of the bananas from the bowl in instead. And now, as she groaned and lifted herself higher to accommodate this unusual offering, he had it lodged firmly, half inside her, half out; he peeled back the skin of the fruit and started to eat it from its position between her legs. As he nipped pieces from the fruit, the part of it trapped inside her jerked, stimulating her until she streamed with wetness.

He took his time. No matter how much she pleaded with him to come inside her, to hurry, she wanted him now, Micky just carried on at a leisurely pace, replenishing the Vouvray that soaked her so that she no longer knew which was her own juices and which the wine, eating the banana – and only when he had finished eating and drinking his fill from her convenient portal did he move his body up over hers.

'Goodness, aren't you wet?' he observed as he dipped the head of his cock down and nudged it against her opening. He pushed it into her, just a little, just teasing her with it when she was desperate and wanting it all. 'What a naughty, wet, lustful girl you are,' he cooed against her ear, making her shiver with sensation. He kissed her mouth, his tongue sparring lasciviously with hers.

'You want some more?' he asked, gazing intently into her eyes.

Venny groaned, nodding.

Micky pushed up, just a tiny bit, and Venny's hips made a lunge for him, trying to drag him deeper. He pulled back, denying her, but stayed inside her just enough to drive her wild with anticipation.

'You're so naughty, I think I'm going to have to cuff you,' said Micky, reaching down to her jacket pocket and bringing out the feather-covered cuffs she had earlier in the evening used on him. He fastened them to her wrists, then held her wrists prisoner in one of his hands, above her head. 'That's better,' he said with a roguish smile. 'Now I can do anything I like with you, Venny. Anything at all.'

And, saying that, he pulled out of her. Venny nearly screamed in rage and frustration. She looked down between their bodies and saw his cock, reddened with passion, twitching with hunger and slick from her juices, still standing perkily upright between his thighs as he reached behind him. He turned back to her holding a ripe, fuzzy peach. Bending over her, he gently lodged the soft furry fruit over her opening, then moved further down the couch so that he could devour it, literally eat it from between her legs.

As he bit into the peach and Venny felt the cool juices flow down over her skin, Micky returned his fingers to her hungry little clit; and this time he was even more tortuous with his caresses. He squeezed her little bud between his fingers, pulling it out from her body, then letting it go. Then he squeezed again, and let it go – and so on, until she was groaning and writhing and begging him to hurry.

Finally the peach was eaten. Micky tossed the stone aside and moved up her body again, slipping his cock back into its hot, wet mooring between her thighs. This time there was no teasing half-measure. This time he pushed up into her until his penis was lodged inside her up to the hilt. He pushed in so firmly that the sensation of him filling her up was sudden and almost shocking. His balls, full and hard, slapped firmly against her.

Venny let out an involuntary scream and pushed down madly to meet him.

'Oh, yes,' she breathed. 'Do me, Micky. Do me *now*.'

'Is that what you want?' he teased, leaning over her, the hot length of his body pressing her down into the couch.

'You know it is,' she whispered, and he kissed her, and she tasted the sweet fruitiness of the peach and the muskiness of her own sex on his mouth.

Slowly Micky began to thrust inside her. The man's control seemed almost inhuman, thought Venny, inasmuch as she was capable of sane thought at all. She was no more than a female fucking machine now; all she wanted was for him to finish what they'd started. But Micky seemed in no hurry. His thrusts into her were deep but leisurely, and Venny cried out again, feeling the glimmering threat of her orgasm hover closer as he did so.

'Good?' Micky murmured against her ear, biting the lobe quite hard.

'Yes. Good,' she breathed.

Micky's hand went down between their bodies to rest upon that ragingly sensitive spot on her belly he had touched to such effect before. He pressed gently, and the sensation seemed to explode through her veins – his hand pressing, his penis thrusting. His hand slid down further still to trap and squeeze her clitoris. With a scream she felt her orgasm begin, her hips writhing in a crazy rhythm all of their own.

Micky was thrusting faster, faster. She felt his cock

thickening and lengthening as her spasms coiled around it, clasping it and releasing it in a frenzy. Every forwards thrust of his hips was met with an equally furious thrust of Venny's own as she sought to prolong her pleasure. Glancing down between their heaving bodies, she could see the thick heavy shaft of his reddened and shiny cock pumping vigorously in and out of her, could see his balls swinging heavily beneath the taut rod of his penis as he moved over her. The muscles in his belly seemed to tighten as he opened his eyes, gasping, to stare into hers.

'I'm going to come,' he warned.

'No, not yet,' moaned Venny. 'I want more.'

'Jesus!' Micky breathed raggedly, burying his head in her shoulder. She could see the sweat standing out on his brow as he clenched his teeth and tried to delay the culmination of his pleasure. With an almost Herculean effort, Micky grew still above her, his cock lodged deep inside her. 'This is torture,' he hissed, his face screwing up with the effort of not spurting into her right now.

Venny lay back with a feline smile. 'I know,' she whispered into his hair. 'Oh, you've got so big, too,' she murmured, moving her hips restlessly against him.

'There's a cruel streak in you, Venny Halliday.' Micky grimaced but almost smiled at her tortuous teasing.

'Big and horny.' She moved languorously against him, pressing her naked rock-hard nipples against his chest, flattening the cushiony pads of her full breasts against him so that he could feel every lush curve. 'But I don't want you to come yet.'

'So what do you want me to do?' asked Micky, his breathing harsh.

'Let me get on top of you,' said Venny, and her own boldness surprised her somewhat.

'OK,' he moaned, and after a second to more fully regain his composure, he straightened, sliding his slick wet cock free of her. He lay down on his back on the couch while Venny clambered up awkwardly onto her knees, using her cuffed hands to lever herself around. Her breasts swung like bells as she repositioned herself. She straddled his hips eagerly.

'God, this is even worse,' complained Micky. 'Now I can see your tits, and you know your tits drive me mad.'

'You like them?' teased Venny.

'They're beautiful.' Micky reached up and clasped each silky globe in his hands. 'When I saw you outside the bank wearing that blue raincoat, I wanted to rip it off you there and then, and suck your nipples.'

'Well, you could have,' said Venny, flushing with pleasure. 'I wasn't wearing anything underneath it.'

'Venny, that's rude,' he breathed, but his cock jerked its approval. 'Not even pants?'

'Not even pants,' she affirmed. 'Just think about that. You could have taken me down an alley.' She wriggled her hips so that his cock was neatly trapped between her thighs. 'Unfastened my coat.' She put her cuffed hands between her legs to find the swollen head of his cock. 'Pushed me up against a wall.' She stroked the red helmet softly. 'And fucked me.'

To demonstrate the delights that might have been

available to him, Venny slid her hands further down until she held his thick slippery shaft; then she guided the tip of his penis up and into her wet and commodious hole, wriggling herself down onto him as if settling into a saddle for a long ride.

'You can suck them now,' said Venny when she'd got comfortable, leaning forwards so that one of her large coral-coloured nipples brushed his lips. Micky's tongue snaked out to lap at her teat; then he lifted his head a little and formed a vacuum around the nipple with his mouth, sucking hard.

'Oh!' groaned Venny ecstatically. Micky's tongue was now paddling the tip of her teat while it was trapped in the hot prison of his mouth. One of his hands gripped her hip, and the other rose to clasp her free breast. He pinched her nipple almost cruelly – perhaps to pay her back for this sweet, sadistic torture she was perpetrating against him. Suddenly the hand that had been resting on her hip was gliding between her legs and pressing hard on her mound so that her clit too was under pressure.

'No, that's cheating,' complained Venny, and she tried to squirm away – but she was too far gone. It was no good. This time her orgasm was less intense but much longer, much sweeter, and her involuntary contractions finally pushed Micky over the edge of reason too. She felt him pumping hard up into her, his hips pistoning violently, felt his cock swell and swell inside her while she rode him. At last he fell back, his arms flung across his eyes in an attitude of exhausted satiation. As the last dregs of her orgasm were drained away, like the Vouvray he had so avidly lapped from her, Venny fell across Micky's chest and his arms came down, pinioning her there in a warm hug.

To the soft sounds of the crackling fire and the swoosh of the waves nearby, they fell asleep.

Chapter Eight

Venny awoke at dawn, just as she always did, her head full of all the jobs she had to do. It was a shock to find herself glued to the back of a hot male body and her eyes opened with something approaching alarm. Micky's shoulders were inches from her face, moving peacefully as he breathed in sleep.

Suddenly she knew where she was, and with who, which should have made everything OK, but it didn't. She was miserably aware of having broken one of her own golden rules – never mix business with pleasure. No doubt Micky would say rules were made to be broken, but to her rules were very much made to be adhered to.

But.

Oh, such shoulders. Her sleepy eyes roved down over his back to the well-muscled buttocks. A red flame tattoo flared on the left one, inviting her fingers to trace its flaring outline. Micky flinched in his sleep at her touch, and she drew away with a half-stifled smile, carefully rose from the couch and tiptoed to the window.

They hadn't even pulled the curtains across last night. Thinking about last night plastered a smile of pure delight on Venny's face. It grew broader as she saw the view from the window. The sun coming up all golden and warm tinted the smooth expanse of the sea to the colour of treacle. The beach looked deserted, except for a few foraging gulls down by the seaweed-strewn waterline. On impulse, Venny went to the door and stepped naked out into the new morning. What she hadn't realised last night in the darkness was that there was a little verandah on the front of the hut, with a hitching-rail like in the cowboy films and two wicker chairs to lounge in.

Enchanted by the chill of the morning against her overheated skin, Venny perched on the rail – watching for splinters – and breathed deeply of the ozone-rich air. Sitting side-saddle, she stared out at the thundering surf and at the birds, and felt something steal over her that, for a moment, she barely recognised. When she thought about it, tried to analyse it, she realised that it was contentment.

'Venny?'

She turned her head at the sound of his voice. Micky was standing buck-naked in the doorway watching her curiously. Almost of their own volition her eyes trailed down the front of his body to where his penis lay in its black nest; and the touch of her eyes upon him had an immediate effect. Venny watched as his cock straightened and lengthened; then her eyes lifted and met his.

'You drive me crazy,' he murmured, as his erection pushed up strongly against his belly.

In two strides he reached her, pushing her legs apart so that he stood between them. Venny gasped at the suddenness of it, automatically raising her arms so that they fastened about his neck as she wobbled precariously on the slender wooden rail. Micky grabbed one luscious buttock in each hand and, with one smooth movement, lifted her up and onto his cock, pushing into her with a hard and hungry motion that forced a cry of surprise and pleasure from between Venny's lips.

This time there were no games, only a fierce, quick and elemental exchange of sexual appetites. The speed and urgency with which he came was almost shocking, and she was a little outraged in some dim, distant, cool part of her brain that he could take her like this, without consideration, without foreplay, without anything. But still, with her clit being buffeted by a series of violent impacts that sent shudders through her, Venny came. Her head went back and a cry escaped her that sounded almost like a howl of despair. It mingled with the wild shouts of the gulls further down the beach.

When she came back to herself, she was a little scandalised at her own behaviour. The other huts were some distance from Micky's, but still – there could have been people walking on the beach even at this early hour. Someone could have seen them fucking like wild animals on the verandah. She was almost pleased when Micky let her go. She slid onto her feet and went hurriedly inside.

'Can I use your bathroom?' she asked over her shoulder.

'Sure,' said Micky, following at a more leisurely pace. 'What's up?'

Venny looked back at him as he came into the little living area and closed the door behind him. He was still flushed from sex, and his penis was still up, still red and rosy and slick from her.

'Nothing,' she said untruthfully, and gathering up her scattered clothes she vanished into the bathroom. She showered quickly, dressed, used his toothbrush to clean her teeth and tried to reassemble the frizzed disaster that was her hair with one of his combs. Finally she emerged and instantly the scent of frying bacon assailed her nostrils. She followed the fragrant trail to the small kitchen area and found Micky there, frying bacon in the buff.

'That looks dangerous,' she said, unable to keep a smile from forming. 'Um – I don't usually eat breakfast,' she added cautiously.

'Venny, you have to eat breakfast.' Micky looked outraged. 'Protein's what you need after last night.'

'A transfusion is what I need after last night,' joked Venny, although it wasn't entirely such a big joke. Her thighs were aching, and she did feel tired. Tired, but also replete.

'Watch this, will you? I'll grab a shower.'

He left her there with the frying pan and the brown,

crisping slices of bacon. Venny looked at it helplessly. 'I can't cook,' she shouted after him.

'I'll be five minutes,' Micky shouted back.

'Hell,' muttered Venny as smoke began to rise from the pan. She hunted out a plate from the rack, grabbed the spatula, and tentatively scooped the bacon onto the plate. Now what? She dumped the pan in the sink and ran cold water into it. It sputtered like mad and she leapt back. She looked at the rashers. Well, they'd get cold. She fiddled with the stove and eventually located the grill. Finding the appropriate control, she set it on a low heat and shoved the plate with the bacon under it.

There.

'OK?' Micky was back, wearing clean jeans and pulling on a white T-shirt. His hair stuck up in all directions. He smelled delicious. His feet were bare.

'No,' said Venny. 'Cooking's for the birds.'

'It's easy when you know how,' said Micky, retrieving the frying pan and cleaning it up. 'Shove over, Venny.'

Venny moved aside and leaned on the counter watching him as he poured oil into the pan and cracked two eggs into it. They started to splash and sputter, and she moved back a little.

'I didn't think chefs would want to cook when they weren't working,' she said, watching as he deftly used the spatula to lift the edges of the cooking eggs.

'Why not? I enjoy it.' Micky shot her a grin. 'Food's more like a religion to me than a way to make bucks, Venny. It's a very interesting subject.'

Venny gazed at him sceptically.

'For instance,' he said. 'Did you know that fish and beans are very good for erections? And that too much red meat can ruin your sex drive while bee pollen can promote it? And hot foods are good for passion – chillies and onions and garlic.'

Venny had to laugh. 'That's always supposing you both eat the garlic,' she pointed out.

'Of course.' Micky flipped the eggs onto two plates, grabbed cutlery, retrieved the bacon and doled it out. He shot her an acute look. 'It frightens you a bit, all this, doesn't it?'

'All what?' Venny asked, stiffening.

'Your own sensuality. The extent of it.' He was staring at her. 'I suppose some lover let you down in the past? Did something to hurt you?'

'I don't know what you mean,' shrugged Venny, but she felt a blush rise into her cheeks. She remembered the disastrous business deal with her first lover, the way he had schemed to swindle her while at the same time whispering love-words in her ear. Business and pleasure, pleasure and business. She hated, in some deep visceral part of herself, to mix the two. It made her extremely nervous to be doing so again; nervous of hurt and disappointment.

'You don't want to talk about it? Well, that's OK. Come on,' he said, and in relief Venny followed him into the living room and sat on the couch with him. They ate the eggs and bacon off their laps in companionable silence. Venny dubiously tasted the salty bacon, and then discovered that she was actually quite hungry. Must be the sea air, she thought. Or maybe all that wonderful sex. Maybe he's right; maybe I do need protein right now. Whatever, she tucked in and cleared the plate just as Micky cleared his.

'Coffee?' he asked when she'd finished.

'No, thanks. That was great. Really.'

Micky looked at her acutely, as if about to speak.

'What?' asked Venny.

'Can I ask you something?'

'Sure,' said Venny with trepidation. What now? Was he going to ask her how come she was such a lousy lay? Stupid. Of course, she wasn't a lousy lay, but she dreaded anything puncturing the afterglow of the night they'd just spent together. One crass remark, and it'd be gone, flat as a pricked balloon after a party.

'Is your flatmate, Dani, sleeping with my brother?'

Venny stared at him. 'Um – you mean Caspar?'

Micky smiled. 'I only have the one brother, Venny. Yes, Caspar.'

'I can honestly say she isn't,' said Venny, relieved that she could at least tell the truth about it, if only by default. She thought of red-haired, voluptuous Flora lying sated in Dani's bed. But then he hadn't asked if Dani was shagging Flora, had he?

'Good,' said Micky. 'Because they're having a few problems at the moment, and I don't think it would help.'

Venny glanced nervously at her watch. 'Look, we have to get back. The restaurant.'

'I know. Give me a moment to clear up, yeah?'

Venny wandered back out onto the verandah as Micky tossed pans about in the little kitchen. She inhaled deeply and avidly drank in the scene with her eyes – the beach, the sun now shining strongly on the cerulean sea, the gulls searching for scraps at the water-line. He probably brought all his women here, gave them that sob stuff about his poor family and this hut being all he had in the world. Got the sympathy vote from each of them, screwed them rotten, and then dumped them like a hot potato fresh from the oven. She'd probably never see this place again.

'All ready, then?' Micky came out onto the verandah and locked the door. Venny watched him soberly as he tucked the key into its place under the pot. For God's sake, hadn't the man ever heard of security? But she said nothing. He turned to her. 'What's the matter?' he asked, a swift frown forming on his brow.

'Nothing.' Venny shook herself. 'Post-fuck blues, maybe.'

He came to her and slipped an arm around her, nuzzling at her cheek with his lips. She swayed into him, inhaling the warm male scent of his skin, feeling the irresistible twitch of his cock as the front of his body connected with hers.

'There'll be plenty more fucks,' he said softly.

Oh, sure, thought Venny. Sure there will. I don't think.

'See this.' Micky pulled her round to face him full-on. He was holding a thin gold-coloured chain, about eighteen inches long and with a small clip at each end.

'What?'

He pushed her blouse up, baring her breasts. Her nipples puckered instantly in the early-morning chill. 'Micky!' she complained, glancing back at the beach. There was a couple down on the shingle, walking a tiny terrier.

'They can't see,' Micky reassured her. He took one of the clips and fastened it carefully to her left nipple. Venny gasped. It was tight, but not painful. More – stimulating, she thought. He fastened the other clip onto her right nipple. Then he gave the chain that dangled between her breasts a tiny tug. 'Oh,' said Venny, feeling her stomach tighten with lust, feeling her juices starting to flow all over again. The clips felt restrictive on her nipples, but the sensation was definitely more pleasurable than painful.

'Wear this at work today,' murmured Micky huskily, bending his head to give each nipple a salutary lick. 'And think of me.' He pulled the blouse back down, concealing her freshly ornamented tits from the curious eyes of the couple with the little dog. 'Now come on. Let's get back.'

The rest of the staff were sitting around the table drinking coffee when Venny and Micky showed up, and Venny was amused to note that it was the sight of Micky, not her, which galvanised the sluggish troops into action. He entered like a whirlwind, setting them all chopping and washing and dashing out for supplies.

'I'm going over to collect my car,' he told her, when he'd got the place moving. Venny was by then sitting at the table, watching all the activity going on around her while she grabbed a coffee.

'Fine,' she said briskly.

He looked at her, and Venny thought that she had surprised him with the coolness of her tone, but he didn't pursue it. There was a full house for lunch and another for dinner; there wasn't time, right now, for love-games. Or even post-fuck blues, Venny reminded herself, picking up the post and heading upstairs to her office with it. She could feel the little gold clips pinching at her nipples as her unfettered breasts swayed with each step she took. She loved the feeling; it was deeply erotic and every time she felt the tug she was reminded that Micky had placed the clips there, with the chain looped between them. Feeling distinctly moist at the thought of the pleasure they had shared, she opened the post. It was mostly rubbish – the usual get-rich-quick flyers, platinum card offers and catering supply catalogues – but one particularly fine white vellum envelope made her pause. She slit it open, read the enclosed letter, gave a shriek and immediately picked up the phone to get the kitchen extension. Neil answered.

'Is Micky back yet?' she asked urgently.

'He's just come through the door.'

'Well, send him up, will you? And Neil, you'd better come up, too.'

They were both up the stairs and in her office within minutes.

'What's up?' asked Neil.

'Yeah, where's the fire, boss?' asked Micky with an insouciant grin.

'Under your arse, if you don't watch it,' said Venny tersely.

'I love it when she's like that,' said Micky to a dubious-looking Neil.

Venny tossed the letter across the desk to him. 'Look at that. The Blue Ribbon judges are in the area. And we're not ready for them.'

Micky looked at her, scanned the letter, then passed it along to Neil. 'Sure we are,' he said. 'No sweat.'

Neil was reading the letter. 'Yeah, Micky's right. Bookings are up. Everything's going fine.' He passed it back to her.

Micky sat on the edge of her desk and looked at her. 'You see? Everything's fine.'

'But we won't know who they are. They'll just book like normal customers,' fretted Venny.

'Does that matter?' countered Micky. 'All our "normal" customers are going away happy – so why shouldn't the judges?'

Venny let out a sharp breath. 'You're right,' she admitted.

'Of course I am. Chill, Venny. Have some fun for a change.' He gave her one of his melting looks. 'Come on, show Neil your chain.'

Venny looked at him in bewilderment. She was still focused on the letter. 'The what?'

'The chain I gave you this morning at the hut,'

Micky reminded her, and his voice had thickened and deepened with the memory.

'Oh.'

For a moment Venny was totally wrong-footed. Did Micky expect her to take it off and show Neil, or lift up her blouse and show him? She looked into Micky's laughing eyes and knew it was the latter. It was a dare, she saw that; he was daring her to loosen up, to have fun, to stop being chilly and over-controlling Venny Halliday. His eyes told her that he expected her to bottle out, and that did it. Despite flushing with a heady mixture of embarrassment and arousal, Venny put the letter down and stood up. She slipped off the oatmeal jacket and dropped it onto her chair. She looked a challenge at Micky.

'You'd better help me with the buttons,' she purred, and was amused to see a jolt of surprise in his eyes as he realised she was actually going to go through with it.

As Neil watched curiously, Venny moved around to their side of the desk and turned her back to Micky. Moving close to her, Micky started to apply himself to the tiny buttons, starting at the top and working his way down; when the blouse was open and Neil could see that Venny was definitely not wearing a bra – something he'd suspected while watching her walk around the place – Micky ran a caressing hand down over her smooth, naked back, then stood back so that she could turn around.

Venny turned slowly, holding one arm across her breasts to keep the flimsy lemon-yellow material of the blouse in place there. She hitched up a shoulder, allowing the blouse to fall down one arm until that arm was free. Then she changed arms and slid the other one free. Now she was holding the blouse up over her naked breasts and both men were watching her with very close attention. Their avid gazes seemed to flood her with an exultant female power. She glanced down the front of their bodies. Micky was already erect, she could see that clearly. He made no attempt to hide the fact. But Neil was shyer, and kept his hands clasped in front of the bulge in his trousers.

'Come on, Venny. Let it drop,' Micky encouraged her. 'Show Neil the chain.'

Obediently and with a thrill of arousal, Venny gently allowed the blouse to float to the floor. She stood naked to the waist before them, her finely rounded breasts glowing like polished marble in the subdued light of the office, her coral-toned nipples big and blushing to a deeper reddish tone where the two clips were fastened to them.

'Oh, wow,' said Neil reverently. 'What gorgeous tits.'

Micky stepped forwards and gave the gold chain a tiny tug, pulling at Venny's nipples in the most delightfully painful way. She groaned, and her sexual juices seemed to flow in a torrent. Micky smiled into her wildly dilated eyes and said: 'Come and look closer, Neil. Look, the clips have made her nipples very sore – and very sensitive.'

Gently Micky unfastened one tiny clip from her left nipple, and rubbed his thumb over the reddened teat as if to soothe it. 'Better?' he asked in a husky whisper, leaning close to Venny.

'No, that's worse,' she moaned, and he gave a low chuckle.

At Micky's urging, Neil stepped closer, and unfastened the other clip. Growing bolder, he bent his sleek dark head and put his lips to the turgid nipple he had set free, and kissed it lightly. Venny's head went back and the white arch of her throat was an open invitation to Micky. He trailed a line of hot kisses down its length, and then on over her collarbone and down until his spike-haired head came to rest at the other breast. His mouth hungrily sucked in her sore nipple. Venny let out a gasp and clutched at Micky's shoulder, and then at Neil's. She looked down, and there were two dark heads tugging at her teats, sucking and licking and biting at them. The feeling was exquisite and incredibly arousing.

'Oh, God, yes,' she heard herself muttering hoarsely. 'Please, yes.'

And it seemed that both men were more than happy to accommodate her wishes. Micky's mouth was rougher, she thought – pulling harder, sucking more firmly, revealing his more forceful personality – while Neil's mouth was tender and gentle, almost reticent. Both were utterly delicious, and she was almost sorry when Micky seemed inclined to want to take this very enjoyable game even further. She felt his hand at the waistband of her skirt, unbuttoning and unzipping. She felt the silk-lined skirt slip down around her ankles. She was wearing no knickers.

Now it was Neil's turn to groan as he drew back a little to stare at the tiny toffee-coloured pelt that adorned her otherwise naked mound. Venny's dewy slit was clearly visible below it, and her legs were curving but long and graceful.

Micky gave her nipple a tiny teasing bite before releasing it. He too stared at her mound, but again he proved the bolder of the two. 'Isn't she terrific?' he asked Neil, and ran one long-fingered hand down over her fluttering stomach, tangling his fingers into her pubic hair before dipping down even further to slip two fingers between the plump lips of her labia. He spread his fingers, opening her wet centre for Neil's inspection.

'Look how wet she is. Touch her,' he invited, like a gourmet bidding a friend to try a truly excellent titbit. Neil seemed only too happy to oblige. He reached out and pushed two fingers into the opening Micky had made ready for him. Surprising Venny with his boldness, Neil then continued, angling his digits upward until they found and penetrated her vagina. Venny opened her legs a little wider to his questing fingers, aware that Micky was still close and holding her open for Neil, aware of her own panting breaths and the hurried, excited breathing of the two men. She looked down the front of Neil's body; as he pushed his fingers in and out of her in a seductive rhythm, his cock inside his tight black trousers reared and sank to the same tune.

'You want to fuck her?' Micky asked him, placing a fraternal hand on the younger man's shoulder.

Neil at once regained his sexual shyness. His pumping fingers slowed, and Venny groaned a protest.

'Don't stop,' she begged, pushing down frantically onto him, her wetness making tiny sucking sounds as she clutched at him.

'Only if she wants me to,' he said reticently.

Does he think I'm going to fire him over this? Venny wondered wildly. Doesn't he realise that I want this just as much as he does, that Micky has orchestrated this just like he orchestrates a sumptuous dinner, and that I'm loving it?

'I want you to,' Venny gasped. She leaned her nude buttocks against the desk so that he could get into her more easily. Neil, released from his restrictive and mistaken belief that he was doing something wrong, plunged yet another finger into her waiting snatch and found this offering to be instantly and gratefully accepted. Venny moved back until she was actually sitting upon the desk, her legs splayed wide. Her naked breasts swung and bobbed crazily as she got comfortable, straining Neil's self-control to its limits.

'See? She wants it,' said Micky. He ran a contemplative finger over the tiny questing nub of her exposed clit, then caught it between two of his fingers and tugged it teasingly. Venny cried out and pushed her hips hungrily forwards. 'Look at that. She wants it desperately,' Micky pointed out. 'Have you seen horses mated, Neil? No? Well, there's always a handler to keep the friskier fillies in order.' He tweaked her clit quite roughly, and Venny leaned back onto her elbows, more than ready to proceed now. 'And if the stallion's having trouble getting mounted, the handler helps him in. Like this.'

Venny watched, panting hotly, while Micky unbuttoned the waistband of Neil's black trousers and then unzipped his fly. He reached into the slit in a red pair of commodious boxers and pulled out Neil's fine, bright-pink, naked cock, which was shorter than his own, but very thick.

'Nice cock,' he congratulated Neil, and had the audacity, Venny saw, to stroke it, running his fingers up it from its base among a jungle of red matted hair up the shaft to its fierce pink helmet which was already opening its little eye and displaying a tiny pearl of pre-come. Neil seemed not to object to this caress; indeed, Venny thought that he rather enjoyed it, to judge from the sudden mad twitching and rearing of his prodigious organ.

Neil's fingers, buried up to the hilt inside her, were quickly withdrawn and Neil moved eagerly between her sprawled thighs to lodge his aroused cock where he wanted it most.

'Ah, not so fast,' Micky cautioned the eager young man. 'The handler has to do the tricky parts, remember? The filly has to be still.' He glanced at Venny, who was writhing with impatience. She grew obediently still. 'That's better,' he praised her. 'And the stallion has to be assisted, to make certain that his cock goes in properly. Now, Neil.'

Micky firmly took hold of Neil's turgid flesh and pushed the swollen head down between Venny's soaking-wet slit. She arched up instinctively, but at a warning look from Micky she grew still again. Venny felt the big organ slip over her clitoris in its little hood, nudging hard at her most tender part. She gasped. Then Micky, taking extreme care and far too much time, she thought irritably, sought out her vagina and with the greatest care pushed the reddened glans up and into her.

'That's it,' he said conversationally. 'Now, Neil, push further up and into her.'

Neil obliged, and Venny was treated to the sensation of his lovely, naked, pink cock filling her completely.

'Now back out again,' said Micky, not relinquishing his control over proceedings.

Obediently, but clearly not willingly, Neil moved his hips back so that the shaft of his thick wet cock emerged from Venny's body. The pink helmet at its tip was still trapped inside her.

'No, right out,' ordered Micky.

With a groan of reluctance Neil obeyed; his penis sprang up against his belly as it came free of Venny's slit with a slurp.

'Now in again,' said Micky softly, and eagerly Neil pushed his big organ back down. In one swift movement he was once more lodged inside the woman sprawled across the desk.

'Good?' Micky asked Venny, his hand going again to her hungry and swollen little bud to stroke it.

Venny swallowed convulsively, almost beyond speech. This was torture, but torture of the most erotic and enjoyable kind. 'Mm,' she managed, biting her lip as his hand smoothed over her damp clitoris; aroused almost beyond bearing, Neil pushed eagerly forwards, raring to go, but again Micky was determined to dominate the situation.

'Out now, Neil,' whispered Micky, concentrating fiercely on stimulating Venny's clit with firm pressure from his questing fingers. Groaning as if in pain, Neil complied. Venny let out a half-stifled scream of frustration and longing.

'Patience, Venny, patience,' chuckled Micky, keeping one hand busy at her clitoris while the other now stroked admiringly up and down over Neil's quivering penis. 'Now let's put this back in,' he murmured, and using his hand he guided Neil's member to Venny's vagina, easing it in with assistance from Neil. The instant Micky had pushed Neil's glans inside her, Neil started to thrust up in desperation.

'No, let's take this steady,' soothed Micky, and Venny thought that it was as if he were talking to a horse, a big horny stallion with a jutting prick and an insatiable eagerness to get on with covering the filly before him.

Again, Neil was commanded to withdraw. Now the frustration was almost pain, and the pressure of Micky's hand held constantly at her clit was teasing the edges of orgasm for Venny. Oh, she wanted, *needed*, to be filled, and filled right now. 'Micky,' she wailed hopelessly.

'In,' said Micky, and Neil pushed into her almost brutally, battering at her; but she was wet, so frantically wet and ready, that there was only satisfaction in his roughness, only pleasure where there might otherwise have been pain.

'Out,' snapped Micky, working her clit with his fingers while Neil fucked her.

Neil withdrew.

'In!' said Micky, and Neil pushed in mightily.

'Out!'

'Oh God,' screamed Venny as the first hot wave of pleasure hit her with all the force of a bomb-blast.

'In! In! In!' yelled Micky, and Neil pushed, pushed, pushed, while Venny cried out wildly and scrabbled at the leather-tooled top of her desk, her thighs trembling, her nipples engorged with her arousal.

Her orgasm engulfed her totally then, her back arching, her legs suddenly stiffening around Neil's body before clutching madly at him. Micky's hand worked and worked at her clit; Venny's eyes opened dazedly and she saw Micky frowning, hesitating, before he ordered Neil out of her once again.

But this time the stimulation provided by Venny had proved too much for the stallion, however willing; and in four hard spurts Neil came, pumping out his come over Venny's heaving belly. At last, the lovers were still. Micky looked into Venny's eyes; she saw that he was still frowning. But he turned to Neil, whose now wilting penis was being tucked back into his boxer shorts, and said: 'Well done. Let's get back to work, shall we?'

Chapter Nine

'So how is it going with the boss lady?' Caspar asked
Micky as he helped carry boxes of Micky's belongings –
and there weren't very many – up the stairs to the now
empty little stockroom beside Venny's office. Micky had
asked her if he could move in there; there was already
a little sink in the corner, and now all the large catering
tins of this and that had been relocated downstairs, it
was easy to see what a nice little room it could be. A
small leaded window with bulbous bits of ancient glass
in it gave a view onto a street that hadn't changed
much since the days of Charles the Second. Caspar
was looking out, admiring the location, thinking what a
clever sod his older brother was to land on his feet like
this. But then, where women were concerned, Micky
always landed on his feet. And Micky was single, free –
and Caspar envied him that very much. He sighed, and
turned. Micky was dumping shirts and jackets onto the
floor.

'Oh, fine. It'll be great when I've got the bed up here,' said Micky. 'It's coming this afternoon.'

'A double, I take it.' Caspar's expression was wry.

'King-sized,' said Micky with a grin.

'Lucky bastard,' said Caspar wistfully.

'Hey, you're a lucky bastard, too. You've got the delectable Flora.'

'So I have.' Caspar's wry expression turned to bitterness. He looked around them at the sunny slant-floored little room. Even the ceiling was crooked, sloping down to the floor at a height of about three feet at one side of the room. There were beams bedded in the plaster on the walls, old and blackened beams that had weathered and taken on the texture of rock.

'I don't know that I should be helping you do this, Mick. They're pussycats when you're footloose, but move in with them and everything starts to change. It's like a landslide. First a tiny bit of dirt falls on your shoe, and you think, hey, so what? What's a little dirt between friends? And then suddenly a shitheap the size of Berkshire lands on your head, and you're buried alive.'

Micky looked at his brother sceptically. Gawd, Caspar was miserable, for all his money. But then, even when Caspar had been plain old Charlie, in the days when they had been poor East End teenagers, even before Charlie had decided that he wanted to climb the social ladder and acquire a well-bred wife, he had still been a dour bugger. Charlie – *Caspar*, Micky reminded himself sternly – had always been the one lounging around looking twisted and tortured and Byronic. While he, Micky, had always been up for a laugh.

Good old Micky Quinn, he thought, ladies' man extraordinaire. Love 'em and leave 'em gasping for more, that had always been his motto. He frowned. So what was he doing, moving in over the restaurant, moving into a room which was right next door to his boss's office, the boss he also just happened to be boffing right now?

Boffing, he thought.

Did that sound any better than fucking?

No, it sounded worse.

Making love, then. Was what they did making love? He thought of Venny Halliday – his boss, his lover too; thought of her prickly carapace of pride and rigidity, and underneath that tough shell was all that hot ripe womanly lust, just waiting for him to tap into it, to strike oil, so to speak, with his nodding donkey.

Damn! He wasn't even being serious now. Nodding donkey, for God's sake.

He thought of her now, her wild dark-blonde curls that frizzed in the heat of summer, her well-rounded body, her toffee-coloured snatch – and yes, his cock twitched with lust and lifted its head with unstoppable interest, but his mind – his heart, he supposed – flooded with another kind of sensation altogether, and it wasn't anywhere near as pleasant.

He'd never felt guilty before with a woman. Not when he'd dumped them, not even when he'd treated them – on very rare occasions, because he adored most women – quite badly. But now he acknowledged this horrible feeling of guilt, because he'd tricked his way into this job, and by so doing he had also, let's be honest, tricked his way into her bed.

Not that she minded – or, at least, she didn't seem to.

But he did. The deception, the trickery, gnawed at him. And that grumbling sense of guilt made him edgy. What the hell, after all, was going on here? He was moving in, and at his own request, not hers. And furthermore – oh, and here came another complete doozy of a realisation – he acknowledged now, almost a week after the event, that the cosy little threesome he and Venny had enjoyed with Neil in her office had caused him to feel something he had never really felt before.

He had felt jealous when Neil fucked her.

He felt so jealous that the only way he could deal with it was to take control of the entire situation, in some childish effort to control her.

Oh, Gawd.

Was he falling in love with Venny Halliday?

He really, really hoped not. After all, just look what love had done to poor old Charlie. Sorry – Caspar.

'Earth to Micky, come in please,' said Caspar, and he was jolted out of his reverie.

'Sorry,' said Micky, slumping onto the floor beside his meagre pile of belongings. 'Miles away.'

'I could tell.' Caspar came over and slumped down beside his brother. He smiled twistedly. 'Daydreaming about the delicious Venny Halliday?'

'Sort of,' said Micky guardedly, because he didn't want to admit to Caspar what was churning around inside him. Bad enough to admit it to himself. And Caspar was so down on relationships at the moment that he would only pooh-pooh the whole thing and tell him to bale out while he still had his balls intact.

'So it's still bad, then? You and Flora?' he asked, anxious to deflect the conversation from his own love-life and onto Caspar's instead.

Caspar's face was suddenly full of unhappiness. 'Christ, yes. Worse than bad, really. Bloody diabolical. She says she's bored with the way things have become between us. I think – Mick, I think she's screwing around.'

Micky digested this and although it was his policy not to interfere in Caspar's tortured lovelife, he felt he ought to say something at this point.

'I thought that you and Dani – Venny's flatmate – were having a bit of a fling. So if it's OK for you, why not for Flora?'

Caspar looked ruefully at his brother. 'Well, it was certainly on offer,' he admitted, 'but I didn't take Dani up on it, because I thought that if Flora found out, with everything being so tricky just at the moment, that it would probably be the end.'

Micky looked at Caspar in puzzlement. 'Oh. Well, if you say so. Only Dani's definitely having a bash at someone, and I thought it was you.'

'Well, it isn't, OK?'

'Fair enough.'

'She's fucking that Scots guy who came to the vampire party in the grey Bram Stoker suit. What was his name? Jamie. So far as I know.'

Micky thought this over. Jamie hung around downstairs in the kitchens sometimes, chatting to the staff, just killing time in between completing commissions for his weird and wonderful artworks in his studio over in Shepherd's Bush. But from what Venny said, Jamie and Dani had suffered a bit of a rift after the party because Dani had been making a pretty obvious play for Caspar. When he had been visiting Flora and Caspar, he had even seen Dani wandering in and out of their flat – but Caspar said, and Caspar wouldn't lie to him, that there was nothing going on between him and Dani. Suddenly it was as if a bright light had been switched on above his head.

'She's not with Jamie at the moment but, Caspar, she's certainly got the hots for someone and I think, Caspar,' he said as delicately as he could, 'that if you give it a bit of thought you'll realise who it is.'

Caspar looked at Micky. Micky looked at Caspar.

'Flora's going over to Dani's tomorrow evening,' said Caspar, his face blank with realisation. He looked like he'd been sandbagged. 'To see a girly video and have a takeaway, she said.'

'And Venny's going to be out,' pointed out Micky. 'Some restaurateurs' dinner or other.'

'The cheating cow,' said Caspar.

Micky thought for a while. 'Actually,' he said at last, 'this could be just what your marriage needs. Spice it up a bit. Don't you think? Maybe you should have taken up Dani's offer. It looks as if Flora has, anyway.'

Caspar considered this. In fact it was quite a turn-on, imagining his red-haired and full-breasted wife being fucked to a standstill by the dark-haired and gorgeous Dani. A hell of a turn-on, actually. He was getting exceedingly hard just thinking about it.

'Jamie has a key to their flat,' said Micky, and grinned. Suddenly he and Caspar were teenagers again, colluding in mischief.

'Let's do it,' said Caspar decisively.

'Why not?' grinned Micky, and watched his brother leave with real fondness and a hope that it would all work out well for him. With Caspar gone, Micky set about unpacking his small amount of belongings. Things that were dear to him, nothing of very much value really; keepsakes from his dead parents, clothes that were of good quality and skilful cut, but not designer, and – he paused over this – a small photo in a silver oval frame, a present from Venny. It was a photograph of her, snapped in the park, her hair flying in a bitter winter wind, her cheeks pinkened by the cold. She looked about fourteen, carefree, reckless. Dani had taken it, she had told him almost shyly when she gave it to him over dinner the other night – it had been a long, slow, sumptuous dinner and had ended with a night of languorous, blazingly erotic lovemaking. But if he didn't want it, she said, worried that this was too soon, perhaps too intimate a gift, then of course she would understand. But he wanted it – of course he did.

He slumped down on the wide old elm floorboards in a patch of warm sunlight and leaned back on one elbow, gazing at her image. He thought that she was growing less cautious, more adventurous, and he was certainly working towards that end and was pleased with her progress as a lover. Thinking of that night of love now, of the way they had feasted on the food and then upon each other, like that bawdy scene from *Tom Jones*, made his cock twitch and fill. And why not? With leisurely movements he unbuckled his belt, freed the metal button on the waistband of his jeans, and slid the zip down, wriggling his hips forwards a little on the hard floor to let his nude penis protrude from the gap. He smiled down at it, rearing up all rosy and filled with lust. Then he looked back at the photo. The sort of photo he would really like of her was one where he could see her naked breasts, and the soft curves of her hips and belly, and her mound with its now thickening patch of toffee-toned hair that was always so soft beneath his fingers.

Whoa, boy, he thought to himself as his cock reared up harder still. Don't let's rush this. He loved to masturbate almost as much as he loved to fuck. Lazily he placed the photo on the floor where he could see it easily, and he lifted his hips a fraction so that he could push his jeans down to his knees; this done, he applied a hand to his own pubic hair, so much denser and thicker than Venny's, so much darker too. Lightly fingering the wiry filaments over his thighs and his tightening balls brought a rush of sweet sensations.

With a hissing indrawn breath, Micky cupped his

balls in his fingers as if weighing them for consideration. They were full now, needy. Softly he slid the hand up and onto his naked shaft, which quivered in answer to the touch. His glans peeped out above his encircling thumb and forefinger as he pushed down, very lightly, almost teasing himself with the pleasure such a movement engendered. The little eye at its centre was winking, exuding a thick teardrop of seed.

He thought of Venny as she had been the other night, her naked thighs straddling him, her cries like that of a madwoman as she impaled herself repeatedly upon his organ – and her excitement had increased his own to fever point, so that the clamouring of all his male hormones made him grip her hips and flip her onto her back on the bed, made him mount her and drive into her with something approaching her own frenzy.

Jesus! She'd been so wild, so creamy. Just remembering the way she'd been made him inhale as deeply as if he were temporarily deprived of oxygen, as if he could smell her skin, her excitement, right now. A shudder of pleasure swept through him. His eyelids drooped as he gave himself up to the pure enjoyment of sensuality.

Groaning, Micky clasped his cock tighter and gazed at the photo. What was he doing here, anyway, masturbating over a girl's photo like a schoolkid before the poster of a pop idol? But he was too far gone to care, too far gone even to question any more. Fatalism was overtaking him. He wanted her, he knew that much; and if it ended tomorrow, or next week, or never, it was wonderful right now, and he wanted to milk the thrill of it for every last drop of sensuality, of eroticism, of good old-fashioned lust. He wanted to know everything there was to know about Venny Halliday – he wanted to know her to her bones, and fuck her until they were both exhausted.

His penis swelled harder, painfully and deliriously harder, so that it was pressed up tight and full against his belly, so that pulling it away, even touching it lightly, was a torment and a delight. But pull it away he did, and he cupped it in his hand almost tenderly and lay back on the floor, pulling up his knees so that his feet were flat to the floor, yanking up his white T-shirt above his dark-brown nipples to keep it free of come.

Near-naked and gasping now, his exposed belly heaving with each hurried breath, Micky gave himself over to the glory of pleasure, pushing his hand down, up, down, up, and then waiting a desperate second or two, not wanting it to be over, not wanting to finish this bliss, this utter, utter bliss. Then again, his hips coming up off the floor as his hand administered each stroke with increasing haste. Down, up, down, up, covering not just his shaft now but his eager, creaming glans too, until he glanced down and saw that the tip of his cock, vanishing and emerging from the cup of his hand, was wet and glistening, red and engorged. Pausing, breathing heavily, delaying again, teasing himself, torturing himself, he saw the veins on his naked shaft standing out like blue ropes before he started again on the road to sure relief.

Up, down, up; harder, rougher; oh, yes; oh, Jesus,

yes, yes. Down, up, the friction so delicious now, so desperately and terribly delicious, and suddenly he was coming, he was coming hard and full and shooting forth like a miniature cannon, shooting white spurts of come up over his belly, over his ribs, almost to where the T-shirt was rolled back to preserve it. He watched it, every tiny second of it, and managed not to cry out and so attract the attention of anyone downstairs in the kitchens. Venny was not in her office – she was out in the market with Dani.

He slumped back with a sigh of release, freeing his cock which now lolled thickly against his come-smeared belly. 'God, Venny,' he murmured, picking up the photo and holding it up in front of him. 'That was so good.'

Camden lock market was full to bursting with people. The beautiful hot weather had brought everyone out in droves to finger the fresh produce, haggle over skirts and shrugs and frilly little cardies, hunt hopefully and usually in vain for Faberge or Meissen among the dross on the second-hand stalls. Dani and Venny strolled at a leisurely pace, fingering and haggling with the best of them.

'I'm telling you,' Dani purred, looking more than ever like a contented little cat as she diverted to a clothes stall and smoothed a hand over a silky fabric, 'Flora is just divine.'

'Caspar's the possessive type, though,' said Venny, although the heat was making her lazy and she was just making conversation; she wasn't seriously worried that Caspar might do anything drastic about Dani and Flora's relationship, if you could call it that. Jamie, now. Jamie was a whole different species. Now there was a possessive man. Something in the Scots blood, maybe; all that marauding and pillaging over the border with your face painted blue, it must upset the hormones or something.

Venny yawned. God, she felt tired. Shagged out, if the truth were told. Micky was a very, very hot lover. And a great chef too. She couldn't believe how well he'd done, turning the business around in the short time he'd been working for her. Bookings were well up, and she was starting to dare to hope that the Blue Ribbon award might be within her grasp after all.

A secret smile curved her mouth upwards as she thought of him; and then as suddenly she frowned and thought that he had actually been a bit stand-offish with her since that episode with Neil. Maybe her willingness to participate in the threesome had shocked him? But he had instigated it, after all. Men were, however, strange moody creatures, and although he seemed just a trifle cool, he still made love to her, still lunched with her in the park, still seduced her body and her palate and her mind. So maybe she was just imagining it.

'What d'you think of this?' She was running a hand over a slim little sheath of a dress with an embroidered hem; it was red, and cut rather lower than she would normally have considered appropriate.

'Not your usual sort of thing, is it?' said Dani in some surprise. She knew very well that Venny's preference was for suits, whatever the time of year; beautifully cut, but stiff and formal and a bit, let's be honest, forbidding. A bit 'hands off', really. Now here she was, looking at a dress that said, in no uncertain terms, come and fuck me. And she had bought a pair of red skyscraper-heeled mules yesterday when they'd been trawling Oxford Street. She'd even started wearing perfume, which she had never bothered with before. Dani looked at her friend and thought, ah-ha. Good old Micky Quinn. And she thought that maybe she could take advantage of all Venny's new-found bounty, too.

'Listen, buy it. It's absolutely you,' she assured her.

While Venny had the dress bagged and paid for it, Dani said: 'You know, I've been thinking.'

'Steady,' said Venny with a grin. It was a devil-may-care, un-Venny-like grin.

'Flora's coming over to our place tomorrow night,' said Dani cautiously.

Venny took her purchase and they strolled on together. 'So that's still going on, then?' she asked.

'Of course,' said Dani smugly. 'That girl is so great. Listen, Venny.' She hesitated, and then pressed on. 'Why don't you join us?'

Venny stopped dead. She turned and stared at Dani, who had the grace to look ever so slightly awkward. 'Do you mean—?'

'Why not?' asked Dani defensively. 'You liked it when I was helping you get ready for Flora's party, didn't you?'

'Well, yes.'

'And what's the alternative? Some boring restaurateurs' thrash where you're surrounded by strangers who'll get drunk and try to grope you? Come on, Venny.' Dani winked at her encouragingly. 'Come and have some fun with us. You can show Flora your new dress, and wear those new shoes.'

Until you take them off me, thought Venny, feeling quite flushed and excited by the very idea. 'OK,' she said. 'Why not?'

They did watch a video together the following night, Dani and Flora and Venny, although it could not really be classified as 'girly'. It was in fact a film that Venny thought Micky would love – *Tampopo*, an erotic Japanese masterpiece full of fucking and food. They drank white wine as they watched the lovers' antics on the screen, but although their attention seemed fixed to the steamy blending of eating and sucking and acres of naked skin on film, each was very aware of the other two. Their thighs touched, and their bare arms too, for it was a hot night in more ways than one and they were wearing thin clothes, clothes just made for seduction.

Venny was, as Dani had requested, wearing her new low-cut red dress and skyscraper-heeled mules. Dani was in her short ice-blue wrap, and Venny guessed that she was probably naked beneath it. Flora wore a brief lime-green chiffon top with a bra beneath it, which Venny thought rather hungrily was a pity, and tight black leather trousers that exuded a rich animal scent. When the film was over and Dani switched off the television, Venny knew that the real fun would begin. She already felt quite hot and ready after watching all that action on screen; and she knew, from the squirming and fidgeting during the unravelling of the ravishingly erotic plot of the film, that both Dani and Flora were ready too.

'That was great,' said Dani, stretching lazily. She straightened and leaned forwards, placing her empty glass on the coffee table and taking up three matches that were lying in a bowl there. Venny had noticed them earlier, but hadn't thought to wonder what they might be doing there; she was relaxed and felt that she just wanted to let the evening unravel as it would.

'Now we're going to strip, one at a time, down to the skin,' said Dani excitedly, bunching the matches into her fist. 'And we'll draw lots to see who goes first.'

Flora's almond-shaped, dark-grey eyes grew wide and she sat forwards, putting her glass down, eager to proceed. Venny put her own glass down. Her heart was thumping a little because she had never done this before: not with women, and certainly not with two women. Flora took the first match, then Dani drew hers, and lastly Venny took one.

They compared matches.

Venny's was shortest.

'Come on then, Venny,' said Dani purringly, lying back on the couch so that she had the best possible view. 'Strip,' she said, licking her lips in anticipation.

'What if I don't agree to play?' teased Venny, already enjoying herself. 'What if I don't want to?'

'Oh, you want to,' said Flora, answering for Dani in the cut-glass accent that they shared. 'You were as excited during that film as Dani and I were. You were nearly burning a hole in the couch, admit it.'

'Well, maybe,' admitted Venny. It was certainly hot tonight, as hot and humid as it had been for every night over the last two weeks, and it would feel good to be naked. Her new underwear chafed her slightly, and yes, she would love to shuck it off, and enjoy the novel experience of two women ogling her while she did so.

'And if you don't strip, we'll do it for you,' threatened Dani, her dark eyes gleaming with awakening lust.

'OK, OK. I'm doing it.' Feigning pique because it was all part of the game, Venny pouted as she stood up and let her hair down. It lay about her shoulder in a wild blonde tangle as she shook it out with a wild movement of her head.

'Maybe we should have music for this,' commented Dani, watching avidly.

'Ravel's *Bolero*,' suggested Flora, flicking back her fiery red hair and tucking her long legs underneath her, her catlike grey eyes gleaming with interest as she looked up at Venny.

'Barry White,' considered Dani.

'I'm not stripping to music,' objected Venny, fiddling with the zipper of her tight-fitting dress. 'What do you two think I am, a lap dancer?'

'Now there's a thought,' Dani said.

'No music,' insisted Venny, and gathered her courage

and pushed the red dress down. The spaghetti straps of the thin dress slipped down her arms as she pushed it down over her hips and let it fall to the floor. She stepped out of it, hooking it onto the toe of one of her high-heeled mules and kicking it casually aside.

'Oh, wow,' breathed Dani, clutching at Flora's arm in her excitement, while Flora simply goggled with amazement.

Expecting action tonight, Venny had come prepared. She wore two things she would never, pre-Micky, have considered as an option. She wore a low-cut black PVC bra which clung like a tight sheath to the full globes of her breasts; it was underwired and cunningly designed to push her tits up and out to their fullest extent. Also, it had holes cut out of the PVC where her hard and excitingly naked nipples jutted louchely out. To add to the show, she wore matching PVC briefs with the crotch cut away so that her toffee-coloured pubic curls were clearly visible to the watching audience.

'You like?' she asked the two women, turning slightly so they could admire the thong effect at the back. Her buttocks were naked, split only by the black line of the briefs to conceal the puckered little bud of her anus and her already dampening sex. Earlier in the evening, she had thought to anoint her lightly tanned skin with a glitter-filled moisturiser, so that now the taut curves of her arse gleamed enticingly in the subdued lighting of the room as she turned and displayed her wares for them.

'Turn back to the front,' ordered Dani, pushing her clenched hands between her thighs to try and subdue her own rising passion.

Venny obeyed, enjoying their attention more than she had ever suspected she would. Would she have even considered being a party to this very enjoyable little game of Dani's, if Micky hadn't come into her life? She didn't think so. She didn't think she would have had the sexual confidence to do so.

'Now take the bra off,' said Flora.

'Oh, no,' objected Venny teasingly. 'Not until Dani takes off her robe.'

'No problem,' said Dani, and she pulled the tie free at the waist of the ice-blue silk robe. She knelt up on the sofa and shrugged the thing off in an instant, and remained kneeling there so that both Venny and Flora could look her over. Again, Venny was filled with admiration for Dani's cherry-nippled and pert little breasts, her petite and neatly curving body, the thickness and lush darkness of her pubic hair. Flora too was clearly enraptured, reaching out a hand to caress a taut little nipple which flaunted a gold ring. Dani swayed into Flora's touch as the redhead's hand drifted from Dani's breast, down over her waist, over her gold-ringed navel, down over the slope of her belly and into the thicket of her pubes.

'Mm, that's good,' murmured Dani, parting her legs for Flora.

'Hey, don't get too distracted,' Venny reminded the pair of them. Now it was Flora's turn to obey the rules, to draw back with regret the hand she had so eagerly reached out to Dani. 'The deal was we all stripped naked, one at a time. So come on, Flora. Give.'

'Ah, but you're not naked, are you?' said Flora, running a catlike gaze down over Venny's curves. 'And until you are, why should I keep my end of the deal?'

Venny had to admit that Flora had a point. Reaching behind her, she unhitched the straps of the PVC bra, then slipped her hands down and leaned forwards. The straps slipped down and over her arms until she freed them, one at a time, always keeping one arm over the heavy fall of her breasts. Finally she tossed the PVC bra aside and let them look.

The edges of the nipple-holes had chafed her teats a little, reddening them most attractively; and the way she was bending towards them, swinging her breasts just lightly, teasingly, made the two watching women think how nice it would be, how utterly wonderful, to just step behind Venny and push that obtrusive thong aside, lick a finger or two and just slip them into her.

'Come on, Venny, get 'em off,' encouraged Dani, her dark-red nipples standing out like crazy with the extent of her arousal.

Venny complied quite happily, pushing the black PVC briefs down her legs and stepping out of them. She still wore the high-heeled mules, and they seemed to emphasise her total nudity to the two watching women.

Naked now, Venny went over to the couch and stood beside the equally naked Dani, who reached up and slipped a rather more than friendly arm around her flatmate's waist. The arm dropped a little, and Dani was fondling Venny's buttocks, fondling the hot peachlike curves of them before dropping down to ticklingly negotiate her bumslit.

'Not yet,' said Venny firmly, stepping slightly away despite the fact that she was enjoying Dani's touch enormously. 'First Flora's got to get naked.'

'Come on, we'll help her,' suggested Dani with a rakish grin. She leaned forwards on the couch while Venny bent over the red-haired woman; between them they shucked off the lime-green chiffon blouse Flora wore, and it was Venny who sat on the arm of the couch and unclipped Flora's white lacy bra; her very heavy breasts spilled out from the confines of the garment in fleshy ripples, and each of the watching women gasped in admiration at such beauty.

'Flora has a party trick too, don't you, Flora?' said Dani excitedly. 'Show Venny, go on.'

Flora cupped a hand under each of her magnificent breasts and lifted them as far as they would go, which was pretty high. She then bent her head and stuck out her tongue – and licked her own cinnamon-coloured nipples!

'That's really cool,' said Venny, slipping her hands around from behind Flora so that she could cup those lovely tits of hers, could feel the hard puckering nipples still moist from Flora's own mouth. Flora leaned back against the pillow of Venny's naked breasts with a sigh of pleasure while Dani leaned over Flora like some dark female satyr and unzipped her black leather trousers.

Eagerly Dani pulled the tight trousers down, baring Flora's lushly curving belly and the brilliant red flame of her pubic hair. With another sigh, a sigh of surrender, Flora lifted her hips from the couch and kicked off her ponyskin mules so that Dani's progress should not be impeded. Her almost luminously white skin glowed richly against her red hair, and her two acolytes looked upon her in wonderment. This, Venny thought, was how a woman *should* look. She was fairly confident of her own attractiveness, and she knew that Dani was confident to the bone about hers, but Flora was truly beautiful, and she could easily understand now why Dani was so enthusiastic about bedding her.

And then they were all three naked and tangling together on the sofa in a bewildering but delicious tangle of arms and legs, breasts and thighs – and it was so different, Venny thought, so very different to making love with men; these two were the other part of her, they were soft, they were yielding, they were women.

'Come on,' said Dani, surfacing from Flora's kiss to grab Venny's hand. 'Let's make ourselves comfy in my bedroom.'

They stood, touching, kissing, fondling in wonder and affection, and made their way to the door leading to Dani's bedroom – Dani only pausing at a drawer near the television to snatch up a huge penis-style vibrator. Giggling excitedly, they linked arms and hugged each other. The bedroom door was opened, and they stood there, framed by the glow of a peachy-toned bedside light, three women, naked and entwined. And then the door from the hall burst open, and in tumbled Micky, Caspar and Jamie.

Chapter Ten

After the first mad flurry of alarm, Venny was able to see how funny the situation was, her and Flora and Dani standing there naked and wide-eyed with astonishment, the three men charging in unannounced. The scene it most closely resembled was Rubens' *Rape of the Sabine Women*, and she found herself very tickled to realise this, for it was a favourite erotic daydream of hers: to be abducted, carried away, kidnapped by some strong, horny Roman god.

She was pleased to note, amid the sudden confusion, that neither Dani nor Flora seemed particularly alarmed by this unexpected development either. In fact, Dani seemed quite titillated by the way Jamie grabbed her and dragged her on into the bedroom, decisively closing the door behind them. While that was going on, Micky had grabbed the rubber penis off Dani and was propelling Venny towards the hall, and her own bedroom. Glancing back as he pulled her

along by the wrist, she saw a very annoyed-looking
Caspar haul the naked and lustfully quivering Flora
into his arms in the instant before that door too was
closed in her face.

'Wait –' she gasped at Micky, half-laughing, half-
serious. Goodness, Micky looked quite annoyed too
as he spun back towards her, his eyes raking over her
naked body almost scathingly.

'I expected Dani and Flora, but not you,' he snapped.
And where was that happy twinkle in the eye, that
devilish, almost piratical glee now? He looked deadly
serious.

Venny shrugged. Her breasts bobbed alluringly as
she did so, and Micky's eyes dipped to them irresistibly.
'Dani invited me to join in.'

'And of course you did,' said Micky scornfully.

'Yes.' She looked at him in bewilderment. 'Why not?
I was curious. I've never done it before with even one
woman, much less two, and I wanted to know what it
was like.'

A glint of humour returned to Micky's vivid blue eyes.
He knew very well that he had started all this, set her
on the road to sensuality; he had awakened her sexual
curiosity, so it was churlish to be shocked, amazed –
yes, even downright horrified – to find that she was
not at her stuffy restaurateurs' do but here, taking part
in a threesome with two other women. She was right.
Why shouldn't she? It was up to him to enjoy her, and
she certainly enjoyed him, but really, if she wanted to

experiment, to broaden her horizons, who was he to tell her otherwise?

Still, there was fun to be had here; fun for both of them in a little play-acting.

Abruptly Micky pushed Venny back against the wall. She hit it with a thump and a gasp of surprise. He followed her, pressing his body hard against the front of hers, staring into her startled eyes from inches away.

Venny could feel Micky's erection pressing against her.

'Do you know,' he said softly, menacingly, 'what I am going to do with this?'

He brandished the imitation penis under her nose. Venny nearly went cross-eyed trying to look at it. Her eyes went back to his.

'No,' she said with feigned wariness.

'Use your imagination,' he suggested, then stepped back and hauled her forwards, flipping her deftly over his shoulder in a fireman's lift. All the air went out of Venny as her midriff hit his hard-muscled shoulder. She often forgot, because he was slim and compactly muscled, just how strong he was, how strong he had to be, to withstand the workload that was an everyday part of being a professional chef. But she was aware of it now, meltingly aware in every sinew and cell of her own body.

Micky went into her bedroom, still carrying her, kicking the door closed behind them. He dropped her across the bed, where she bounced judderingly. He stood over her, watching the quiver of her breasts until the motion was stilled. Venny looked up at him. She was panting and her breasts rose and fell agitatedly with each quickened breath. She was enjoying herself, eager to see what he would do next, but she had to admit that the three men's unexpected entrance had been a bit frightening, and she was using the adrenaline rush of fear to stoke the fire of her own lust for gratification, playing the weak and helpless female to his marauding warrior – and enjoying every second of it.

'Please don't hurt me,' she whispered pleadingly, while her eyes danced and played lusty games with his.

'Maybe I ought to,' said Micky roughly, playing along too as he tossed the vibrator onto the bed and quickly stripped off his white shirt. Venny gazed admiringly at his sparingly muscled but gorgeously well-toned torso, his strong well-defined arms. Her eyes slipped lower.

'God, you are such a randy little bitch,' said Micky, seeing where her eyes were resting. They both looked down. His upright cock was pressing against the material of his trousers with an urgency that surprised neither of them. 'You want it, don't you? You want it up you, hard and hot.'

Venny nodded slowly.

'Say it,' hissed Micky.

'I want it,' said Venny softly, gazing up at him with her eyes all slumberous with desire.

Holding her eyes with his own, Micky undid the button at the waistband of his trousers. With a sharp movement he pulled down the zip on his fly; then he kicked off his shoes and pushed the trousers down and off. When he straightened he was naked, but one hand concealed his balls and his tumescent cock from her hungry eyes. Cupping himself, Micky came down onto the bed, opening her legs with a rough movement and moving up between them. Exposed and wet with longing, Venny lay there and waited to see what he would do now. Still Micky kept himself hidden from her, and she wanted, wanted desperately, to see him, to touch him.

She reached out as if to do so, but Micky snapped: 'No. Turn over.'

Hesitatingly, Venny did as she was told. She shivered with a delicious sense of dread at how cold he sounded, how very controlling. Almost brutal. She shivered again, her nipples rising to urgent peaks that tormented her so that as she turned face-down on the bed she rubbed them furtively on the dark red velvet throw that served as a bedcover. Um, she loved velvet. Particularly on her nipples when they were so hard, so desperately in need of stimulation.

'Say it all. Say you want it up you, hard and hot,' ordered Micky, yanking two pillows from under the cover and thrusting them under her pubes. Hopelessly aroused, she ground her pudenda into the pillows. 'And stop that,' he said. 'I'm going to pleasure you; I don't want you pleasuring yourself. Now say it.'

Venny squirmed, feeling his hard furred thighs moving in close behind her where she lay spread-eagled, her bottom hiked up in the air by the pillows. If she was any the less rabid for sex from him she would have felt incredibly embarrassed. He must be able to see everything – her anus, her snatch, her lust-swollen labia, even surely a teasing glimpse of her clit, swelling hungrily within its little hood.

Suddenly she heard a steady humming start up. She saw Micky reach out for the lubricating jelly she kept on the bedside table, but she couldn't see what was going on behind her and it was starting to worry her slightly. What was he going to do with her?

'Say it,' he ordered again, his voice husky with passion.

'I want it,' groaned Venny into the velvet cover. 'I want it up me, hard and hot.'

'Take it, then,' he murmured, and she felt him slip between the widespread cheeks of her bottom. Oh, he was big. Hugely, satisfyingly big, and she wriggled back as far as she could, ready for him, more than ready. Micky easily found the waiting wetness of her and pushed in a little; and as he did so Venny abruptly realised from the strange rubbery feel of him that this in fact was not him at all, that this was the vibrator. She let out a faint moan of protest and pleasure as the steadily thrumming thing went deeper into her, deeper, and suddenly Micky pushed it hard, all the way into her, so that she was filled utterly, and the tiny protrusion at the base of the vibrator pressed firmly upon her clitoris.

She gasped and squirmed as the thing moved against all her most sensitive places, tears squeezing out from between her lashes as she screwed her eyes tight shut, becoming nothing but an entity designed for receiving sensation. And such sensations. The vibrations from the fake penis seemed to generate sparks from everything it touched. Micky pushed it relentlessly in and out of her, as if this huge cock was his own, as if he personally was fucking her. At every thrust her clitoris was bombarded with startling shafts of pleasure.

Her soft inner walls, flowing with moisture to more ably accommodate this rubbery intruder, were pounded by wave after wave of almost unbearably exquisite feelings. Her G-spot was assailed time after time by the most excruciatingly intense stimulation until she couldn't bear it a moment longer and her climax gripped her. She screamed once, loudly, and then caught in the grip of her orgasm pushed back in a desperate rhythm to milk every last drop of pleasure from it.

Finally she lay still, spent; but Micky had only just started. He eased the vibrator out of her; Venny moaned, missing it instantly, wanting it back inside her, but helpless to do anything right now but lie there and wonder what the hell he was going to do next. The humming stopped. Distantly she heard a wail.

'What the hell?' asked Micky.

'It's Dani,' she mumbled into the coverlet. 'Come inside me now, please, Micky. Right now.'

'God, haven't you had enough yet?' he whispered, bending over her back, slipping his hands between the overheated skin of her midriff and the coverlet, then easing them up until they cupped her breasts.

Venny moaned again, squirming pleasurably back upon the pillows until her still needy cunt connected with Micky's hard, muscular thigh. She rubbed herself against it like a cat, and like a cat she purred with pleasure as she did so.

'Hot little bitch,' said Micky, his body curving over her back as he smoothed his hands over the big pale globes of her breasts. He tweaked her nipples almost painfully as he kissed and bit at her neck, making Venny squirm even harder with lust.

She could feel his rough, crinkly pubic hair tickling her left buttock as he leaned hotly over her; she could feel the rigid, heavy length of his erect cock resting upright against her bumslit. Micky squeezed her nipples harder, and Venny experienced a fluttering echo of her first orgasm. Her fingers clawed madly at the velvet throw. One of his hands left her breasts and slipped back between their sweat-sticky bodies. He pushed his penis down, reversing its cosy position between her legs, and she moved back eagerly, expecting him to come inside her vagina; but instead Micky pressed his damp glans to the little puckered ring of her anus, and pressed forwards, moving with extreme gentleness until he was lodged just a little inside this forbidden place.

Venny considered protesting. She had never been buggered before, and wasn't entirely sure that she really wanted to be buggered now, but Micky was being so excessively careful with her, easing in, just easing so smoothly, so steadily, and then tickling her clitoris with the fingers of one hand, arousing her all over again, overcoming her doubts, overcoming the sudden restrictive tightening until he was in, completely inside her, and she found to her amazement that she loved it.

'Oh, you like that?' Micky cooed against her shoulder, kissing her hot skin as he gasped, mustering all his self-control so that he should not climax too soon while lodged inside so deliciously forbidden a place.

'You're so tight,' he complained aloud, groaning as he fought for restraint, keeping still for long tortuous moments until the urge to come, and come right *now*, had passed.

'Tighter than in the front?' asked Venny almost shyly; she wasn't used to talking during sex, but Micky seemed to see it as part of the pleasure, and could talk dirty enough to drive her completely insane with desire.

'Much tighter. Feel that.' And he pushed in, right up to the hilt, but so gently, so carefully, before drawing back his swollen rod. A droplet of sweat dropped from his brow onto Venny's back, and he licked it away with slow enjoyment, tasting her sweet milk-scented skin, his own saltiness. 'Tight, see?'

'Mm, tight,' groaned Venny, sprawled on the bed without a movable bone in her body. She felt as limp, as spineless and relaxed, as a jellyfish.

'That's it, relax. Chill,' he said encouragingly. Too late, thought Venny. This was wonderful. Her tightness and the huge dimensions of his penis combined to generate a heady elixir that she found she couldn't get enough of. She was so sensitive to every move he made, and he was just as badly affected; she could tell that by his tortured breathing, by the heavy pushing of his rock-hard balls against her buttocks, by the spasmodic movements of his hands as they grasped her waist, held her still for him.

'Jesus, I'm going to come,' Micky gasped through clenched teeth. Venny didn't care in the least. She wanted him to come, she wanted to feel that happening to him while he was in her forbidden place. She turned her head, smiling lazily, enjoying this so very much; and caught sight of their reflection in the mirror on her dressing table through the wild tangle of her hair.

With a careless movement she swept her hair back, and looked at the tableau so unexpectedly revealed to her. She could see herself lying prone on the bed, could see her raised hips resting on the pillows and the full soft undercurves of her breasts. She watched, fascinated and aroused, while Micky pushed his hands under her thighs and lifted them up on either side of his waist, creating a wheelbarrow effect, her as the barrow, him as the pusher.

And push he did now as she subtly altered shape inside, allowing him even greater access. Venny watched him, his straining shoulders as he held her up gleaming under a gloss of sweat, his head scrunched down onto his neck and his face screwed up in intense concentration. His buttocks were clenching and unclenching furiously as he pushed, withdrew, pushed and withdrew from his tight nest. The flame tattoo was clearly visible, glowing red and angry and seeming almost to ripple and come alive as his muscles moved restlessly under his skin.

But again his control was amazing. While she was all but biting the coverlet with the extent of her excitement, he paused again, paused and pressed hard on that slow-down spot that was situated between his anus and his cock. He threw back his head and his face was momentarily contorted as if in pain. Turned on by the sight, Venny moaned and writhed briefly, but he had her totally in his control, holding her immobile while he set the pace.

'Oh, Micky, please finish me,' moaned Venny.

Micky's contorted face softened into a grin as he paused and stared, panting, at her tousled head. Seeing which way she was facing, his own head turned fractionally, and he saw the mirror. Their eyes met in the mirror.

'Why, Venny Halliday, what a wicked girl you are,' he murmured. 'You've been watching me.'

'Mm,' said Venny, having to lick her terribly dry lips before she could speak now. She could feel a thunderous, cataclysmic orgasm hovering in the pit of her belly, in her breasts, in her clit and her cunt and her arse, her soft arse where he was lodged as hard and unbending as a maypole thrust up in spring.

'Say please, then,' said Micky, holding her gaze in the mirror before glancing down almost admiringly at the thick root of his cock, settled so cosily against the puckered gate of her anus.

Venny squirmed and then relaxed hopelessly. 'Please, then,' she muttered. 'Please! Please, you bastard, come on, do it, finish me – *please*!'

Even before she'd finished hissing her wanting and needing at him like a curse, Micky moved, pulling out from her almost completely. Venny, watching in the mirror, saw the slick and thick redness of his heavily lubricated cock slip out of her, and then she saw it and felt it plunge back in. Again and again he drew right back, then launched himself into her anew. His hands dug almost painfully into her waist but she hardly felt it. Her entire being was focused, completely centred, on the building sensations he was causing her to feel. She seemed to open and open ever further for him, like a flower opening to the sun. Finally she collapsed forwards onto the coverlet, clutching at it, muffling her own screams with the thick red velvet as she came again, ferociously, wave upon wave of acute bliss that left her feeling wrung out and as lifeless as a rag doll.

'Jesus,' moaned Micky, and she felt him coming too. His cock grew harder, fuller, and then she felt the wild pumping of his ejaculation. Every muscle in his body seemed to be straining towards this final victory. When at last he relaxed, sinking back onto his knees behind her, he let her thighs drop back to the bed and then put his arms around her waist, pulling her up against his body so that she knelt in front of him. His hands slid up and cupped her breasts, and his hot mouth kissed the curve of her neck, his chin scratching at the ravishingly sensitive skin there in the most delightful way.

'Darling, darling Venny,' he murmured against her feverish skin, letting his penis slip free of her at last. It lay heavy and wet and still stiff against her buttock. Irresistibly Venny reached a hand behind her to stroke it, admire its size, its strength. 'Don't even think about it for the next ten minutes,' said Micky on a half-stifled laugh, his voice muffled by her neck.

'I can't promise not to at least think about it,' Venny chuckled, warmed by the way he was cuddling her so close. So many men were remote after lovemaking, yet Micky loved to cuddle, to hug and sleep close after coition, then wake in the morning and start all over again. And he'd called her darling. Darling Venny. She thought that was sweet, really nice. Of course it didn't mean that he didn't say exactly that to every other girl he slept with, she reminded herself sternly, but, somehow his saying it made her feel special, appreciated.

'Well, maybe I can give you something else to think about. To distract you,' said Micky, kissing her, making her shiver all over again with the feel of his mouth against the ultra-sensitive skin of her throat.

'You can try,' she whispered happily, sinking back against him as he linked his arms around her waist. His cock was still remarkably full, but sinking to half-mast now. She snuggled her buttocks against it.

'Only I was thinking,' said Micky, biting her ear, 'that I might sell the hut. You're right. The market's buoyant, demand's high. I'd get a really good price for it.'

Venny glanced back over her shoulder at him in surprise. 'But you said—'

'I know what I said. I said it was more important to me than money, and it was. It is. But I've been thinking that it could be good for both of us to get things on a more equal footing. So look. I could sell the hut, and sink some of the cash from the sale into the restaurant, we can agree a sum between us. I can buy myself into a partnership with you. I know you've got cash flow problems, anyway, and I thought—'

Venny stiffened. 'What do you mean, "you know".'

'Well, of course I know,' said Micky mildly. 'I see the takings, and you tell me they've doubled since I've been here.'

'They have.' Venny was beginning to get a horrible creeping feeling about all this.

'There you are, then. And you were at the bank when we had that little shunt, weren't you?'

'And you jumped to the conclusion that I was having cash problems?' He'd jumped to the right conclusion there, thought Venny with rising irritation. And it was true what he was saying; he had seen the number of covers they were doing now, and she had told him that takings had doubled, and maybe she had brought this whole damned thing on herself by being loose-lipped with him, but she had trusted him. She had thought he had integrity. She had thought that what they had together was something rather more than a business opportunity.

'It showed up on the computer, too,' said Micky, nibbling delicately at her earlobe.

Computer? thought Venny. What computer? He couldn't mean her computer? There was only a till link downstairs, and all her accounts and personal information files were blocked by passwords. No. He couldn't mean her computer.

'Do you mean the computer in my office?' she asked

numbly, thinking that she really, really didn't want to hear the answer, but she had asked the question now, it was too late, too late. She thought of Caspar, his brother, the IT specialist. Oh, no, she cringed. Oh, no. Micky was trying to screw his way into a partnership with her – just like Bill Thompson had, just like that very first rat of a man had. That was what men did, in her experience. Screw her, get their hooks into her money, then dump her. She had thought Micky was different. She had certainly hoped so. But she had very obviously been wrong.

'Look, I'll own up to the fact that I had Caspar help me check out the accounts,' said Micky apologetically, perhaps feeling the sudden chill wind of Venny's disappointment.

'My accounts,' said Venny flatly.

'Right, your accounts. And why not? I was checking out a business investment, and I think it would be a good one, Venny, so why not? I'll sell the hut, sink some cash into Box of Delights; we'll get a proper partnership agreement drawn up. What do you say?'

'What do I *say*?' Venny twitched away from him and was up and off the bed in an instant. She had to gulp down a few steadying breaths before she could trust herself to speak. 'I say you're a treacherous, underhand bastard, Micky Quinn,' she blazed at him, 'just like every other man I've ever known. So no, don't sell your damned precious hut, and don't even think about partnership deals, because there isn't going to be one.'

'Venny!' Kneeling naked on her bed with his flaccid

cock now dangling down between his legs, Micky was looking at her in amazement. She felt a treacherous twist of sensation in her guts as she looked back at him, but she fought down the rising tide of desire, because it was desire that had tricked her into this situation in the first place.

'Now sod off out of my bedroom and out of my restaurant and out of my life, will you?' She flounced over to the door, snatched her robe down off the hook behind it and struggled into the garment, nearly tearing the delicate apple-green fabric in her anger. Then she flung the door wide open. 'Your services are no longer required.'

Chapter Eleven

Within two weeks Venny had found herself another chef. They were, she reminded herself, ten a penny, and she had really thrown herself into the job of finding a replacement for Micky Quinn, scouring the catering agencies and ignoring the petulance of the rest of the staff over the fact that Micky, as she very firmly and coolly told them, was a thing of the past.

As she sat in her office late one evening while the restaurant busily hummed along downstairs, she congratulated herself on her diligence. And on successfully putting the Micky episode behind her. Some odd things had come out of that night when he'd burst into the flat with Jamie and Caspar in tow. For instance, and this was perhaps the biggest surprise of all, Caspar and Flora were now behaving like regular lovebirds, cooing over each other in the most sickening manner. Dani was pleased that she had been instrumental in healing the rift in their marriage.

'Sexual counselling,' Dani had joked to Venny about it. 'Maybe I should set up shop. What do you think? Fucking both partners seems to work wonders.'

And that was what Dani was doing. Often Venny came across Flora with Caspar and Dani, enjoying a threesome in the flat. If the spark had gone out of their marriage before, there were enough sparks now to set alight the entire building. Once, she had even joined in, and they had gone three-on-one with Caspar lying on the bed; tied to the bed, actually. She sighed and felt her crotch moisten hungrily as she thought of Caspar, but really, the physical similarities to Micky were a little too pronounced for her to feel entirely comfortable with him.

It was Caspar who told her that Micky had sold the hut. Venny was surprised by the sharp stab of sadness she felt when she heard that news. She'd so loved it there. And Micky had loved it too. Still, life went on. And so, apparently, did Micky's career. He had set up his own place, called Beurre Blanc, over in Shepherd's Bush near Jamie's studio, and Jamie had told Venny – not without a certain bitter satisfaction, she thought – that Micky was going to enter for the Blue Ribbon awards. Unlike Bill Thompson, Micky was pretty powerful competition, and Venny knew it. They had a fight on their hands. Well, she felt fine about that – now that she had Anton.

Someone was clattering up the stairs. Venny snapped out of her reverie and waited expectantly. One of the waitresses, Kate, almost fell into the office in her haste. Her face was excited but with a garnish of anxiety.

'Venny,' she said urgently, 'we think we've got one of the judges in downstairs.'

Venny felt panic clutch at her. Well, they'd known that the Blue Ribbon judges were in the area. They'd had enough notice to prepare. Hell, they were prepared. She stood up, taking a deep calming breath.

'Are you sure?' she asked, dismayed by how thin and strained her voice sounded.

'Well,' said Kate in a rush, 'pretty sure, yes. Neil's seen him making notes.'

'Maybe a critic on one of the papers. Or a magazine.'

'Neil doesn't think so. Come to that, neither do I. Do you know the way examiners look when you take your driving test? Sort of bulky and austere and taking note of everything?'

'Yeah, I remember.' Venny even managed a smile at the memory of what a nervous wreck she'd been on the day she passed her test on the first attempt.

'Well he's like that. Exactly like that. And he's had the chef's selection, so he's been sampling a lot of different dishes.'

'And he seems happy with everything?' asked Venny anxiously.

'Hard to tell with that sort. But he's taking his time over coffee now, and I did tell you I had to get off early. Anton's already left, and so have Neil and the others, so can I leave him with you?'

'Sure,' said Venny, straightening her shell-pink suit jacket as she prepared for the fray. She had gone back to wearing suits after Micky's departure, but suits with a softer edge to them – more low-cut, tighter, shorter, and in softer pastel colours rather than severe black, navy and burgundy like she used to wear. All right, Micky was a rat, but she acknowledged fairly that he had done her a favour, cast his influence over her, made her more aware of herself as a woman.

'Right, you scoot off, Kate,' said Venny briskly, because after all she had promised that Kate could leave early tonight to meet her boyfriend, Jez, and it wasn't Kate's fault that a Blue Ribbon judge had picked tonight to call. 'I'll see to our guest.'

As Venny went into the almost deserted restaurant, she was checking that the place was tidy, even though there had been a good evening's trade, and some spillage was inevitable, but even she had to admit that it looked pretty good, nice and neat, just maybe needing a little work here and there. Picking up a dropped napkin on her way, she walked over to the man who was seated in one of the cosy plush corner booths sipping at a coffee.

He watched her come towards him, and Venny felt her cheeks pinken slightly at the open male appreciation in his eyes. Soft music was still being piped through the sound system. She heard the outer kitchen door close as Kate departed. And Kate had been right, she thought. He did look like an examiner, a judge. He was a thick-set man in his forties, with dark hair peppered with grey at the temples, which added a note of distinction to his overall appearance. His face was heavy and slightly florid, but handsome. He was a man, she guessed, who enjoyed food and all other appetites too. His hand, clasped around his cup, was so big it made the cup look like a piece from a child's tea set. He had grey eyes under heavy black brows. Yes, handsome, she thought. And despite the aura of reserve she sensed about him, his eyes were very bold as they looked her over.

'Good evening, sir,' said Venny, arriving at his table. 'I'm Venny Halliday, the owner. I hope you enjoyed your meal?'

He looked up at her with a smile that assessed her as well as her restaurant. 'It was very good,' he said guardedly, and stretched out one of his huge hands. 'Robert Fielding,' he introduced himself, and they shook hands. 'This is a charming building. How old?'

'Parts of it are seventeenth century,' said Venny. In any competition this would be her restaurant's main strength, she knew; its lovely old-world ambience.

'Won't you join me for a coffee?' He indicated the banquette on the other side of the table.

'Thank you, I'd like that.' Venny went to a nearby station and fetched herself a cup and saucer. She returned to the table and sat down as he had indicated.

'Trade seems good,' he said, pouring coffee for her and more for himself from the cafetière on the table. He offered her the mints. She shook her head.

'Trade's never been better,' said Venny, knowing that this was not the time for false modesty. She wanted, needed, to impress him, and if she had to gild the lily to do it, embroider the truth a bit, fair enough. She was determined to win that award, whatever it cost her.

'I think I'd like a brandy,' said Robert Fielding.

'Of course,' said Venny, taking a sip of her coffee. She half-rose.

'But I'd like it brought to me properly,' added Robert with a smile.

Venny paused, frowning in bewilderment. 'Properly?' she asked.

'Yes. There's a little place in Soho where the waitresses wear frilly little waist-aprons. I'd like it brought to me like that.'

'I'm not a waitress,' Venny pointed out, just a little coldly.

'You're not refusing, surely?' he asked, and his eyes challenged her to say yes. One hand fingered the closed notebook that was still on the table – awaiting his next observation, thought Venny with a rush of anxiety, and it was now up to her whether that observation was good or bad. Kate had already left, so she was going to have to play waitress, and really, what could it hurt to do that just this once?

'No, I'm not refusing,' she assured him with a conciliatory smile. 'You just surprised me, that's all.'

'Good.' Robert sat back with a happy sigh. 'There's no hurry. I'll wait while you get yourself sorted out. Just the apron, then. Oh, and keep the heels on, of course.'

Venny looked at him. 'Just the apron?' she echoed incredulously.

'That's right. That's how they do it in this lovely little place in Soho – haven't you been there? Gorgeous waitresses wearing nothing but these tiny aprons. I suppose you do have such an apron? Only I thought I saw the waitress wearing one earlier. With a black dress, of course, so that I was forced to imagine how she might look without the dress underneath.'

'Well, yes, we do have waist-aprons for the waitresses,' stammered Venny, torn between outrage and excitement at his unexpected proposal.

'Good,' said Robert with an expansive smile. 'There's no hurry. You go and get changed, and bring me my brandy. I'll finish my coffee.'

And he sat back like a man expecting a treat. With a last wondering glance at his perfectly composed face Venny went off to the now empty kitchen and snatched up Kate's discarded apron. She had a feeling that the old Venny, the Venny she used to be, so cold and controlling, would have told Robert Fielding exactly where to get off, and in so doing would have also blown her chances of winning the Blue Ribbon. But now she could admit to herself that the new Venny was titillated by the idea of serving a man in a state of near-nakedness. In fact she already felt quite creamy and aroused at the thought, her wetness beginning to flow, her nipples puckering with excitement under her suit.

Smiling to herself, Venny quickly unbuttoned her jacket, beneath which she was naked. Her breasts dangled heavily as she bent over and pushed her skirt to the floor. No pants, either. She ran a hand languorously over her pubic hair, tickling her mound and biting her lip quite hard as pleasure forked up from her twitching little clit. When Micky had been here, she hadn't wanted to wear anything that could impede his progress to her skin. But now, she reminded herself with a slight frown, Micky was gone; and there were other men to satisfy her – men like Robert Fielding, who was waiting for her now. She picked up the small white linen apron. It was a scant half-moon of fabric with a frill around its curved outer edge and a waistband and ties along its flat side. She put it around her waist and tied it in a big bow at the back. Craning around, she could see the bow flopping in a most provocative fashion above the bare peachlike curves of her arse. She glanced down at her front. Her naked nipples were outrageously hard; the tiny apron covered her crotch with about three inches to spare; the high heels she wore accentuated the length of her legs.

Taking a deep breath for courage, she passed back through the swing door, with its little circular window, into the restaurant. Not looking at Robert Fielding – although she could feel his eyes resting hotly on her – she went to the little bar, pressed a glass to the brandy optic, set out a saucer and a coaster, then came back around the front of the bar with Robert's brandy and carried it over to him. With every step she could feel her tits bouncing louchely. The feeling of his watching eyes on her was exceedingly sexual. All at once, Venny saw why those girls in Soho didn't object to performing this service. If it excited the watching men, it almost certainly drove the half-naked girls crazy with lust.

'Your brandy, sir,' she said sweetly, and bent from the waist, her naked breasts hanging inches from his eyes, to place it in front of him.

'Thank you,' said Robert with equal civility, but the

huskiness in his voice betrayed the depth of his arousal as he stared at her.

'Is there anything else I can do for you?' asked Venny politely.

'Mm, you can attend to this,' said Robert, leaning back on the banquette and turning a little towards her, so that she could see the heavy bulge of his upright penis, clearly outlined beneath his twill trousers.

Venny looked down at this tempting sight, and decided that it would be rather exciting to play the frightened virgin to his domineering patron. She averted her eyes delicately.

'Goodness, what can you mean, sir?' she asked nervously. 'You can't mean that you want me to take it out?'

'That's precisely what I do mean,' said Robert, reaching up to give one of her nipples a lustful tweak. Despite her intentions to play the frightened little servant, Venny let out a tiny moan as he did so, and Robert chuckled deeply. 'I mean that I want you to take it out, and suck it dry.'

'But it looks so big,' breathed Venny as his hand dropped to her hip, caressing the hot silky skin there before progressing lower to cup one luscious buttock. His hands were so big that his fingers intruded into her slit, not enough to please but just enough to tease. Venny could feel another moan building in her throat, but she bit it back. Her labia felt hot, swollen, almost indecently wet. Her heart drummed in her chest like a brass band.

'It is big,' Robert admitted, not without an edge of boastfulness. 'Unzip me and see.'

'What if it's too big for me to manage?' quaked Venny, now thoroughly enjoying their game.

'Too big for you to take it in your mouth?' asked Robert. Venny nodded. 'Then we shall have to use some other orifice to relieve it, won't we?'

'Which orifice would that be, sir?' asked Venny with fake trepidation.

'Your cunt,' said Robert, dipping his wandering fingers deeper so that one found its way into her. Venny moved restlessly, pressing her thighs together to relish the intensity of her own excitement. 'Or perhaps your delicious little arse,' he added, and another finger found the delicate puckering ring of her anus, and pushed in very gently.

'Do you want me to unzip you now, sir?' she half-gasped.

'Right now would be good,' said Robert encouragingly.

Venny leaned forwards as his hand continued its exploration of her nether regions. His eyes rested salaciously on her ripe, naked tits as they dangled right in front of his eyes.

'Glorious tits,' said Robert in congratulatory tones. 'Never thought they'd be this big when I first looked at you.'

Venny meanwhile was busy unbuckling his brown leather belt, and unfastening the button at his waistband – which was straining a bit over his well-filled belly, she noted. He was a big man, big all over. Perhaps his cock really would be too big for her. Holding her breath in anticipation now, she slowly slid down the zip of his trousers. Nothing too alarming happened. A white-clad bulge loomed into the opening, poking from beneath his pale-blue shirt-tails. Now Robert caught his breath, too. His hand on her buttock tightened almost to the point of pain.

Delicately Venny continued her task. She smoothly pushed aside the shirt-tails, and concentrated on the white parcel that awaited her, ready to be opened and enjoyed. Hooking one thumb into each side of the widened gap in the front of his trousers, she looked at him and smiled.

'Lift up, please, sir,' she requested.

Robert eased his hips off the banquette and Venny was then able to pull his trousers down to his ankles. His thighs were vast yet well-muscled, and covered in dark hair. A warm, musky male scent arose from his skin. With a sigh of pleasure Robert slid his hips a little forwards and opened his legs for her to continue.

White Y-fronts, thought Venny, almost smiling. Hardly stylish. But this wasn't a stylish man. His sports jacket was quite old, with leather patches on the elbows. This was a fairly conservative, probably rather staid sort of man. Probably he hadn't even bought those Y-fronts. It was far more likely that his wife had, but Venny wasn't looking for wedding rings at this stage. All her attention was focused on the bulging rod under those excessively unattractive pants.

Now the decision was: whether to take him out of

the slit at the front, or bare him completely? She was not a woman for doing things by halves, after all.

'Lift up again, sir, will you?' she asked him in a whisper.

Again, unable to stifle a little groan of arousal, Robert lifted his hips. Without hesitation Venny hooked both thumbs into the elastic waistband of the unlovely briefs and yanked them right down to join his trousers at his ankles.

'Oh, that's better,' she breathed.

It certainly was. She eyed the huge purple prick revealed to her with awe. It was of medium thickness, but it was very long. If she tried to take it too deep into her mouth he would choke her. And as for her cunt! She thought about how that enormous length would feel up inside her and her wetness immediately became a flood of desire.

His pubic hair was very thick, and gingery in colour. She ran a curious finger over the springy mass that clothed his fatly lolling testes, which were pushed up invitingly by the hard foam of the banquette underneath them. Robert groaned and strained his naked hips up towards her hand. His hands came up and clutched at her breasts, squeezing them almost cruelly. She was pulled inexorably forwards, almost overbalancing onto his lap, while he brought one turgid nipple to his mouth and sucked desperately.

'Oh,' moaned Venny, cradling his big head with her hands, enjoying the warmth of him, the male sex smell he exuded so strongly now. She allowed her own hand to drop and to lightly stroke up over the shaft of his prodigious organ. Before her trailing hand reached its straining, quivering head, she pulled away, freeing her breasts from his crushing grip. She pulled his legs round to the side of the banquette so that the table should not impede her progress, and sank to her knees between his widespread legs, her eyes fixed with admiration on his penis.

'So big,' she murmured as it twitched and swelled even more. 'It's too long for me to take it right inside my mouth. But I'll suck the head, yes?' she suggested, reaching out a finger to smear the moisture from its little open slit around the top of his glans.

'Yes. Do it,' said Robert through gritted teeth, watching her with feverish eyes.

Venny carefully applied her mouth to the silky-smooth tip of his cock. She licked the salty head assiduously, and sucked it, while Robert moaned and tried desperately to thrust against her. To accentuate his arousal, Venny pulled the skin on the shaft of his penis back towards its base, her thumb and forefinger circling his big cock quite forcefully, thus making every touch on the tip of his cock feel even more intensely pleasurable. But this trick only made Robert strain and thrust harder, seeking release. Finally, Venny had to admit defeat. She drew back.

'I think, sir,' she said throatily, pulling his hands back onto her breasts and encouraging him to knead them while he gazed down at them lasciviously, 'that I had better accommodate you some other way. I think your arousal would be better served if I allowed you to put your beautiful cock into my cunt. I'm very ready, I assure you. Hot and wet enough to give you very great pleasure.'

'Right up?' asked Robert gruffly. 'You won't make me pull out? You'll let me thrust, you'll let me come?'

'I want you to come,' Venny assured him, wondering if his wife routinely objected to so massive an organ invading her. 'If sir will just lean back a little?'

This sir was more than happy to do, bracing his hands against the plush seat of the banquette while Venny kicked off her shoes and knelt upon it. Daintily she stretched a knee across Robert's naked lap and then knelt there, steadying herself with her hands on his shoulders and smiling into his wildly dilated pupils. He was sweating lightly, full of good food and ready now for good sex.

'There. All ready for you, sir,' she said sweetly.

Robert glanced down at her naked, heaving breasts, her wide-stretched legs. He moaned aloud. 'Lift up your apron,' he ordered roughly. 'I want to see it go into you.'

'Oh, sir,' said Venny with pretend coyness. 'You're so rude.'

'Do it,' husked Robert. 'I want to see me fucking you.'

As if reluctant to do so – when in fact Venny found that the act was extremely arousing – Venny lifted the little apron up to reveal her wide-spread and vulnerable centre, her swelling mound with its toffee-coloured curls, her softly curving belly above it, all naked and exposed to him just as he wanted.

'So lovely,' panted Robert, fumbling with his cock to dip its head down between her parted legs.

'If sir will allow me?' said Venny helpfully, and she pushed his hands aside and took his penis into her own hands, having to pull the head down very firmly because he was now exceedingly aroused.

Luxuriously Venny eased his prick between the moist lips of her swollen labia, enjoying the touch of its silken heat against her clit, pushing it hard up against the little bud and then on until the head was positioned ready at the entrance to her vagina. She pushed down carefully, admitting the big organ by an inch or two at first; then with extreme pleasure she pushed down a little further, until it was halfway inside her. Robert's eyes were closed in ecstasy as he leaned back against the banquette and, emboldened by his obvious delight, Venny took him in still deeper, and there was still ample cock to spare. How deep could she go with this enormous thing of his?

She wanted to find out. She pushed down even more boldly, feeling herself open ever wider to accommodate him. Her progress was gentle and steady, and finally she found that she could settle right onto the base of his shaft. Perhaps she should recommend that his wife try it on top, as she was, to facilitate entry? Because it felt wonderful, quite arousing and stimulating in fact, and as she started to move up and down on Robert Fielding's lap Venny found that his penis was causing her nothing but the most intense pleasure, touching her so deeply and setting fire to her most sensitive places.

'If sir will just put his hand there?' she gasped, guiding one big mitt to her clitoris.

Robert happily obeyed, enjoying his own passivity as she moved energetically up and down on his pole. His eyes were open now, dwelling lasciviously on her bouncing breasts and then moving lower to her wetly glistening slit to watch himself being repeatedly enveloped by its hot, velvety clasp.

Venny threw her head back in abandon as she felt the first glimmer of orgasm start to dart from her engorged nipples to her clitoris. Sensing her building excitement, Robert tightened his grip on her mound and rubbed faster at the hot bud between her legs, keeping up a rhythm that matched the one she was setting by her movements on his cock.

Sweat and love-juice melded their groins together in a heady, slippery alchemy as they lost, found, regained their mutual rhythm and finally, when it grew too intense, too much to bear, Venny cried out madly as climax after climax crashed over her.

Stimulated by her cries, Robert came too, issuing his own cries, masculine echoes of her own. His gigantic cock swelled and swelled inside her as he pushed up, desperate for release. Venny felt his cock twitch as it shed its load, and she slumped against his shoulder, spent, exhausted.

For a few moments there was only the soft beat of the music, and the steadying thuds of both their hearts.

'Well,' said Robert finally, just a little hoarse from his exertions, 'that was most satisfactory, Miss Halliday.'

'I'm so pleased you liked it, sir,' said Venny, with a smile. Ha! she thought vengefully. Just let Micky Quinn try and compete with *that*.

Micky moved quietly back from the circular window in the swing door that led into the restaurant. He wasn't quite sure what he felt about what he had just witnessed. Angry, he supposed – angry that she seemed to have gotten over him so thoroughly, and so quickly too. And aroused. Fiercely and desperately aroused by the spectacle he had seen, by the huge dimensions of the man at the table, by the way she had serviced him, her tits bouncing crazily, her orgasm – if he was any judge, and he thought he was where Venny was concerned – perfectly genuine. His own cock was up and full in sympathy for the man's arousal. And maybe he felt a bit – just a teensy bit – jealous?

No. He was never jealous.

Was he?

'I really shouldn't have let you in here, you know,' hissed Kate, who was waiting for him by the back door that led out into the yard behind the kitchens. 'Venny'd have a fit if she knew you were here. Come to that, she'd blow her stack if she thought *I* was still here too. What she does with the customers is her own affair, Micky.' Kate's tone became petulant. 'Anyway, I had things to do tonight. Jez was going to meet me here.'

'Well, he hasn't shown up, has he?' Micky pointed

out in a whisper, moving away from the tempting, tormenting scene in the restaurant and going over to where the waitress stood.

'Look, that isn't the point,' pouted Kate. 'I shouldn't have let you talk me into any of this. You shouldn't even have come here. And when Venny came in here to strip off, we shouldn't have hid in the larder and – and spied on her like that.'

'Look, guilty on all damned counts, all right?' snapped Micky with an ill temper that was quite unlike him.

Kate was absolutely right. He had come here to see Venny, to rebuild broken bridges, hopefully to restart their affair. After all, they might be rivals now, but they could still be lovers. And what had he found? That she was busy seducing a judge for the Blue Ribbon awards, busy pushing her business forwards, and quite clearly she had forgotten about him already. She had even got a new chef already – some Swiss control freak called Anton, according to Kate, who had hung a bloody cuckoo clock on the wall over the door and who did everything by the clock and by the book. Hell, the guy himself sounded cuckoo. But Kate said he was a good chef – if a little unimaginative.

Micky felt the pressure of anger and sexual frustration building up such a head of steam in him that he felt he might very well burst. God, he needed a shag. He looked at Kate, who had obviously been stood up. She was a good-looking girl, with straight blonde hair cut in a bob, a petite fair-skinned body and snappish blue eyes.

They were snappish now, certainly. Well, he supposed her loyalty to Venny was to be commended.

His eyes dropped to the front of her red T-shirt, under which she was very obviously not wearing a bra. Her nipples stuck out proudly, so Micky could tell that what had gone on tonight had aroused her too. She was looking back at him now, little tight-arsed and small-breasted Kate, and the look was speculative and overtly sexual. Well, why not? he thought to himself. One woman was much like another. All cats, after all, were grey in the dark, and all cunts were wet and warm.

'We may as well get out of here,' he said quietly, but their eyes were exchanging other messages now. Kate quickly passed her tongue over her lips as she stared at him. She turned and Micky followed her on tiptoe to the door. With extreme care Kate let them out into the yard and hot summer night, then as quietly as possible locked the door behind them. She dropped her key back into her bag, then turned and was suddenly in Micky's arms being shoved up against the restaurant wall, his mouth hotly welded to hers, his hands roaming her body in a frenzy of lust.

'Steady, lover,' she chuckled breathlessly when she could get her mouth free. She reached down to his jeans and unzipped him; Micky's naked cock sprang out like a siege weapon, ready and armed. Kate gave it a salutary rub with both hands, and Micky cursed, his face screwing up with his hunger for her. She ran a finger over his cock-head, and felt him creaming and ready for her. Quite a compliment, she thought. And ignored the fact that it was Venny who had aroused him so violently.

Micky slipped his hands under her thighs and lifted her up against the wall, spreading her legs so that they surrounded his waist. Pants! he thought in irritation. Here he was ready to roll and she was wearing pants.

Micky ripped them away. The sheer fabric tore loudly, and Kate let out a squeak of protest, which Micky ignored. Ramming his cock up between her soaking sex-lips, he found the opening he wanted and pushed hard, entering her in one heavy thrust. Kate cried out and her legs jerked around him. Micky put a hand over her mouth to keep her quiet.

'Creamy delicious little bitch,' he whispered against her ear, and thrust into her hot and hard, ramming his cock home time after time, relishing the slurping sounds that her dripping sex made as he had her. It was true, after all. Women were all alike. But it was the image of Venny, naked and glorious as she paved her way to first prize in the Blue Ribbon awards by so sweetly fucking one of the judges, which floated in his brain as he shut his eyes and sought his orgasm. And when he came, in three short, hard jolts of sensation that seemed to come from his thighs, his scrotum, his arse and his prick all in one delectable moment of time, he had to bite Kate's neck quite hard to stop himself from calling out another woman's name.

Chapter Twelve

Next morning, Venny came into work early. She told herself that everything was going just fine and that she did not feel even a tiny bit down. She had laid the foundations for success in the Blue Ribbon competition by obliging Robert Fielding last night; she was just about to catch up on all her paperwork before the staff arrived, and she relished the unusual peace of the place; she had a good chef – oh, all right, he was unimaginative, some might even say a bit pedantic, and he'd hung a cuckoo clock in the kitchen, for God's sake; what the hell was that all about? But he was good; and the troublesome Micky Quinn was out of her life. This was, she assured herself, a plus.

Now there were no tantrums over organic fruit and vegetables. Anton didn't care if the produce was coated in every pesticide known to mankind or even if it was radioactive, so long as it wasn't actually rotten. Although the staff did whinge a bit about Anton doing everything by the clock, and being a humourless bastard, and although the kitchens did seem very quiet, even subdued, since Micky's departure, nevertheless Venny was moderately pleased with her new chef. Box of Delights' warm ambience, her spadework and Anton's perfectly competent cooking would combine to win the Blue Ribbon. She just knew it.

She was engrossed in feeding figures into the Sage program on her computer when she heard a clatter downstairs. Someone else was obviously in early. Or were they? She paused and looked thoughtfully out between the slatted blinds on the window at the bright new day. It was just that she'd had the oddest feeling last night when she was with Robert Fielding, almost as if she were being watched. Strange things did happen. Someone could have got hold of Neil's spare key, or Kate's, and made a copy. She hadn't reset the alarm system after she'd come in, so it was entirely possible that some unauthorised person could have used a key to gain entry downstairs. Or maybe they had forced their way in, broken the lock, who knew?

Venny picked up her pretty but very substantial St Louis floral paperweight and hefted it in her hand as she rose from her chair. Carefully she crossed the room, trying not to make the boards creak too much. She passed by the open door to what had been Micky's room. It was empty now. Anton had his own loft apartment across the city, and she was glad about that. She didn't want another man under her roof – or under her skin.

Stealthily she went downstairs. At the padded

burgundy door she paused, frowning, listening intently. Her own heartbeat was the loudest thing she could hear now. She pushed the door open, just a little.

It was Anton.

He was setting out pots and pans, pausing occasionally to consult a well-thumbed book which lay open on the counter. Venny let out her breath and relaxed. Knowing he hadn't heard her approach, she took a little while to study him. Actually, she thought after several minutes' consideration, he was pretty damned good-looking. He was about five feet eleven, but looked taller because he always wore the full chef's regalia while he worked, and that included not only chef's whites but also the chef's high traditional hat, the toque. He was solidly built, neither running to fat nor too muscular. His thick mat of pale blond hair was cut close to his well-shaped head, but small curls peeped out from beneath the toque. He had a moustache – which was also blond – like a dedicated follower of fashion fresh from the Seventies. His brown eyes were intense and rarely sparkled with any sort of humour, but their very intensity was attractive. Hm, she thought. There was a lot of the stern disciplinarian about Anton; and that was an attractive trait to a lot of women – including her.

Venny pushed wide the door and walked into the bright strip-lit kitchens. She put the paperweight down on a table. 'Hi, Anton,' she said casually, because he couldn't know that she had been eyeballing him with extreme sexual curiosity for some time. 'What's on for lunch today?'

Anton turned and gave her a formal half-bow. He was so quaint, she thought. But nice.

'Good morning, Venetia,' said Anton cordially. Damn! thought Venny. Why the hell did he always insist on calling her by her full name? And what jerk had told him her full name? She hated the thing. She felt her warm smile cool a little as he spoke.

'I am going to concoct a fondue,' said Anton, showing her the incomprehensible but excessively neat jottings in the book. Neat was the word that defined Anton, she thought. He was probably an anal retentive. 'Also some rosti with a pepper sauce, yes? And of course the sachertorte, very rich, very chocolatey.'

'Sounds good,' said Venny encouragingly. She liked his accented English. It was sexy. She glanced over his shoulder as the cuckoo clock over the back door chimed out. The cuckoo, painted in garish colours that no real cuckoo had ever flaunted, shot out and chirruped. There were two chains hanging down below the ghastly contraption, and big lead weights shaped like fir cones dangled at the end of each chain. Maybe this gross little item reminded him of home in the Alps, she thought. It must have some sentimental value, surely, because it certainly was not a thing of beauty.

'Perhaps you can help me?' Anton was asking.

Venny's attention snapped back to him. 'What? Well, I don't cook.' She smiled. 'House rule. The boss doesn't have to cook if she doesn't want to. And I never want to.'

'But this is such a shame,' said Anton as if her words

were the cause of deep dismay. He went over to the cuckoo clock, stood on a chair, and made some sort of adjustment to it. Then he came back to her. 'Come, help me here, Venetia.'

'Please call me Venny,' she said with desperation, but she knew he wouldn't. She'd said the same thing before, half a dozen times; the man was just so formal that he had to use one's full name. Anything less probably seemed like sacrilege to him.

Anton nodded; but he didn't call her Venny. Sighing inwardly and feeling that a wicked twinkle in the eye and a broad grin would be a pretty welcome sight right now, Venny approached and stood facing the worktop. There were weird-looking nobbly little potatoes laid out ready for peeling. I don't believe this, she thought. This guy is going to get me peeling potatoes. At least Micky had never done that. Not that she missed him being here – no way. She picked up the scraper, stifling another sigh. Well, let's get it over with, she thought glumly.

'Now you hold the scraper like so,' said Anton, coming up close behind her and putting his arms around her like a golf pro showing an amateur how to hold the club.

Venny stiffened in surprise. His hot male body was pressed up tight against her buttocks. And was that a rolling pin in his pocket, or was he rather more pleased to see her than she had anticipated? He picked up the scraper and showed her how to scrape away the skins from the potatoes. 'These are Pink Fir Apple,' said

Anton right beside her ear. His breath tickled her lobe almost unbearably. She could smell that he was very clean – no surprises there. The sweet odours of soap and cologne drifted around him.

'Oh,' she said, not very intelligently. She was more interested in that rolling pin. She discreetly wriggled her arse back just a little and came to the conclusion that this was not a rolling pin, but a very erect penis.

'You like that, yes?' asked Anton, scraping away at the potatoes while his pole-like cock moved against her buttocks. 'My penis, yes?'

Goodness, thought Venny. Maybe not so anally retentive as she'd thought, after all. 'Your penis, yes,' she echoed faintly, swallowing convulsively as the manic desire to laugh gripped her.

'Good. You try now. Hold it tight.' He handed her the scraper, lying his large blond-furred hands on her forearms to guide her. Oh, well, thought Venny, and started scraping. She would much rather hold his cock tight, but she was humouring him here.

'No, no!' burst out Anton suddenly. 'You are scraping too deep. Wasting too much potato, yes?'

'Yes,' allowed Venny. So what? she thought acidly. Hardly a hanging offence, was it? Hardly a matter for judge and jury.

'I think you are a very bad girl,' Anton scolded her in his sexily accented English.

'Guess so,' said Venny lightly.

'Bad girls have to be punished, yes?' Anton's warm

body drew away from the back of hers. 'Now you pull down your pants, Venetia, and I will punish you.'

Wow! Not anal retentive at all. By this time she was starting to get quite seriously aroused. She wished he'd put his body back against hers, but she felt very stimulated by his unexpected request and more than happy to play along.

'I'm not wearing pants,' said Venny breathlessly.

'But such behaviour is shameless,' said Anton, looking genuinely scandalised. 'You will prove this. Lift your skirt. Show me.'

With *a frisson* of pleasure Venny complied, lifting her suit skirt very slowly, so that he first appreciated her lace-topped hold-up stockings, and the fine contrast between the tan of the thin nylon mesh and her own much paler, finer skin. Her well-shaped thighs had the translucent sheen of silk pulled tight over a pad of the finest down. She heard Anton catch his breath in appreciation. Then she proceeded until the lower swell of her arse became visible to him. Proceeding further, and leaning forwards against the worktop as she did so, she slowly bared her bumslit to him. At last she held her skirt up around her waist so that the whole of her delectable buttocks were exposed. Feeling extremely turned on at the thought of him watching from right behind her, she gave her naked bottom a little wiggle, teasing him with it.

'Ach!' said Anton. 'Such a very bad girl.'

To Venny's surprise, a stinging slap was administered to her private parts. She squealed in pain, and the tender skin of her arse throbbed hotly. Venny glanced over her shoulder and saw that Anton had taken up an icing ruler; it was obviously this that had been whacked across her buttocks. She could see the outline of his aroused penis even more clearly now, rearing up underneath his chef's whites, and he was breathing hard. He looked up at the clock. Venny looked up at it, too, in curiosity, while wincing a little from the stinging pain Anton had inflicted on her. The clock chimed as another minute passed, and out popped the cuckoo with a chirrup.

Smack.

Venny let out a cry as pleasure and pain warred within her. Oh, that icing ruler hurt. It really hurt. And yet at the same time, standing here half-naked before an aroused man while he slapped her backside was wildly exhilarating, hugely exciting. Her nipples were suddenly standing starkly to attention. She craned her head around and saw that he was watching the clock again. The seconds were ticking swiftly by. Venny watched the clock too; and then there came the chime, the cuckoo's ghastly call, and she was slapped again, whacked right across her tender butt with the icing ruler. She groaned.

'Ah, that hurts you, yes?' Anton crowed. 'And so it should, such a wicked girl you are. No pants – and wasting the potatoes.'

'I'm sorry,' gasped Venny, joining in the fun. 'I'll try to be good, Anton.'

But he was clock-watching again. Venny's nerves tingled enjoyably as she too looked at that monstrosity he'd hung on the wall. She wondered vaguely if she was going to be phobic about horology for the rest of her days, after this. Suddenly, another minute was up. The second hand seemed to be whizzing around the dial now, unstoppable. The thing chimed. The cuckoo squeaked. Anton's arm swung, and Venny let out a shout of pain. Her buttocks seemed so hot that she felt they must almost be glowing. She glanced back, and down. They were very pink, but no welts had been raised. He was perhaps being careful with her. She looked at Anton. He had paused in lambasting her, and while the icing ruler hung in one fist, his other hand rubbed busily against the hard outline of his erection.

And oh, the clock was still ticking, those seconds were racing by like a whirlwind.

Again, the cuckoo cried out.

So did Venny as the ruler hit her backside again.

It was almost too much for her now. Her buttocks felt quite sore. Also, her slit felt very damp. She was sure that he must be able to see the snail-trail of desire that was wetting her thighs with juice now. As if to confirm this, she felt Anton's hand touching her lust-swollen crotch. He spread his fingers and by so doing pushed the cheeks of her arse open wide. Leaning over the worktop and breathing heavily, Venny imagined the picture she was presenting to her sadistic employee. She could feel her anus clenching, puckering with excitement; her labia were hopelessly soaked and swollen; her clit was leaping and twitching hungrily beneath its concealing hood; and her cunt felt so empty, so juicy, so unbearably open that she felt he must be able to see right up inside her. Of course he couldn't, but it certainly felt like that.

The cuckoo clamoured again, and she tensed in anticipation of the blow, her hands clenching into fists on the worktop, her nails digging into her palms. Her teeth caught her lower lip almost hard enough to draw blood.

But the blow never came. Instead Anton was moving around the worktops again – no doubt fetching some new instrument of torture to torment her. With a groan of acute arousal, Venny felt the pressure of his body hard against her own once more, his still-clothed cock pressing desperately against her, and then his fingers were delving down between her legs, pushing them wider, inserting something – please, let it be his penis soon! she thought – into the wide-open depths of her wet vagina.

It wasn't his penis. Venny felt a weird fizzing sensation in her pussy and straightened in alarm. What was he doing to her now? But Anton kept her pinned there against the worktop with his body when she would have squirmed upright. And as the seconds passed, and the damned cuckoo let out its ugly squawk again, she began to feel that the fizzing was in fact very pleasurable. It tickled and teased at her soft inner surfaces; she felt more wetness trickling from her as her body responded to the stimulation.

'What?' she gasped out.

'Alka Seltzer,' said Anton beside her ear. 'Feels good, yes?'

'Yes,' groaned Venny as Anton's mobile fingers

started making incursions into other more forbidden places. One finger wriggled inside her anus, and then another pushed a tablet up there too. Again, there was that unbearably arousing sensation, like champagne shooting from a bottle after it had been vigorously shaken, like cascades of foam frothing around her most secret parts and tickling them with an intensity that made her wince and cry out. Her heart seemed to be beating its way right out of her chest, and her nipples felt as hard as bottle tops. Moisture flooded her now.

'Ah, now you are ready, yes?' asked Anton.

Too ready, thought Venny, thinking that orgasm was only a heartbeat away. Furiously she pressed herself against the edge of the worktop, seeking relief.

'Yes, ready,' Anton noted, and it was as if she were a recipe he had whipped up and was now ready to taste for seasoning. She felt him fumbling with his trousers beneath his chef's whites, and pushed back with even more desperation than she had just a second ago been pushing forwards.

'Steady, *liebling*,' breathed Anton, and now, at last, the blunt head of his penis was presented at the foaming gate of her cunt. Venny let out an involuntary cry and pushed herself down onto it. Anton slipped easily into her, pressing forwards until his delightfully full organ was lodged deep inside her.

'Now we thrust, yes?' he said.

Get on with it! thought Venny desperately. Yes, thrust!

But he paused.

He paused until the cuckoo emerged from its hiding-place and squawked. And then he slipped his penis back out of her, almost until he was dislodged from her but not quite; he paused again, waiting, waiting.

Waiting for the clock.

Venny leaned against the worktop in a groaning heap of hopeless arousal, listening to the unbearable tick-tock of the infernal thing until the cuckoo was catapulted from its nest once again. And at that instant Anton's penis surged back up into her so suddenly, so violently, that her breath was expelled on a gasp.

'Bastard,' she said weakly. 'Oh, you bastard.'

'Ha! Such a very bad girl you are.' Anton was clearly enjoying himself hugely. Huge was a good word for it. His cock was long and full and hot, and Venny wanted more of it, far more, right now.

But again he was watching the clock. Finally, the cuckoo sang its ghastly song. Anton withdrew, almost completely. Then the waiting, the terrible waiting, and the cuckoo singing again, and then the violent, delicious, longed-for thrust of his hips and the glorious feeling of his fullness deep inside her.

'Ha, now we are cooking on gas, yes, *liebling*?' chuckled Anton.

'Yes,' choked Venny weakly, barely able to utter over the tumult of her pulse. Every nerve in her body was rioting now, anticipating pleasure upon pleasure until she could stand no more. 'Ah!' she squealed as he withdrew. 'Oh!' she moaned as he plunged back in up to the hilt, ramming the base of his shaft right up against her so that she felt his crinkly pubic hair and his engorged balls.

Anton was panting now as he laboured behind her, and she sensed that it was taking every ounce of his self-control to carry on with this. She felt him clutching at the stem of his cock to slow himself down. Even so, she knew he could not last much longer. *She* certainly couldn't, either, and she was relieved and gratified when at last Anton seemed to lose his rigidly self-imposed rhythm and give in to the animalism of the moment.

Enthusiastically now and without restraint he ignored the clock and fucked her furiously. Fizzing and throbbing and filled with cock, her clit pressed hard up against the worktop, Venny felt her orgasm begin and let out a wild cry just as Anton cried out too. Their cries mingled and echoed in the empty kitchen, and the cuckoo joined in too, as if mocking them.

Anton pumped like a maniac as he emptied his cock of seed. With no hint of his former restraint, he clasped her hips roughly and drove into her with a vengeance while she throbbed and clutched and cried in the throes of her pleasure.

At last, they were still. After a few moments to compose himself, Anton slipped his penis out of her wet depths. It came free with a resounding slurp. Venny turned a little, still breathless and weak in the knees, and saw him drop his apron back over his still upright pink penis. It glistened with her juices. She was quite sorry to see it vanish beneath his apron.

'You liked that, yes?' panted Anton, smiling at her.

'Um, yes.' Venny put a hand to her hair, then realised her skirt was still up around her waist and that he was eyeing her exposed pubes as if considering another bout. She wasn't sure her bottom could take the strain. Hurriedly, she pushed her skirt back into place. Her abused buttocks throbbed and burned, and she was still fizzing away like a drunk's morning-after cure down there. She needed a shower, she thought. She was sweaty and wet and she smelled very strongly of sex.

'I'm popping back home for an hour or so,' said Venny, managing to straighten without wincing. Slowly, her heartbeat was getting back to normal. 'I need a shower after that'

'I will take care of everything here,' Anton assured her.

I just bet you will, thought Venny, watching him as he went to readjust the mechanism on the cuckoo clock. His cock was still tenting the front of his apron; he hadn't yet put it back inside his trousers. She felt her cunt throb briefly at that thought. Now, whoa there, girl, she thought. After all, she thought as she went to get her bag from upstairs, she was going home to shower – to wash the scent of Anton's sex off her body. And it did occur to her, briefly and annoyingly, that if that had been *Micky's* come now leaking out of her and wetting the tops of her stockings, she would have let it dry on her skin, and relished the smell of it throughout the long, hot day.

Chapter Thirteen

It seemed like the worst kind of coincidence – or maybe it was just fate – but when she got back to the apartment by the lock, there was a man stepping into the elevator just in front of her. Venny felt a rush of nervous perspiration spring up on her brow. Her nipples swelled and rose to hardness. Her clit twitched. Oh, God; oh, God. It was him. The spiky dark hair, the slouch suit cut loosely to hang from the broad shoulders and so accentuate them. Micky turned and his eyes swept over her at first without recognition; then his mouth curved up in a swift smile, and the blue eyes twinkled at her just as boldly, as intimately, as they had ever done.

'Um – what are you doing here?' she asked him as he pressed the button for her floor and hauled the clanking wrought-iron safety cage closed behind them. Venny leaned back against the wall just as far away from him as she could get. By so doing, she pressed her sore buttocks back against the hard interior surface of the lift, and started forwards in a hurry, only just managing to stifle a yelp of pain.

Micky was watching her curiously. She felt at a distinct disadvantage here. He looked so cool and collected, and she was frankly ruffled, and wet from sex, and his well-trained chef's nose was so sharp that she was sure he could smell it on her.

'Just visiting Caspar,' said Micky casually. 'My brother, if you remember.'

'Of course I remember,' snapped Venny.

'Actually, I'm glad I've run into you,' said Micky thoughtfully, coming closer.

'Actually,' said Venny sarcastically, 'you did run into me. With your car. If you remember. And you haven't paid me yet.'

'I'll put a cheque through the door today,' said Micky. 'Good.'

'But there was something else I wanted to say to you.'

Why was this damned lift so slow? wondered Venny irritably. Being true to the character and atmosphere of the building was all very well, but would a good modern high-speed lift really have been such a bad thing when they renovated the place?

And it wasn't only the slowness of the thing. Venny couldn't help remembering that the last time they had been in this lift alone together, she'd been as good as naked apart from a belt or two and he had been giving her a very enjoyable pussy-licking. And of course he was remembering that too. She could see it in his eyes.

'Right, go on, then,' she said, folding her arms and

instantly hating herself for the unconscious gesture. It made her look defensive, as if she were under attack. She unfolded them quickly.

'What I wanted to say was this.' Micky had walked forwards, hands in trouser pockets, until he stood right in front of her. A whiff of his cologne and the musk scent of his skin teased at her nostrils and she almost moaned aloud with suppressed longing. Micky's blue eyes had lost their laughter and were deadly serious now. 'Venny, I shouldn't have done what I did. I shouldn't have got Caspar to help me tap into your private files. I should have realised how offended you'd be by that. All I can say is that I did it because I was desperate to know you better. You are a very self-contained woman, and I found your reserve frustrating, so I cracked and hacked in. It wasn't done out of any sort of malice. It was just to get closer to you. The irony is, by trying to get closer to you I drove you away, didn't I? Well, I'm sorry. That's all.'

'Is that it?' asked Venny faintly. He was apologising! Well, miracles would never cease.

'No. It isn't.' Micky drew closer, placing a hand on either side of her head. His breath tickled her face now. And she had retreated to the lift wall again, and her buttocks were smarting horribly. 'The Blue Ribbon awards, Venny. Beurre Blanc's doing fine, and I hear you've got a good chef now, so Box of Delights is in with a good chance too?'

Venny nodded cautiously.

'Well, I'm pleased for you. Really.'

He really did look as if he meant it. Venny suddenly felt like a complete heel, because he had sold the hut in Whitstable, his precious hut, to fund his restaurant, and if she hadn't been so bloody awkward he would still have it, plus a partnership with her. This was a very generous gesture he was making, and she didn't deserve it, because she hadn't been generous with him, not at all.

'I don't see why this should come between us,' said Micky, gazing deep into her troubled green eyes. 'The best man or woman will win, whether we fight or not. Agreed?'

'I suppose so,' said Venny guardedly, thinking of Robert Fielding the judge, and the rather special treatment he had received at her hands the other night. Micky, of course, didn't know about that. And she certainly wasn't going to tell him. The Blue Ribbon was as good as hers, but if Micky wanted to feel he was in with a chance too, who was she to tell him otherwise? She hoped he'd be runner-up, at least. He deserved that, if he couldn't be the winner; and he would still get a huge amount of publicity from second place, enough to fill his restaurant for months on end, get him a column in one of the food magazines, perhaps even – who knew? – secure him a television deal. He had the sort of quirky ebullience and self-assurance that television producers seemed to like.

'So can we let the whole thing go now? Put it down to a misunderstanding and be pals again?' asked Micky hopefully.

Venny stared at his face. And oh, it was true, she'd missed him and she wanted him back in her life.

'Why not?' she said at last. Grinning happily, she surged forwards to kiss him. Micky's hands went straight to her ass and pulled her in tight against his burgeoning erection, and Venny let out a squawk of pain.

'Poor sore baby,' said Micky ten minutes later as they tumbled onto her bed together. He was touchingly careful not to tumble on top of her and so exacerbate her discomfort, Venny noticed. Oh, he was sweet.

But how could she explain her sore arse away?

'Are you going to tell me how you hurt it?' Micky asked, nuzzling luxuriously at her neck, sending bolts of pleasure zipping around her body like wildfire.

Venny thought hard for a few minutes. 'No,' she said finally, smiling into his eyes.

'Aha,' said Micky, returning her smile and running a hand up under her skirt to where her lace-trimmed hold-up stockings curved around the soft flesh of her inner thighs. 'Then I'm just going to have to play detective, Venny darling, and find out for myself. Let me see now.'

Micky's hand burrowed warmly between her legs. Venny gasped aloud with delight as his fingers whispered over her pubic hair, then found the sticky moistness she had come home to wash away. To her embarrassment, Micky quickly snaked down her body, lifting her skirt to bare herself to his curious gaze. His fingers splayed open, parting the lips of her sex. He sniffed.

'Oh, I see,' he murmured, dropping a featherlight kiss onto her crinkly toffee-coloured hair. 'Turn over, Venny.'

Lazily Venny rolled, and again he pushed her skirt up. This time he peered closely at her naked buttocks. If she glanced sideways – she did so now, surreptitiously – she could see him in the mirror, staring at the lush roundness of her arse, which was so pink from Anton's beating that it almost seemed to glow in the subdued light of the bedroom.

'Mm, I see,' he said again, softly. 'He's good, then, this new chef of yours?' he inquired.

'Well up to standard,' mumbled Venny against the pillows.

'Well up, anyway,' drawled Micky, kissing the alluring dip at the base of her spine. 'He's been up you, Venny, and today. You liked it?'

'Mm,' admitted Venny. She'd loved it, and she saw no need to deny the fact, either. After all, it was chiefly Micky's arrival in her life which had opened her up to new experiences; she felt he would understand her need to satisfy her awakening appetites. Anton had been a revelation, whether he was a control freak or not. She was a control freak herself, most of the time. She saw nothing wrong with that.

'I'm not going to apologise,' Venny warned.

'Did I ask you to?' queried Micky.

'Some men might expect it,' she shrugged.

'I don't.' Micky eased himself up off the bed. Venny scrambled up onto her elbows, wondering where he was going. Had he changed his mind now? Was he jealous, possessive, boring as most men were about their women? She looked at him anxiously.

'I'm just going to the kitchen. You need something to ease your poor little arse,' he said with a smile. His eyes glittered. 'Get naked, Venny. I'll be back in a second.'

He went out, and presently she heard him rummaging about in the kitchen. What was he after out there? Shrugging, she took off her suit jacket; her breasts swung loose and naked. Straining back, she undid the zip on her skirt and wriggled out of it. She kicked both garments onto the floor. Then she slid down the lacy hold-up stockings and tossed those too to one side. She sat up, wincing, naked now, arms clasped around knees, and awaited Micky's return.

She didn't have long to wait. Micky came back in, closing the bedroom door behind him. He placed a towel and a bottle containing some greenish liquid on the table by the bed, and took off his jacket to reveal a cream silk Cossack-buttoned shirt underneath it. He rolled up the voluminous sleeves of the shirt above his elbows.

'Perhaps I should shower first?' asked Venny worriedly. She was sure no man would appreciate smelling another man's come on the woman he was about to seduce. Or was he going to seduce her? She looked at the bottle. It was extra virgin olive oil, from Dani's comprehensive store cupboard. Dani dashed it over stuffed roasted purple peppers when they were hot from the oven, or used fresh crusty bread to mop it up from a saucer. Venny almost laughed aloud. Perhaps he was irritated by her antics with Anton, after all. Perhaps he was going to baste her arse like a joint of meat, and attempt to stick it in the oven to cook.

'Come on, roll over on your belly,' said Micky, taking up the bottle and unscrewing the cap. Venny obediently bounced herself over onto her front, aware that her breasts swung outrageously as she did so, aware too that the erection which was so well hidden by the generous cut of his trousers was still there, faintly outlined. She heard the harsh intake of his breath as he looked at her tits, and again as her high-coloured buttocks were presented to him.

He wants me, she thought. He wants me desperately. And secretly she pressed her sex a little harder into the softness of the mattress, relishing the sensation of pressure it brought her. She felt the slight chill of the oil flow onto the dip at the base of her spine. A little gasp escaped her. The oil flowed between her bumcrack and down either side of her waist, wetting the sheet beneath her just a little. Then Micky's hands skimmed over her skin, following the path the oil had taken. Into her slit, then back out and up to her waist, then down one side of it, and back and over to the other side of it; then again his hands slipped into her slit, and back again to her waist. Venny gasped and writhed as his hands delved between her legs, then bit her lip with frustration as they left her and caressed her waist instead.

Then, when she was just about to protest at this

torture, Micky poured more oil from the bottle. It rolled glutinously over her hips and again into her already very moist slit, and then his hands very gently began to massage the olive oil into her bruised buttocks.

A lush scent rose from the oil as it was warmed by the friction of his hands; it was the scent of olive groves on baked Mediterranean hillsides, of the crushed fruit as the presses went to work on the precious little juice-packed orbs.

Micky's hands moved over her tender buttocks with a smooth but not overly gentle action. He knew, of course, that this caused her a slight degree of pain, but Micky knew all too well that a little pain is an aphrodisiac when combined with a great deal of pleasure.

'Good?' he murmured, dropping a kiss on the lower slope of her back.

'Mm,' said Venny dreamily, feeling that her whole lower body was suffused with heat and hunger. In the mirror she saw him take up the towel and wipe his hands briefly; then he unbuttoned the neck of his shirt, tugged it out of the waistband of his trousers, and in one swift, graceful movement pulled it up and over his head. He tossed it aside. His torso was tanned from the English summer sun, from Sundays in the park and naps on Caspar and Flora's balcony. Venny stared at him in frank admiration. He was so lean, so toned. The curtains were still pulled over in the bedroom and the sun's vivid light was softened and diffused by their dark red fabric.

Caspar and Flora, thought Venny.

'Are they expecting you next door?' she asked him, as he tipped more oil into his hand.

'No. I was just dropping in,' said Micky. He grinned to himself. 'They were probably in bed anyway. That's where they seem to spend most of their time, these days. Dani's worked wonders with their lovelife, I can tell you.'

'Good old Dani,' said Venny lazily.

'Caspar thinks she should take up couple counselling. Sex therapy.'

'She'd be good at that,' admitted Venny, thinking of Dani stark naked but for a few body piercings and a cowgirl hat, counselling nude couples while refereeing their lovemaking and joining in with her usual enthusiasm. 'She'd enjoy it, too. Oh, that's so good.'

Micky's hands strayed from her buttocks into her wet cleft again, anointing her with the oil until she really couldn't tell where her own wetness ended and the oil began. His fingers slid lower, bypassing the achingly open mouth of her pussy to dip between the swollen lips and brush tantalisingly over her overexcited little clitoris. It twitched and strained hungrily with every sweeping pass he made. Venny groaned.

'Oh,' she gasped, and then her legs stiffened, her toes digging into the mattress, her fingers clenching and bunching up the soft Egyptian cotton as orgasm gripped her. 'Oh!' she cried out, as Micky's fingers rubbed even harder and the delicious throbbings became almost completely overwhelming. She shuddered and clung to the bed as the last luscious quiver died away.

'Good?' asked Micky.

'Oh,' gasped Venny, and heard him chuckle.

'Turn over now,' ordered Micky. Feeling almost boneless with satiation, Venny rolled over and lay there like a landed fish, gazing up at Micky as he applied the towel to his hands once again. When they were free of oil, he unfastened the waistband of his trousers and unzipped himself. His erect penis sprang out of the opening like a cosh, and Venny stared at it, feeling, incredibly, that she was ready for more from him, as much as he wanted to give.

Micky was kicking off socks and shoes and squirming out of his trousers as he knelt up on the bed between her wide-open thighs. When he was finally stripped, he took up the bottle of oil again. Holding the base of the shaft of his big cock with one hand so that the skin was pulled right back, he dribbled a little of the oil onto its pink and quivering head.

Venny watched as Micky caught his breath. She could imagine how that must feel, the cool of the oil on the hot tip of his penis. With admirable control Micky placed the bottle on the table once more, and then softly ran a fingertip across the opening slit in his glans, rubbing the olive oil into it; then he swirled the oil all around the tip with hypnotically slow movements. His breathing was quickening, Venny noticed, as he caressed himself. Then he took the shaft of his penis between the thumb and forefinger of one hand while holding the skin back at the base with the other. With a hard upthrust of his hips, he smoothed the oil all the way down the shaft, then released the base and rubbed upwards, taking the foreskin up and over his ultrasensitive glans as his hand slipped over the tip. Then he pulled down, tugging the skin furiously back against the crinkling black hair and the bulbous hardness of his balls.

'Is that good?' murmured Venny, enjoying the show enormously.

'Lovely,' sighed Micky, as he continued to masturbate between her open legs. He was panting now, very near to losing control. The movements of his hand were becoming a blur of speed. Venny felt her own sex heat and twitch with the excitement of watching him pleasure himself.

Finally he could take no more; but to Venny's surprise, instead of bringing himself off in a jolting fountain of come, Micky moved quickly closer between her thighs, pulling her legs up and over his shoulders. She gasped a little in surprise, but couldn't pretend that she wasn't ready. Her nipples were almost as red as Dani's in the scarlet-toned light of the bedroom, and Micky could see how swollen and hard they were. When Micky started to penetrate her, she let out a little groan of pleasure. With her hips lifted high as they were and her legs up around his neck, she knew that he would be able to get into her very deeply – particularly as she was so very wet, and he was slathered in oil.

Hungrily Micky thrust his hips hard against the undercurves of her buttocks, pushing his cock deep into her. The feeling of exposure, of an almost unbearable depth of penetration, drew a startled cry from Venny, but the sensation was intensely pleasurable, not painful. She breathed again as he drew back a little, but within an instant he was pushing inside her up to his limit again.

Micky paused a moment while his cock was lodged deep inside her. When she was in this position, thought Venny, Micky's full penis felt every bit as big as Robert Fielding's big purple baton. But she wouldn't have liked to risk such deep penetration with Robert, who was a stranger and who might thrust too hard; with Micky, she felt that he would always consider her comfort and satisfaction, even at the expense of his own.

Oh, the feeling of him so deep inside her was just too delicious! As he pushed his lust-driven stalk into her again, Venny groaned with the extent of her pleasure. She tried to wriggle against him, to satisfy the building tumult of desire that was starting to flood over her; and Micky read the signs. Keeping one hand on her thigh to steady her while he was pushing in and out of her, he applied his other hand to her damp thatch of pubic hair. From there, he pushed three fingers down into her wet cleft. The tips of his fingers touched his slick cock as it pistoned in and out of her, and the fleshy pad at the base of his fingers pressed hard against her clit's little hood.

Venny lay back and just let the whole thing happen. She wished it could go on forever, this madly building climb towards an explosive ending; their mutual climax. And this time her control proved better than his. Micky came in an orgy of thrusting and grunting, pushing his cock so far into her that she felt she was going to explode. A cry that was almost a sob escaped her, the feeling was so sweet, so very intense. His pumping cock delivered its tribute of seed and he was beginning to slow down in his movements when the plateau she had been gliding along towards the goal of her second orgasm suddenly sheered away and she fell in a shower of sparkling sensations, crying out, clutching at his hips, taking him into her so crazily that she felt they might be welded together forever.

Finally Micky slipped his juice-covered and reddened cock out of her. He fell to one side of her on the bed, like a bee that had stung and then expired. He was panting in the enclosed heat of the bedroom, trying to draw breath. So was she. Her whole skin felt slick with sweat; a miasma of sexual steam hung over the bed, scenting the air with their exertions.

'Venny Halliday,' said Micky when he managed to breathe again, 'you are the best fuck in the whole of London, do you know that?' His head turned on the pillows and his eyes met hers. Their blue looked darker, almost black, in the low light.

'You too,' said Venny. Her legs felt like jelly. The muscles all along her inner thighs were shaking from the force with which he'd spread her legs. She rolled over so that her naked tits rested upon his sweat-slippery chest. Playing lazily, Venny guided one of her full teats with her hand, until their nipples kissed. She brushed her nipple, broad and swollen, against his smaller, chocolate-brown medallions of flesh, and bit her lip a little as sensitivity made her tit shiver, made her nipple tighten into a bud of lust.

'No!' laughed Micky, displacing her hand on her tit with one of his own. He weighed her fleshy globe with every appearance of enjoyment. 'No more, you crazy woman. I'm finished, I'm done. Turn over.'

She was pretty well finished herself, so Venny was happy to oblige. She turned her back to him, and still keeping his hand on her breast Micky cuddled in against her back, his whole long hard body curving in around hers, so they lay like spoons in a drawer. She sighed and felt strangely happy and content. His penis was at half-mast now, dribbling against her buttock, and Micky tucked it down between her legs.

'Comfy?' he asked, his teeth grazing the nape of her neck. His head was lying on her hair, keeping her trapped there – pleasantly trapped, she thought. Nothing she would object to.

'Yes,' she said, wriggling down against his flagging cock.

Micky chuckled. 'Go to sleep,' he murmured and, to Venny's surprise, she did.

Venny was awoken by something hard pressing against the base of her spine. Something hard, and silky, and hot. She stretched, coming out of a very pleasurable doze, and wiggled her bottom down onto the offending object. She heard a groan behind her, and a hand skimmed over her breast, the palm lightly brushing against the point of her tit until it became more pointed still. She opened her eyes, and remembered where she was, and with whom.

'Oh . . .' She yawned. 'What's the time?' The light filtering through the closed curtains looked dimmer, she thought.

She felt Micky move, straining around so that he could see the glowing numerals on her little alarm clock. 'Ten to three,' he said, and kissed her shoulder.

'Ten to *three*?' Venny sat up suddenly. 'But we've been here since half-past ten,' she complained. There were things to do. She'd abandoned her paperwork. Micky had to get back to his restaurant. Dani would be back at any minute. She was amazed that she had slept so long. She never usually slept during the day.

Guess I was just relaxed, she thought, sinking back onto the bed again. Micky was here; she was friends with him again; everything was fine.

'Tell me everything's fine,' she groaned, putting an arm over her eyes.

'Everything's fine,' said Micky obligingly. 'Let's take the rest of the day off.'

Venny took the arm away and looked up at him as he leaned over her, his upright penis nudging her hip now.

'OK. But is everything really all right? Really?' she persisted.

'We're all right again, aren't we?' said Micky reasonably.

Venny stared up at him. 'I missed you,' she said.

'Missed you, too,' said Micky with a grin. 'Particularly your lovely wet little pussy. Self-abuse is overrated as a pastime, you know.'

'I'm glad you've got your own place.' Venny thought and then added: 'I'm not glad that you're not working at my place. I mean that I'm pleased it's worked out for you. It has, hasn't it?'

Aware that until they had got this conversation out of the way, a fuck was going to be out of the question, Micky leaned back on an elbow and gazed into her eyes.

'Sure it has. We're doing up to forty covers a night, which isn't bad for a new restaurant. And the patrons seem happy – at least, they keep coming back, and they tell their friends to come, which would suggest that, don't you think?'

'Sounds good,' smiled Venny.

'The only slight problem I'm having, and it's so slight it's hardly worth a mention, is that there's been a bit of petty pilfering in the kitchens.'

'Oh?' Venny frowned. 'Like what?'

Micky shrugged and glanced off down her body. 'My blowtorch, the one I use for caramelising, has gone missing. So has one of my knives.'

'Have you told the police?'

'Nope.' Micky looked back at her concerned expression. 'Hey, don't get it out of proportion! I haven't reported it to the police because that seems like an overreaction. Two items, that's all. It's possible I might have mislaid them myself somewhere, and I don't want my perfectly good staff getting jittery by plod walking around the place in their size twelves and accusing them of pinching things.'

Venny's mouth twisted. 'I can see your point,' she admitted.

Micky glanced down with a grin. 'I can see it too,' he mocked. His voice dropped to a rough caress that shivered over her skin like the brush of cobwebs. 'The question is, what are we going to do about it?'

Venny showed him.

Chapter Fourteen

Later Venny and Micky took a walk down to the park, stopping on the way to linger over coffee in a canalside cafe. They sipped the bitter brew and chatted while they sat out on the pavement under a yellow parasol, watching others pass by.

Already, Venny was feeling very excited. After they had showered, Micky had been very insistent about what she should wear for their little outing. He selected a thin crop-cut pale blue top, and a long, loosely cut summer skirt for her. No underwear, though. Venny painted her finger and toenails a pretty frosted pink, and pulled her long heat-frizzed dark blonde hair – which was developing fetching white-blonde streaks as the sun bleached it – up on top of her head in a loose knot. She didn't bother with makeup. Her skin seemed to have an inner glow today, the glow of very satisfactory sex. Micky was wearing his loosely cut trousers and his Cossack shirt, but with the sleeves rolled up and the neck undone. His jacket he left in her bedroom.

As they walked she could feel moisture welling between her legs; and overlaying the fragrance of the light flowery perfume she wore was a deeper, meatier tang, the animal scent of her sex. Beneath her unsupported breasts she could feel a line of perspiration. Her armpits too were damp, from a mixture of excitement and heat.

In the park the sun was beating down upon people spread-eagled upon the yellow grass, hungrily soaking up the sun's welcome rays. Older people strolled and chatted. Children clustered around a parked ice-cream van, holding up their thin brown arms to the man inside.

Micky sat down on a wooden park bench beneath the shade of a tree, and when Venny would have sat down beside him he shook his head and held out a hand.

'Sit on my lap,' he said, and pulled her down, carefully rearranging her voluminous skirts around her.

A little puzzled but pleased by the intimacy of the gesture, Venny complied, and linked her arms around his neck. Micky kissed her hungrily, nipping her tongue with his teeth, slipping his own tongue into her mouth. Venny felt her senses freefall into dizzy willingness, felt her juices spurt with an answering hunger. But they were in the park, in public. People were passing by just feet away.

'No one's interested in a couple kissing in a park,' said Micky against her lips, as if he had read her mind.

'No,' she breathed, thinking that she wanted so much more than to kiss him.

'Or in a woman sitting on a man's lap,' added Micky.

'No,' agreed Venny with a quavering sigh. She could feel his hand moving beneath the enveloping folds of her skirt. She moved restlessly on his lap, and realised abruptly that what she could feel beneath her bottom was not the material of her skirt, but of his trousers. When she'd sat down, he had lifted her skirt out of the way. Feeling the powerful surge of his erection trapped beneath the fabric of his trousers but still nudging greedily at her naked pussy, Venny groaned.

'What are you doing?' she asked, feeling the surreptitious movements of his hand. Suddenly she heard the whirr of his trouser zip coming down. His hand nudged warmly at her inner thigh. So, to her intense pleasure, did his freshly released, extremely horny and totally naked penis.

'Fucking you,' murmured Micky, lifting her a little so that he could get his cock exactly where he wanted it. It pushed energetically up against her soaking slit.

'But people will see,' pointed out Venny, scandalised and delighted all at once. She looked around nervously as he tried to prod his cock into the hole that so longed for it.

'No they won't. That's why I told you to wear this skirt. It covers everything.' Micky found her and lunged upwards.

'Oh,' moaned Venny, clinging to his neck as he pushed right up inside her. The worst of it was, she couldn't react as she wanted to. She couldn't scream, or claw at him, or pump him as she desperately wanted to do. She had to sit here, outwardly decorous, just a woman sitting on her boyfriend's lap in the park, while Micky Quinn had his hugely erect cock buried right up inside her.

A couple passed by, glancing their way. 'See?' Micky said, his voice shaking a little with the effort of control. 'They don't realise we're fucking right in front of them.'

Venny looked around. She was painfully aware that under the revealingly thin top her nipples were very erect. And, like Micky, she was finding it hard not to gasp out loud or to push with her hips. He was right, though. The couple passed straight by, obviously suspecting nothing. But there was a young man with a tumble of long corn-gold hair sprawled on his back on the grass a few yards away. He wore very faded denim jeans, and he'd taken his shirt off and was using it as a pillow. His torso was very tanned and well muscled. He was watching them, using his hand to shield his eyes from the glare of the sun.

'*He* knows we're fucking,' said Venny, indicating the watching man with a nod of her head.

Micky looked over with interest at the Viking-like young man.

'So he does,' he drawled, and Venny felt appalled as he pulled down the low-cut front of her top so that one of her heavy, naked breasts spilled out. There was no one else passing for the moment, but the young man saw this unexpected treat and turned with interest towards the copulating couple under the trees, propping himself up on one elbow as he did so.

'Micky!' she complained mildly, but the glinting interest in the young man's eyes and the way that Micky was now kneading her exposed breast silenced her protests. How could she protest, really? She was loving this. She had Micky's cock up her, and another handsome man was watching her and clearly – she could tell this from the unruly bulge he sported at the crotch of his jeans – wishing he could join in the fun.

As more people approached, walking along the nearby pathway, Micky deftly popped her tit back beneath the top. The young man briefly passed a hand down to his crotch, pressing to ease the ache there, then he eagerly returned his attention to Micky and Venny.

'God, I want you to move,' panted Venny as Micky's cock twitched and swelled hectically inside her. Her juices must be wetting the front of his trousers, she thought, and didn't care. She didn't even care, right this minute, if anyone did see what they were doing. A most unVenny-like recklessness was taking her over. As the people moved on, she looked the watching blond hunk in the eye and lifted the top herself with both hands, exposing first her belly and then her weighty, big-nippled and very clearly aroused tits for the young man's inspection. She held the top above the full upper curves of her breasts and let him look. And she was delighted to see how his penis leaped and waggled at the front of his jeans. She felt wonderfully powerful as she beheld the discomfort his erection caused him.

'Oh, look,' said Micky by her ear. 'He's got a stiffy.'

'Are you surprised?' gasped Venny. 'Oh, can't you push a little?' she pleaded.

'If I push at all, I'll come,' warned Micky. He glanced down at her naked frontage. 'Your tits look pale in this light,' he noticed. 'Like big white meringues with two *marrons glacés* stuck on.'

'Good enough to eat?' teased Venny, feeling that this was delicious, but a torment too.

'Mm,' said Micky. He glanced at the watching man. 'Look. He's coming over.'

'Should I cover these up?' asked Venny, although she didn't want to. No one else but the man was close enough to see her semi-nudity now. She watched him get up, snatch up his shirt and walk towards them.

'No, don't,' said Micky. 'Let him look. It's turning me on like crazy.'

Venny was more than content to let this handsome blond Viking look at her nude breasts. As he drew closer, staring avidly at the big globes, she swung them a little, letting him see how ripe they were, how full and inviting.

'Hi,' he said huskily as he reached their bench.

Micky gave him a friendly grin. 'Hi. Want to join us?' he asked.

The young man's eyes were still glued to Venny's naked glory. Demurely, she now allowed the top to fall back into place.

'Oh wow, don't cover them up,' he said in a strong Australian accent. 'Such gorgeous titties should be on show all the time.'

'I'd get arrested,' quipped Venny, but with a quick glance to either side of them she obligingly lifted the top up above her breasts once again.

'Ha! If you did, the cops'd only fuck you in the back of their patrol car on the way down the station.'

Micky saw some more people coming along the path; so did Venny. Regretfully, she dropped the top to conceal her boobs again.

'If you stand in front of us,' suggested Micky, 'no one could see what we're doing at all.'

'Right.' The blond man, sweat from the sun's heat rolling down his hairless and muscular torso until it dampened the low-slung waistband of his jeans, moved so that he stood right in front of the entangled couple. Venny watched as if hypnotised as a bead of sweat ran slowly into his navel and then on down into the sprinkling of pale-gold hairs that feathered down under the front of his hipster jeans.

'Good, that's better,' approved Micky, allowing himself the luxury of one deep, delicious thrust up into Venny's wet depths.

'You in her?' asked the Viking interestedly.

'Mm.' Micky lifted Venny's skirt where it rested against the open front of his trousers. 'Have a look.'

As casually as if Micky had offered him a drink in a pub, the blond man leaned forwards and looked at Venny's naked thighs, resting slightly open across Micky's lap. As he peered closer, he could see the stem of Micky's cock pushing up into her slippy-wet vulva.

'She feel good?' he asked.

'Magnificent,' sighed Micky, and gave another, unstoppable thrust. Venny let out a little shriek of enjoyment.

'She looks wet,' said the Viking.

'Oh, she's wet all right. Feel.'

Eagerly the Viking reached down one big calloused hand and eased his fingers between her swollen lips.

'Juicy,' he said admiringly, dipping his fingers in her moistness and then lifting his hand to his mouth. He sucked the slickness from his fingers like a gastronome slowly relishing a superb dish. 'Nice and wet. Want to see my dangler now, girl? Only I have to tell you, it's not dangling at the moment, it's sticking up as ready for a fuck as a stallion's prick on mating day.'

'I can see it already,' said Venny, realising all at once and with a little thrill of excitement that she could. The maroon-coloured glans of his agitated cock was displaying itself just over the low waistband of his jeans. Its eye was open, and wetness oozed there. On impulse Venny darted her head forwards and stuck her tongue into the inviting little slit, returning his compliment.

'Oh, wow,' he breathed, his compact belly sinking in with the breath. With renewed eagerness he unbuttoned the fly on his jeans to give her better access to his rampant penis.

Venny gazed at the revealed column of male flesh with open admiration. The tip glowed as red as a ruby, but the shaft was quite pale – strikingly pale, like the band of white skin around his hips where he obviously wore bathing briefs. But it was pleasantly thick, and not too long for sucking. His pubic curls were white-blond, like the down on a baby's head. Enraptured, Venny set her lips to the childish curls, darting her tongue into the crinkly depths until she found the twin mounds of his balls in their protective sac of hairy skin. Sucking vigorously, she took one ball into her mouth. When the Viking gave voice to rapturous sounds and caught at her hair to keep her doing just that for as long as possible, she attended to his other ball too.

Venny then discovered that by leaning over to apply her mouth to the Viking's erect phallus, she could more thoroughly enjoy the sensation of Micky's cock, which was still lodged in her pussy. She could move more freely now, and push her hips up and down so that her juices merged with Micky's and created wet sounds of love.

Above them in the trees, birds sang; pigeons cooed and mated with flapping wings and frantic sounds. It seemed incredibly wicked but very stimulating to Venny that no one in the park knew that she was here on the bench servicing two men at once. And it was so sexy, doing this in the open air, with the breeze whispering over her face and arms and probing around her uncovered pubes.

Hungrily she fastened her lips around the hot shaft of the Viking's naked penis, sliding her head slowly up and down to stimulate him. She heard him groan, and quickly grasped the base of the big twitching organ to slow him down. Then she started the leisurely movements of her head once again, caressing his shaft with her lips, then fluttering her tongue against its heated surface in a series of butterfly caresses. The Viking threw his head back and groaned. His cock seemed to swell to new heights. Venny moved her mouth up to his come-sticky glans, enclosing the shaft with her hand so that she could continue rubbing him. Carefully she took the top of his rod into her mouth, slipping it deep but controlling the depth with her encircling hand.

Falling into a seductive rhythm on the Viking's cock, she was then able to attend to her own satisfaction, and to Micky's; she plunged her hips up and down on Micky's lap, milking his rigid penis until he quickly lost control. She felt his wild pumping inside her as his seed spurted, and she groaned with pleasure as he bit down quite hard on her shoulder to stifle his cries of delight.

The Viking was only a little way behind Micky, clutching at her head as her mouth sucked him voraciously now, urging him on towards his goal. With a wild cry that made a few heads turn across the park, the Viking came, spilling salty juices into Venny's mouth. She swallowed quickly and then, when he was done, slipped her mouth off the end of his prick and gave his glans one last hungry lick. Her head went back as she swept her tongue around her lips to savour the taste of cock. She smiled up at the panting Viking.

'Good?' she asked.

'Great,' he said, awestruck at his own unexpected luck. He glanced down at his drained and drooping penis, and as if suddenly coming back to himself, he tucked it almost pruriently back into his jeans, and buttoned them up. 'Thanks,' he said bashfully.

'That's OK,' said Venny sweetly, and Micky chuckled as the Viking quickly walked away and out of the park. Able to concentrate more fully upon her lover now, Venny put her arms around Micky's neck and kissed him warmly. The Viking's salty come was still on her lips. Micky licked them lasciviously, and their kisses deepened and grew passionate while he hardened again inside her.

This time the pleasure was Venny's; Micky was careful to caress her clit beneath the folds of her skirt with one hand while he held her up a little with the other. By doing this, he could move inside her to their mutual satisfaction, and the intensity of their orgasms shook them both.

Panting, gasping, wrapped together on the bench, a warm feeling of familiarity and closeness enveloped them both. At last Venny was able to say the words she'd been longing to say all day.

'I'm sorry you had to sell the hut,' she murmured against his spiky dark hair. 'I know how much you loved it, and I blame myself.'

Micky looked at her in surprise. 'Well, don't,' he said huskily as his cock once again diminished inside her.

'But I do,' Venny fretted.

'No really, don't.' Micky looked at her quite seriously. 'What you obviously haven't been told is that Caspar bought it off me.'

Venny drew her head back and stared at him in surprise. 'No, I didn't know that.'

'Well, he did. So I've still got the use of it more or

less whenever I want. Caspar's such a workaholic that he hardly ever goes down there.'

'Oh.' Venny smiled with relief. 'I'm so pleased.'

'Yeah, well, since we're spilling secrets, there's one I've got that might not please you. But I think it's fair you know.'

Venny nodded complacently. Nothing would seriously discountenance her at this moment. She had Micky's penis wilting inside her, his arms around her, he was back in her life and he had not lost the hut. Nothing else mattered. Well, not much else. Except of course the Blue Ribbon.

'Go ahead then,' she said jovially. 'Shock me.'

And Micky did.

'Did you realise,' said Venny to Jamie when she arrived at his studio in Shepherd's Bush two days later, 'that Dani has not only been fucking both Flora and Caspar? She's also been balling Micky.'

'What, Caspar's brother Micky? The chef with the place just round the corner from here?' Jamie looked suitably perturbed by her news.

'The very same.' Venny wondered why she felt so angry about that – and still so shocked.

She had been so shocked in fact that she had told Micky that she needed time to take his confession in, to think it over. To come to terms with it. She knew very well that Dani would fuck anything with a dick, and of course Dani had had a perfectly good excuse for muscling in on Venny's man.

'Dear heart,' she'd said to Venny when Venny confronted her with it. 'Sure I slept with Micky. Well, maybe not slept. We kept rather too busy for that, as I recall. But I thought you two had split. Correction, you *had* split. So I thought, why not? And I took advantage of the guy. What sane woman wouldn't?'

It was all very reasonable, Venny knew that. It all made perfect sense, when Dani explained it to her. And Micky had confessed, had come clean, after all. He hadn't made any sordid attempts to cover up their affair, however brief it had been. And there was always the nagging thought at the back of her brain that she had very nearly succumbed to Dani's seductive powers herself. But still, she felt betrayed. And angry. And so the very first thing she did – after she had dismissed Micky from the flat and spoken to Dani – was to phone Jamie, Dani's Glaswegian sculptor protégé, who was very possessive of Dani. She supposed she was looking for a shoulder to cry on, or maybe even just a chat with someone who would feel about the situation as she felt – betrayed, and angry.

Or at least that was how she'd felt a couple of days ago. Since then she'd cooled off a bit. Now that she stood in the middle of Jamie's midden of a studio with its weird metal mobiles hanging from the ceiling, its paint-splattered wooden floor, its stacks of oils, water-colours and bare charcoal sketches leaning against the walls, its overwhelming smells of turps and linseed oil, she was beginning to wish she'd kept her grievances to herself. But it was too late for second thoughts now.

'I knew she was playing around with other guys,' said Jamie, frowning heavily.

And girls, thought Venny, but didn't say it. She was sorry she'd come here now. It might mean more trouble with the temperamental Scot for Dani. She tried to backpedal frantically.

'Well, I suppose it's a free country,' she said lightly. 'After all, you two aren't in what you would call a committed relationship, are you? I mean, it's pretty open, wouldn't you say?'

'Not to me, it isn't,' said Jamie broodingly.

He looked pretty damned handsome when he was petulant, thought Venny. He had straight dirty-blond hair that he wore flopping over his grey eyes. He had a trim, tanned body although he wasn't particularly tall. He looked as if he had just tumbled out of the unmade bed in the corner alcove, thrown on combat trousers and an open shirt – between the sides of which she could see his very tasty torso – and answered the door to her. He looked like he should be home where his mother could keep an eye on him.

And that was the point, she supposed. Jamie was only – what? – nineteen? And when love, or something very like it, hit at that age, it hit very hard.

To distract him, she looked around the studio, slipping off her fuschia-pink cardi as she did so to reveal a paler pink shift dress beneath. She could feel his eyes following the movement, following the heavy sway of her breasts in their push-up balconette bra as her arms moved, and thought, ha! One rule for the boys and one for the girls, as usual. He could look at her tits and want to touch them, but Dani had to be virgin pure, repelling advances from other males as if her life depended on it.

'You know, you've got some very interesting work here,' she said, although if she was honest the work wasn't really to her taste. It was, frankly, weird. Otherworldly and a touch sinister. Jamie's stuff reminded her of Dali's melting clocks, of Van Gogh's madly intense use of primary colours, of that strange picture by the other chap of a crazy, screaming face. Frankly, it gave her the shivers, but she was trying to put Jamie in a good mood and repair some of the damage she'd just done, so she was prepared to apply a little bullshit, like a poultice to his wounded male pride, if it helped.

'Thanks,' he said guardedly, but his face did brighten.

She spotted a sordid-looking sink in the corner, where a kettle and several dirty chipped mugs were laid out on an old wooden draining board beside a leaking bag of sugar and a catering-sized can of instant coffee.

'Hey, I'll make us a coffee,' she offered, and headed right over there.

It certainly was a day for wishing she'd kept her mouth shut, she thought as she peered with distaste into the sink's begrimed depths. Gingerly she picked up the mugs and gave them a vigorous sluicing under the tap. In the absence of hot water, she used cold. There was no tea towel in view, so she opened the small cupboard under the sink. She found herself looking at several bottles of washing-up liquid, a single bottle of bleach, and a small diamond-gripped blowtorch. The blowtorch had MQ marked on the grip.

Venny's lips thinned as she looked at what was obviously Micky's chef's blowtorch. That would come in pretty handy for making metal mobiles, she thought. And she'd be willing to bet that Micky's knife was here too – probably being used to smear paint onto canvas, if she knew Jamie. The light-fingered little toad.

She shook the mugs out over the sink, negotiated the horrors of the semi-solidified bag of sugar and the sticky-rimmed coffee can, boiled the kettle, filled the mugs, and returned to Jamie.

He was sitting on a beanbag in the centre of the studio now, holding a poster-sized block of good quality artists' paper. He was scribbling away on the top right-hand corner of the block with a stick of charcoal.

'Thanks.' He looked up at her as she put his mug on the floor beside the beanbag. 'You know, I'd appreciate some help here,' he said.

'Help?' Venny looked puzzled. She sipped at her coffee. It was just as dire as she'd expected but, what the hell, it was coffee. And what could he mean, 'help'? The only help he needed was from a shrink, to thrash out the reasons for his obsessive personality and his kleptomania. 'Like what?' she asked cautiously.

'You know Dani's commissioned an ice sculpture from me for the Blue Ribbon awards bash next week?'

Venny nodded. Of course she knew. Dani was talking about little else at the moment. It was all the awards menus, the seating plans, the sculpture for the centrepiece, and what about the flowers? What colourway should she be going for? Blue seemed too obvious and anyway it was too awkward to get truly blue flowers in the types she wanted. How about peach? Peach and purple – or lime and purple, how about that?

Yes, Venny knew all about Dani's plans for the catering, down to the last boring detail. What with Dani's constant wittering and her own rapidly escalating nerves, she felt she knew more about the Blue Ribbon award night than she actually wanted to know, right now.

'Well, you've got a good body, haven't you? I've been looking around for suitable models for the ice sculpture. I thought an embracing couple, melting together in passion like Rodin's *Kiss* and melting together for real as the evening passes – what do you think?'

What Venny thought was that, in typical Jamie style, he was leaving it all rather late. The melting in passion bit sounded quite lyrical and poetic, for him. But then he was an artist, and she supposed all artists were a touch on the mad side, really. And she was flattered that he should ask her.

'I've got someone in mind for the male part, but I've been having trouble with the female.' Jamie looked down at his doodles, and for a moment he looked like a bashful twelve-year-old. Then he looked up at her and gave her both barrels from those cute baby-grey eyes of his. 'So would you sit for me? Today? Um – now?'

Venny shrugged and put her mug aside on a shelf. It was still half empty. 'Well, if you like,' she said.

Jamie grinned. 'Yes, please, Venny.'

'So – where do I pose?' She looked around. Every surface in the little room was covered with junk, or dirt, or both.

'On the stool there.' Jamie jumped up and dusted down the tired-looking wooden stool that was placed by the north-facing window to catch the best of the light.

'All right then.' Venny walked over.

'But you need to get changed first.'

Venny stopped and looked at him in surprise. 'Into what?'

'Well. Into nothing.' Jamie looked bashful again. 'I thought you understood what I meant. The couple melting in a passionate embrace. They'd have to be naked, wouldn't they? It wouldn't make sense otherwise.'

'Oh! I see.'

Venny hesitated. Was she really happy about stripping off with Jamie? She thought he was about as stable as Semtex. On the other hand, he was very sexy. And she quite enjoyed the idea of sitting there in the buff while he sketched her. It was titillating.

'Have you got somewhere I could change?' asked Venny. 'That's the drill, isn't it? The artist provides a wrap or something, so the model can preserve her modesty?'

Jamie looked perplexed. 'Well, no. There's only this room. And anyway, surely you don't care about stripping off for me? It'll be fun. For us both,' he added, and Venny could certainly see that he was getting in the mood for fun already. She could see his cock standing up beneath the loose-fitting combat pants.

'I don't know,' said Venny uncertainly, although she could feel her crotch growing moist at the thought of it. Propped up by her sexy new balconette bra, her breasts felt suddenly sensitised, her nipples tingly.

'Hey, I'll strip too, if it makes you feel any happier,' offered Jamie.

'Well, I guess that might make me feel a little less conspicuous,' allowed Venny doubtfully. And it would enable me to get a better look at that trim young bod of yours, she thought privately. She liked that idea very much.

'Great!' said Jamie enthusiastically, and reached for his fly.

Chapter Fifteen

Venny stood frozen in fascination as Jamie shucked off his combat pants. There was no hint of shyness about Jamie. No vestige of underwear, either. His erect cock was waggling around like a bowsprit as he bent and kicked the pants to a corner of the room. He shrugged off the shirt, too, and looked her straight in the eye, spreading his arms wide.

'How about that?' Jamie asked her. 'Look, I'm nude, too.'

Venny was smiling down at his looming penis. 'The state you're in, that's hardly a reassurance,' she pointed out.

Jamie looked down at his twitching appendage regretfully. 'What can I say? It's got a mind of it's own. Sorry.' He snatched up a paint-covered rag. 'How about this?' He draped the rag over his lusty protrusion and looked at her hopefully.

'That just looks ridiculous,' said Venny, trying hard

not to laugh out loud. She had this gorgeous, hard-bodied, hot-headed young man standing naked in front of her, except for a little square of fabric that actually seemed to flaunt rather than conceal the fact that he was erect. The fabric didn't even completely cover his balls, she noted. And she wasn't particularly sorry about that; he had very nice balls. He was looking at her so pleadingly that she felt her resolve melting. Well, what could it hurt? It was quite flattering, really. She had never been sketched before, not even wearing all her clothes. And being sketched naked might be exciting.

'All right then,' she relented.

'Oh, great.' Jamie turned away from her to take his seat on the beanbag again. In so doing he displayed to Venny a fetchingly broad set of shoulders and an alluringly taut male bottom. As he dipped down to pick up his artist's block, she got a flash of his anus, and his balls swung heavily. She felt herself starting to salivate – at both ends.

Down, girl, she thought. This is business. This is art.

Jamie had now taken up the sketch block and charcoal. He had flipped to a fresh page of paper and was looking up at her expectantly. Actually he needn't have worried about the rag over the genitals, thought Venny. The sketch block more than covered his cock. Sadly.

Venny leaned over, grasped the hem of the pale pink shift dress, and pulled it up and over her head with one swift, smooth movement. She tossed it aside with her cardi, then turned and looked at Jamie, whose eyes were out on stalks despite his efforts to appear the dispassionate artist.

She put her hands on her hips and glanced down her body. Well, she had to admit that the lacy balconette bra was quite something. She wasn't exactly short in the tits department, and this well-constructed little purple gizmo made the very most of the curves she had. Her tits were hiked up to amazing heights by the bra, so that the upper curves of the big globes were very pronounced. Her nipples sat squarely on the lace-covered upper edge of the bra, half-revealed, half-covered. They looked like twin half-moons perched there, she thought, looking down at them. Jamie was looking up at them. He fidgeted awkwardly, and Venny shot him a secret smile. She guessed the rag was under a bit of strain.

Something devilishly provocative seemed to rise in her. She was in this situation, so why not enjoy it? She turned a little, placing one foot in front of the other to accentuate the long line of her legs and the elaborate cut-away edges of the pants she wore.

'What do you think of these?' she asked the squirming young man. 'They're new; do you like them?'

She turned around further to display the purple pants to him. She'd taken ages selecting them a few days ago while shopping with Dani and Flora. The pants, like the bra, were a work of art, a masterpiece of engineering. They were fastened at the sides with tiny bows, and cut away into a thong at the back – as Jamie was now beginning to appreciate – to showcase both silky buttocks.

'They're – um – great,' said Jamie, a bit hoarsely.

Venny decided she was going to have a lot of fun with this. She strolled over in her high-heeled pink mules to Jamie's beanbag and smiled innocently down at him.

'The trouble is, the bows are very difficult to get undone,' she said with a sigh. 'Can you help, Jamie?'

'Oh. Sure.'

Jamie put the block down on the floor. Venny glanced down; the rag was definitely under an acute strain. His cock was leaping about, trying to get out from under there. Decorously Jamie straightened his little square of concealment before reaching up to assist his model with her disrobing.

His fingers shook slightly as they plied the tiny ribboned bows. And he seemed puzzled that they were in fact quite easy to unfasten. He unfastened the right, then the left; coyly Venny caught the fabric at her crotch in one hand when the unfastened pants would have fallen away to the floor.

'Whoops,' she breathed. 'Thanks, Jamie.'

'That's OK.' He picked up the block again, swallowing awkwardly.

And to think that she had thought there was no shyness there, no boyish awkwardness! His tender years probably accounted for his overreaction to Dani's playing around, Venny considered. At nineteen, it was easy to be obsessive – like a child with a favourite toy, unwilling to share. Maybe his problems had something to do with his impoverished background too. That couldn't help. Poverty could easily make one hoard objects like a manic magpie, even if those objects belonged to other people. And poverty could make anyone cling on to any sort of security with a sort of desperation. Dani had been Jamie's only point of reference when he had first come to London from Scotland; and his fierce possessiveness where she was concerned was only natural, when you thought about it.

Venny had never thought about it before. She guessed that Dani had never thought about it at all. If she had, she would maybe understand Jamie a lot better – and treat him with more circumspection. Poor Jamie, thought Venny. She resolved that today was going to be fun for him too. He deserved some fun.

'I suppose you want me to . . . ?' she asked, indicating the little scrap of fabric that constituted her pants. She was holding them in front of her crotch like a maiden protecting her virtue. From Jamie's uncomfortable movements, she guessed that her reluctant virgin act was driving him wild with lust.

'Um, yes. Sorry,' he gulped.

'No, don't apologise,' said Venny. 'That was our agreement, after all.'

So saying, she let the little scrap of fabric drift to the floor. Jamie stared at the tender mound with its now lusher covering of toffee-coloured curls. Venny gave a girlish giggle.

'Oh goodness, this feels so exposed,' she said, wriggling her hips and putting a hand back over her mound. 'So naughty. And I suppose you want my tits bare too?'

'Please,' whispered Jamie, dry-mouthed with wonder as he stared up at her – naked except for her fuck-me shoes and that outrageously sexy bra.

'Well, you'll have to just help me with the fastening, it's quite stiff,' said Venny. Just like you, she thought with an inward laugh. With apparent artlessness she turned her back to him. She could feel his eyes crawling all over her pearly nude buttocks and could feel her own wetness seeping from between her legs in sympathy for his arousal. She knelt down with her back to Jamie, and lifted up her hair. She was careful to sit with her abdomen pooched out a bit, to accentuate the lush inward curve of her back. One leg was tucked beneath her slit and getting damp as she felt Jamie's fingers tentatively start to fumble with the bra's back fastening. She rubbed her swelling clitoris lazily against her own leg, enjoying the pressure. She could hear Jamie's breathing, harsh and shallow. God, he was ready. She hoped he didn't shoot off too soon. She hoped she wasn't overdoing this.

'There,' he rasped, having freed the catch of the bra. 'It's open.'

'Thanks, Jamie.' Venny stood up, unhooking the bra from each arm as she went. Turning back towards Jamie, she smilingly imparted, 'You know, these things may look good but they aren't very comfortable. Look how red my skin is beneath my tits from all that underwiring.'

She bent down to Jamie with her naked breasts dangling almost in his face, and lifted them up a little so that he could see the faintly pink line the bra had left on the skin beneath them.

'Yeah,' said Jamie, looking dazed as he ogled her deliriously coral-coloured nipples, her full fleshy mounds, her rounded curves leading his eye down to that other mound, that secret mound dusted with hair the colour of burnt sienna and sporting beneath that a pair of fleshy lips that all too easily he could stick his tongue – or his cock – between. 'Oh God,' he moaned.

'Will I do, then?' Venny straightened as if totally unaware of the inner battle that was raging in the artist. She turned away from him and walked over to the stool. She hitched herself up onto it, her breasts swaying as she did so, and beamed brightly at him. 'Is this how you want me?' she asked, knowing full well that how he wanted her was on her back, right now, with her legs wide open and his cock buried up to the very hilt between them.

Still, he had some professional pride. Venny admired him for the way he bit back the extent of his passion and instead – somehow – managed to get his mind back on the job in hand.

'That's fine,' he said, only sounding half-strangled now instead of completely unwound. He took up the block and started sketching her, a frown of very intense concentration on his face. Venny watched his penis bobbing up under its little fabric cover as he lifted the block to make some minor adjustment to her outline. Still as hard as ever, she noted with satisfaction. And then, as he really got into the job and stopped thinking about wild and immediate sex, she saw the outline of his cock start to droop under the cover.

'Oh, dear,' she sighed.

'What?' Jamie looked up at her in surprise.

'Your lovely cock's going down,' she pouted. 'Can I help it stay up, Jamie? Should I maybe shake these for you: would that help?'

Venny stuck her chest out and gave a little shimmy; her breasts wobbled. She saw Jamie's cock quiver and start to reassert itself more boldly.

'That's much better,' she sighed happily, and sat still as he tried to reapply himself to the sketch.

There was silence in the studio for all of fifteen minutes, and then Venny started to feel stiff from sitting in one position.

'Can I move now, Jamie?' she asked.

'Just a moment,' he said, and scribbled furiously away at the sketch for another five minutes.

'Now I've got to move,' said Venny, and stood up and stretched with a luxurious groan.

'All right.' Jamie put the sketch block aside and stood up. 'Thanks for being so patient,' he said.

Venny's eyes travelled down his body to where the little square of fabric concealed his manhood. She strolled towards him and deftly lifted it off. Still hard, she thought. Wow.

'That's a lovely cock, Jamie,' she complimented him truthfully. Thoughtfully she ran a fingernail from the tip of his glans down over the shaft of his penis until she reached his curly nest of golden hair. She tweaked his pubic hair playfully.

Later, she thought that touching his naked cock had been a little like unleashing a whirlwind. She had never actually been swept up in someone's arms before, but she was now: swept up and whizzed across the room and summarily dumped on the tiny unmade brass bed in the corner of the studio. And she found that she was too ready for him to even worry about the state of the sheets. Jamie was all over her, kissing and biting and sucking with such a frenzy of released passion that for a few moments she felt nervous of him. And when he started to fasten her hands to the bedstead using her own bra and pants as bindings, she started to feel distinctly uneasy.

Oh, she loved a spot of bondage. She really did. But preferably with a lover she knew and trusted, and Jamie did not come into either category.

'We ought to have a release word,' she managed to pant out.

'A what?' Jamie was panting too, manhandling her limbs into a position where he could plunge his cock into her.

'Release word. Or words. Something non-sexual, so that if either one of us wants to be untied at once, we just say that word, and it's done.'

Jamie sat back on his heels between Venny's legs and said distractedly: 'Right. What word?'

'Um.' Venny thought frantically. Yeah, what word? Micky flashed into her brain, Micky and his buttock tattoo. And Micky's nicked blowtorch. 'Naked flame,' she said.

'Naked flame.' Jamie paused in the act of stroking her inner thighs. His sharp grey eyes held her green ones. 'Isn't that sexual? Naked?'

'Not when applied to a flame,' said Venny, squirming pleasurably beneath his touch. 'Oh, keep doing that,' she pleaded, straining against her bonds.

'Right.' Jamie gave a smile and concentrated his attention upon her soft inner thighs once again. To her surprise he suddenly sat back on his arse and pushed the heel of one large, well-shaped foot against her vaginal opening. It felt good. She moaned. It felt like an improbably huge penis trying to gain entry, and she was amazed by how stimulating the feeling was. She pumped herself enjoyably against his heel, and was quite sorry when he drew his dampened heel away; but other delights were in store. Jamie reversed his foot and pushed his big toe into her vagina instead of his heel. It penetrated more deeply, and while his big toe waggled away like fury inside her, his other toes tickled at her clit.

'That's good, don't you think?' gasped Jamie.

'Mm,' said Venny.

'You know geishas?'

'Not personally, no,' panted Venny.

'No, I mean, you know *about* geishas and what they could do with their feet? Those awful bound deformed feet that looked a bit like pigs' trotters? Well, the front of the foot was pulled right down, and so was the back, and that left a cleft in the middle where the instep should be.'

'Oh, yuck,' said Venny with a grimace of distaste. 'Oh, yuck, yes, but the cleft was very handy. They used the cleft as another vagina. A man could slip his dick in there if the geisha had the curse or whatever, and get off just fine.'

'You're a mine of information,' gasped Venny, discovering that a man's big toe was actually a very useful thing to have around the place. 'Do that a bit harder, Jamie. And that little toe, move it just a bit . . . oh, that's better. That's it.'

Venny was straining and pushing down onto his foot madly now, chasing the elusive tingle that forewarned of her climax. But again Jamie changed his position, removing his foot from her crotch and going back onto his knees between her legs.

'I want a fuck now,' he said brusquely.

'Fuck away,' said Venny obligingly, because right now that was exactly what she wanted, too.

Jamie pushed closer. Venny looked down between their overheated bodies and saw that he had another surprise in store. He had slipped what looked a bit like a condom over his cock, but it was something a bit more elaborate than that. Venny looked at it in trepidation. It was more like a large dildo, covering his cock. Now when had he put that on? she wondered. Sleight of hand seemed to be Jamie's forte. It was bright red, about ten inches long, and covered in knobbly excrescences. She could see that it was quite a snug fit as it sat over his penis; and she guessed it would feel pretty good once it got inside her, but for the moment she was a bit shocked by it. Should she call out the release words?

No, maybe not.

Why not try it and see if she liked it?

Jamie pushed his cock in its chunky vermilion covering down until the tip of the dildo was just nudging into her slit. He pushed his hips up towards her, and the thing sank deeper into her. The sensation was immediate and amazingly enjoyable. The knobbly growths all along its length gave an extra dimension to her sensitivity, stepping up the action by leaps and bounds until she was panting as if she'd just run a marathon, and straining against him to get the maximum amount of thrills from the encounter. She felt almost sorry for Jamie, because the thing was so thick and so long that he must be feeling very little with his penis trapped inside it.

Still, he was obviously a more considerate lover than she had expected him to be – and she was determined to do him an extra special favour after this, to return the compliment. The big red dildo sucked and pushed and thrust at her like the cock of a giant; her wetness flooded her now as with every mad push from Jamie her breasts shook, her stomach clenched, her fingers clawed at the brass bars her wrists were tied to. This was heaven but it was also hell. Satisfying though the big dildo might be, what she really wanted was hot, surging, living cock, not turgid plastic. And oh, it was big. So incredibly, hugely big. Bigger even than Robert Fielding had been, and she had been on top that time, in control of the situation. The dildo was perched on Jamie's phallus above her, filling her to almost indecent lengths, causing her darts of wild excitement and a sensation that was almost, almost pain.

So as she came, screaming and crying with the intensity of it, she was also shouting out the words that would get her released from this bondage.

'Naked flame!' she sobbed out. 'Naked flame!'

But Jamie was out of control now. Oh, he did stop fucking her with the dildo; he pulled out of her instantly and threw the sopping-wet thing aside. But with equal speed he nosed his cock back inside her, eager to feel her heat and wetness against his own shaft, his own glans, eager to feel her womanliness against the male core of him.

Jamie was pushing and thrusting and slapping against her with greedy enjoyment now, and to her shame Venny felt her second orgasm build to almost obscene heights as he blatantly ignored her pleas to be released and all but raped her.

Heaven, she thought, but also hell.

Heaven in the hard thrust of his cock and his balls against her. Hell in the soreness that the huge dildo had caused her, causing her to wince at his crazy lunging.

But soon it was over anyway. Jamie was far too turned on by this sort of game to wait for long. With a shout of satisfaction he threw back his head and these final thrusts he gave were even more violent, more uncontrolled in their wild passion, than those that had gone before. And Venny came again.

And again.

Heaven and hell, pleasure and pain.

'Naked flame,' she sighed limply, feeling faintly ashamed of the extent of her own arousal now. Jamie pulled his wet penis out of her. She watched it wavering like a one-eyed cobra about to strike as he leaned up over her and freed her from her bonds.

'You wanted that,' he said smugly as he flopped back onto the bed beside her.

'I asked you to stop. We agreed,' said Venny with a touch of sullenness.

'Yeah, you asked me to stop. But you didn't want me to,' said Jamie.

And he was right, of course. Also very wrong, because they had agreed what they would do, and he had broken that agreement. He was mad, bad and dangerous to know, like Lord Byron, and although she had enjoyed him very much, she thought that in future she would leave his sort to Dani, who was pretty wild herself.

'So who's going to be the man in the ice sculpture?' she asked him, feeling replete and well content in spite of all her misgivings.

'Hm?' Jamie looked at her with those acute grey eyes. They were sort of icy themselves, those eyes. 'Oh, I thought Micky Quinn.'

She found Micky over at Flora and Caspar's flat later that morning, enjoying an early lunch with them on their balcony. He answered the door at her ring, wearing a towel around his waist and nothing else. Venny looked him up and down in surprise.

'Venny!' Micky was already pulling her inside, his blue eyes twinkling with pleasure at seeing her. 'Come in, sweetheart. Have you come to make up?'

Well, had she? Venny wondered. All right, she had behaved like a prude when she'd discovered he'd been balling Dani after their split. It was true.

'Yes,' she said simply. 'And to tell you that I sat for Jamie's ice sculpture this morning. His take-off of Rodin's *Kiss*. And he tells me you're going to be the man in the sculpture.'

'That's right.' Micky had closed the door and was leading her across to the balcony, from where she could hear Flora chatting away in her high cultured voice to Caspar. 'He's been sketching me at Beurre Blanc.'

'He's been doing more than that at Beurre Blanc,' said Venny.

Micky stopped walking and turned to look at her. 'Like what?' he asked with a quick frown.

'Like stealing your chef's blowtorch and maybe your knife too,' said Venny. 'I saw the blowtorch at his studio.'

'The light-fingered little git,' said Micky.

'I'd put it down to experience if I were you,' Venny advised him. 'Jamie's really not worth upsetting. He's a bit unstable, I'd say.'

'I guess you're right,' said Micky, and although he didn't look too happy about it, he let it go.

'Sorry to interrupt your lunch,' said Venny.

'No, come and join us,' invited Micky, and he pulled off the towel at his waist and tossed it aside.

Venny had thought they were out there on the balcony in bathing trunks and bikini, but Micky to her surprise was naked. She stared down at his revealed cock and it started to raise its head as if about to return her stare.

'We're having a naked lunch,' explained Micky with a grin. 'No one can see us out there – at least, not without a high-powered telescope, and if they're going to go to that sort of bother then they're welcome to a peek.' He turned and led the way out onto the balcony.

Strange days indeed, thought Venny as she walked out onto the balcony while watching the twitch and roll of Micky's naked butt.

'Oh, hi,' said Flora warmly, sitting there in the sun with her massive tits slathered in sunblock. Her nipples were drooping perilously close to her salad, Venny saw with a tiny feeling of amusement and a large measure of burgeoning excitement. Goodness, that woman could turn any strictly hetero woman into a raving lesbian overnight!

She couldn't see what Flora was wearing on her bottom half because the food-laden table blocked her view, but she guessed that it was absolutely nothing. She felt her cunt throb hungrily. And it throbbed even worse when she glanced at Caspar's naked upper half, and started conjecturing about what lay beneath the table on his side.

Micky sat down beside Flora to resume his meal and dish up for Venny.

'Hello, Venny. Come and join us,' said Caspar encouragingly.

Venny was about to sit down when Caspar held up an admonitory hand. 'House rule. Naked lunches mean naked. That's all the participants, latecomers included.'

They wanted her to strip too. And why not? She quite enjoyed the thought. She was clean from the shower, she had exchanged the clothes she had worn to Jamie's for a more casual aquamarine crop top and tightly clinging stone-coloured shorts, and sneakers. She felt cool and comfortable in this ensemble, but right now she was itching to join in the naked fun with these three. Micky was dishing her up a plate of salad and a slice of quiche. Caspar and Flora were drinking and laughing over some absurd joke they'd heard on the radio. No one cared that she was about to get naked, and she felt quite easy about the situation herself.

She pulled the dainty little crop top over her head, allowing her nude breasts to spill out. She tossed it aside onto a spare chair. Then she unbuttoned and unzipped her shorts, and deftly pulled them down around her ankles and stepped out of them. She tossed those too onto the chair. Aware suddenly that conversation and movement had ceased on the balcony, she kicked off her sneakers and put them neatly to one side.

Naked, she stepped forwards and took the chair next to Caspar. She sat down, nude breasts swinging, and Caspar approvingly poured her out a glass of red wine.

She picked up the glass and sipped the wine. She hoped she wasn't dampening Flora's beautiful seat cushion too much. This felt exceedingly erotic. And now that she was sitting beside Caspar, she could glance down while she was talking to him, and see that he was just as well hung as his brother, and that his thatch down there was black like Micky's, and that his balls were pleasingly big.

She looked up and realised that Caspar had caught her staring at his naked cock. 'Sorry,' she said with a rueful smile.

'Don't apologise,' said Caspar. 'It turns a man on something rotten, having a woman ogling his tackle. As you can see.'

Venny could. His penis had roused up and was now standing erect, as if curious about their lunchtime meeting and eager to join in.

'I'll get the pudding,' volunteered Flora, standing up. Both men looked with interest at her lushly curving body, her ginger pubic curls, her outrageously heavy breasts.

'Your wife's gorgeous,' sighed Micky to his brother.

'I know,' said Caspar proudly. 'Venny is, too.'

'Thank you,' said Venny.

'Pleasure,' said Caspar, and it was clear from the expression in his dark, brooding eyes as they looked at her that pleasure was exactly what he intended.

Flora returned shortly with summer pudding and cream on a tray with some pudding dishes and spoons. She bent over the table beside Micky and placed the tray upon it. Micky stood up to help her, displaying a vast erection. As Flora busied herself with slicing up the raspberry-coloured pudding which oozed fruit and rich juices, Micky stepped behind the luscious redhead and leaned past her to pour out the cream. That accomplished, he pushed the head of his rampant penis down between her bumslit, found her vagina, and thrust up into her.

'Sorry,' he said as he pushed up further into his sister-in-law's very willing body. 'Couldn't wait. It's all these bare tits. Too much temptation.'

'You're right there, brother,' said Caspar, leaning across to tweak one of Venny's nipples. It hardened obligingly as he did so. Pleased with the effect, Caspar reached for the cream and dipped his finger into the jug. He smoothed the cream onto Venny's turgid nipple, leaned across and proceeded to lick it off.

In delight Venny clutched at Caspar's dark head while his lips and tongue worked industriously at her breast. Her eyes met Micky's over Flora's shoulder. Micky's hips were pistoning busily. She looked at Flora, whose eyes were closed in ecstasy as she clasped the edge of the table to steady herself against Micky's thrusts. The redhead's breasts were swinging steadily as she was taken from behind. Venny felt suddenly so wet that she wished Micky was in her, not Flora. But there was always Caspar.

Dropping her hand from his head, she guided his hand to her succulent crotch, leaning back in her chair so that he could gain access to her wet folds. Caspar seemed very happy to do this, and before long she had his fingers exactly where she wanted them, rammed up inside her so that she was being as effectively fucked as Flora was, and she could look across the table at the copulating couple, and imagine that Micky's cock was up inside her, instead of Flora.

And so lunch passed in a cheerful and enjoyable medley of eating and fucking and sucking and drinking. Later, after pudding, Micky and Caspar changed sides, and Micky was able to shag Venny to a standstill; while across the table his brother pulled Flora down across his lap so that she straddled him, and then fucked her with abandon.

Later still, they all retired to bed with another bottle of wine, and the two men watched while Flora and Venny enjoyed one another – and became so aroused by the performance that they fell upon the women again, and fucked them, and brought them to rapturous orgasms until late afternoon, when the four of them were sated and exhausted, and fell tangled together into a soft, refreshing sleep.

Chapter Sixteen

Do you ever wonder whatever happened to Bill Thompson?' Micky asked Venny as she lounged in a brief yellow bikini in a wicker chair out on the verandah of the hut at Whitstable.

'What?' Venny didn't even bother to open her eyes beneath the protective shades she wore. Bill Thompson? She should care. She was having a blissful day off, the sea was swooshing up onto the pebble beach with a sound that was gently soothing her into sleep, and the sun was beating down on them while a refreshing breeze blew softly against their skins. This was bliss. Tomorrow was the day of the Blue Ribbon awards ceremony; she was trying to chill out here, for heaven's sake. What would she be worrying about Bill Thompson for?

'Bill Thompson. You remember? That useless chef you used to employ, the one with the taste for all things Italian?'

'Well, of course I remember.'

Venny sat up reluctantly, and pushed her shades up onto her head. She looked across at Micky, who was sitting at the other side of the little verandah in the other wicker chair, wearing brief black trunks and nothing else. He was looking tanned and healthy and devilishly attractive, she thought, with his feet lazily propped up, ankles crossed, on the little hitching rail at the front of the verandah. He was looking at a copy of *Caterer* magazine.

Venny had told Micky all about the departed – and unlamented – Bill Thompson. How he had wanted to go into partnership with her (Micky had winced a bit at that, because he had suggested the same thing), how he had taken all her staff with him, how they had parted on the worst possible terms.

'Why do you mention him?' she asked.

'Oh, no reason,' said Micky, idly flipping through the pages. 'Only I thought he threatened to set up close by as serious competition?'

Venny let out a noise halfway between a laugh and a snort. 'The words "Bill Thompson" and "serious competition" don't exactly go together,' she said with asperity. 'Both you and I know that restaurants open and close in London all the time. Even if he had set up on my doorstep, he'd probably be out of business by now, and we wouldn't even have noticed his going. Or his coming, for that matter.'

'Yeah, you're right.' Micky tossed the mag onto the deck.

'What's up?' Venny looked at him curiously. 'Getting

edgy about the awards at last? I thought that was my bag.'

Micky blew out his cheeks and leaned back, staring out to sea. 'The best man – or woman – will win, right?' he asked her. 'There's a new Italian place called Fantoni's, that's all. It's getting good write-ups. *Very* good, actually.'

'So what?' Venny replaced her shades on her nose and settled back too. She had no worries about the awards now, none at all. She had even bought the dress she was going to wear – a gold glittering sheath that skimmed over her lush curves and made her feel a million dollars.

'So you think it's going to be Box of Delights, or Beurre Blanc, right?'

'Absolutely.'

'Box of Delights has a lot of ambience. A charming hostess, an excellent Michelin-starred chef, good staff.'

'All true,' sighed Venny with a smile.

'Whereas Beurre Blanc has an even better chef, a cutting-edge ultra-modern atmosphere, and the staff are pretty damned good too.'

'I expect Terence Conran's quaking in his shoes right now,' quipped Venny.

'Well, he ought to be,' grinned Micky.

'Modesty never was a fault of yours, was it?'

'Can't say it was, no.'

Venny lifted her shades a fraction and smiled across at him. 'Oh, come on, Micky,' she urged him sweetly. 'Let it go, will you? Let's just enjoy today, and worry about all that tomorrow.'

Micky's blue eyes opened wide in mock amazement. 'Live for the day and worry tomorrow? Who can this person be? Surely not Venny Halliday, all-round control freak and advance worrier extraordinaire?'

'I'm learning from you,' said Venny primly, setting her shades back on her nose.

'You could do worse.'

'That's what I thought.' Venny considered for a moment. 'Dani says that Jamie's finished the ice sculpture for tomorrow night's centrepiece. He's got it in his local supermarket's freezer room for now. Imagine it. You and me in a clinch, carved into the ice. Immortalised.'

'Well it's hardly immortalised,' said Micky mildly. 'We'll be a puddle of water by the end of tomorrow evening.'

'Hey, don't disillusion me.'

Venny snuggled back onto her chair with a sigh of happiness. She didn't doubt that she was going to win the award, but now it didn't somehow seem to matter so much as it once had. Even if she lost, she could live with that, shrug her shoulders and just carry on. Maybe even sell Box of Delights, move into some other business. Maybe not. She knew very well that a few weeks ago she could not have been so casual, so adult, about the results of the Blue Ribbon awards ceremony. Micky had been a good influence in her life.

Later, after a lazy lunch out on the deck, they went to bed and made love again, then dozed, entangled,

until mid-afternoon. Micky awoke first. He was a light
sleeper, unlike Venny. He was sprawled on his back, and
she was glued to his side like a limpet, one of her arms
across his chest, her breasts resting against his ribcage,
their skin almost welded together by sweat. One of her
legs was hitched across both of his. This was a favourite
position of hers. And he kind of liked the way she clung
to him, her nose burrowing into the curve of his neck,
little snuffling noises escaping her as she slept.

Micky glanced down at the disarrayed curls of her
blonde head. No doubt about it, Venny Halliday had
got to him in a way few women had before. He thought
of taking Kate in the alleyway outside Box of Delights,
fucking her up against the wall. Thinking that all women
were the same, or trying to convince himself that this
was so – a cunt was a cunt was a cunt, yes?

As it turned out, no.

And pushing his cock into the luscious Flora at that
exciting lunch with Caspar and Venny. He was pleased
that Flora and Caspar seemed to have resolved their
differences. He liked Flora. And there had been so
many others, too many to count. He loved sex. Sex and
food, almost – but not quite – in equal measures.

And he guessed that he maybe also loved Venny
Halliday.

And he wished that she would wake up so that he
could get his rocks off again. He had a hard-on like a
steel bar down there. But he was prepared to wait, if he
had to.

Later, they swam in the sea. Micky was surprised by just how strong a swimmer Venny was, ploughing a lively breast-stroke back and forth on a line parallel with the beach, then collapsing in a laughing heap in his arms, gasping and panting and splashing him light-heartedly. They played for a while, and then inevitably the play became more serious as they churned and splashed in the chest-high water. Venny's top was stripped off her. Her breasts were concealed by the water, but she was worried about what would happen when she had to walk up the beach. There were other people about now, walking along the beach, enjoying the sun.

'So you sunbathe and swim topless,' said Micky in cavalier fashion. 'So what?'

Before she could protest, Micky had dived again. Venny felt something tugging at the bottom half of her bikini, and tried to dart away, but Micky was too fast. He pulled the tiny garment free and surfaced, grinning hugely, pushing his hair back with one hand and holding both parts of her apparel in the other.

'Micky!' Venny complained laughingly. It felt very erotic, exceedingly sensual, being naked in the water. She looked more carefully at what he held in his hand. His black briefs were there too. They were both naked.

Micky moved towards her, the current lifting them and brushing their bodies against one another. Venny felt Micky's erect penis pushing at her belly. Her nipples, rigid from the slight chill of the water, teased at his chest. Micky pulled her closer, and before she knew it he was opening her legs, hitching her higher with his hands around her buttocks, and nosing his naked cock between her thighs, nuzzling it against her slit, searching for – and suddenly, with a victorious upthrust that lifted her high and drew a muffled shriek of gratification from her – finding her.

The chill of the water and the fact that they had been making love for most of the day slowed Micky down so that the experience was a steady, unhurried one. He pushed into her so slowly but so firmly, then withdrew just a little, and then he was in again, surging up into her with a powerful upthrust, and then back – it was like the ebb and flow of the tide that supported them so that they floated, weightless and enfolded by total bliss, mating like wild sea creatures at full moon. When Micky's orgasm came, he buried his head in her shoulder and bit her quite hard. Then he slid his hand down between their bodies as the water sucked and pulled at them, and gripped her clit between his thumb and forefinger, tugging it rhythmically until she too came, stifling her cries of pleasure against his waterlogged hair.

They stayed like that, locked together, until Venny started to shiver as the water chilled her; then, giggling like irresponsible teenagers, they struggled back into their swimwear – although Venny didn't bother with the top; Micky kept hold of that – and climbed up the beach, sprawling out on the shingle to dry off in the sun.

People were walking past, and others were out sunbathing too; the sight of a woman sunbathing topless wasn't exactly unique, but Venny's breasts drew quite a few admiring male glances and caused more than one unexpected erection.

Finally they went back into the hut to shower and change for dinner at the Old Neptune pub; and then they wandered back to the hut, loitering down Squeeze Gut Alley to kiss and fondle each other before home, and bed, and more leisurely lovemaking. Venny thought that it actually *was* lovemaking, what they were doing together now. She fell asleep as blamelessly as a child, snuggled into Micky's muscular chest, her head tucked into his neck, one of her legs thrown across both of his.

Chapter Seventeen

'So – what do you think?' Venny asked Micky anxiously when he came to collect her the next evening.

Micky eyed her up and down, and let out a low whistle.

'Wow,' he said reverently.

'Does my bum look big in this?' asked Venny, turning slightly so that he could see the plunging back of the long red gown. She looked at him nervously over her shoulder.

Micky considered the question. Her bum did look big in the dress, but only in the same way that Jennifer Lopez's bum looked big: in a voluptuous and decidedly alluring way. He guessed that this was a man thing. Men liked a generous bottom on a woman; but other women decried that same bottom as too big, too prominent, too fat. Which was rubbish in this case. Venny's bum looked wonderful and he wanted to grope it instantly.

'No, it doesn't,' he lied diplomatically. Venny turned

around with a smile and he thought that she looked gorgeous with her frizzy blonde curls all loose and corkscrewed, her tits obviously naked under the gown. Below the hemline he glimpsed dinky gold sandals and gold-painted toenails. She carried in her hand one of those tiny *pochette* things. What the hell did they keep in a tiny little thing like that, a lace-edged hankie? he wondered.

'Oh, good,' said Venny, relaxing, accepting the lie. She looked at Micky as he stood in the doorway. He seemed to suit clothes of any sort. His long, slender frame made him a perfect clothes-horse. She envied him that. He could wear a frock-coat or even a *djellabah*, and look like he was born to it. She, on the other hand, had to be circumspect about what she wore because of her sticking-out bum and her larger-than-strictly-normal boobs. Micky was wearing a very proper DJ tonight, black with a crisp white shirt beneath, and he looked great and smelt even better. His dark hair was still stuck up in gelled spikes in its usual punky fashion, and he still sported that cavalier grin and the laughing blue eyes that seemed to find something terribly funny and enjoyable in every aspect of life.

'Dani gone already, I suppose?' he asked, picking his jaw back off the floor.

'Ages ago,' nodded Venny. 'She was still muttering about the flower arrangements and the table placings when she went out the door. And she's phoned Jamie three times today about the ice sculpture. She's been driving me crazy.'

'It'll all be fine,' Micky reassured her.

'I'm getting jittery,' Venny confessed.

'I can tell.'

'How can you tell?' challenged Venny.

'There's a curler still hanging in your hair.'

'*What?*' Venny shrieked, and turned to look for the mirror.

'Hold still; I can get it out,' said Micky, trying not to laugh at her panic. As she turned, he studied the back of the gown – or the lack of it. It plunged away to just above her bum. In fact, he thought he could see the little peachlike slit at the centre of her bottom, and the whiter, fatter curves of her buttocks too, just peeping above the gown's daringly cut back.

'Don't laugh,' warned Venny as he stepped forwards and started to unravel the little yellow cylinder. His breath was brushing her cheek, the front of his jacket was brushing her breasts through the thin fabric of her gown, and her nipples were responding to his closeness in the way they always did. 'Oh, God,' she wailed. 'I can't go out of here with my nipples sticking out!'

'Yes, you can,' said Micky calmly, tossing the curler aside as Venny ran a shaking hand through her hair. 'It's expected with a dress like that. Almost obligatory. Every man in the room will be able to see that your nipples are hard, and they'll think what a hot foxy little number you are, and they'll envy me like mad. There. All ready now, yes?'

'Yes,' said Venny faintly, feeling slightly sick now that the Blue Ribbon awards ceremony was actually upon her. Of course she was going to win, but even so, it was a nerve-wracking occasion.

They rode down in silence in the lift. No horseplay this time. No cunnilingus and no sudden delicious fucks. Even Micky seemed quiet, and Venny was getting steadily more and more freaked out.

Outside, the evening was coming down very softly like a purple velvet cover over a cage of blue. Lights were winking on all over London, and there was a massive car at the kerb, a uniformed driver holding the door open for her.

'Micky!' Venny yelled out in surprise.

It was a limo, a real stretch black limo with heavily tinted windows just like the mobsters used in the movies. Just like the ones the stars stepped out of at the Oscars. She looked at Micky and laughed aloud in delight.

'Like it?' he asked, grinning.

'I love it,' she enthused, and was handed into the car by a very hunky-looking young chauffeur who was also smiling, because with Venny looking so damned pleased about the whole thing it was impossible not to smile with her.

Micky piled in after her, and the door closed behind them. It was like sitting in someone's lounge. There was thick white carpet underfoot, and the seats were squashy and obviously covered with the softest, the most supple, real leather. There were two more seats at the side; you could cram eight people into this baby with room to spare, Venny thought. There was a television. There was a little walnut-panelled cupboard which was probably a fridge. There was a drinks cabinet. There was a soundproof sheet of thick tinted glass between them and the chauffeur. There was everything you could possibly want in here.

As the driver climbed in and the huge eye-pulling car eased out into the traffic, Micky popped open a bottle of Bollinger and let the froth cascade into two flutes.

'I had no idea you were planning this,' said Venny, taking a flute from him and sipping blissfully, all but hugging herself with enjoyment.

'It's a surprise,' said Micky. 'After all, it's a big occasion. Why not celebrate it?'

'Whoever wins?' Her eyes held his with a glimmer of anxiety in their green depths.

'Whoever,' said Micky positively; 'You or me, who cares?'

'I'll drink to that,' said Venny, and clinked her brimming glass against his. They drank, their eyes caressing each other. Finally Micky took the glass from her hand and put both safely aside.

'Give me a kiss for luck,' said Micky.

Venny leaned against him and gently touched her lips against his.

'Not there,' said Micky. He leaned back against the sumptuous leather and unzipped his fly. 'Here.'

Venny looked at him in surprise, but her sex was already throbbing treacherously with excitement despite the fact that she was thinking they couldn't, the driver would see. She glanced over her shoulder at the young man's impassive head, seen only faintly through the thick tinted glass between his compartment and theirs.

'He's not interested in what we're doing back here,' Micky assured her. He leaned back with a luxurious sigh and pulled his naked cock out from under the long flaps of his white shirt. It was completely pumped up with heat and excitement, totally erect. Venny could not resist fondling it in an affectionate fashion with her hand.

'Kiss it,' said Micky.

Venny bent her head to the smooth red helmet of his penis, keeping her hand upon its stem while she dropped a kiss onto the top.

'Nice,' sighed Micky, pushing up against her mouth, his cock's little slit opening to release a tiny bead of come.

Eager to co-operate, Venny put the tip of her tongue to his slit and lapped the salty droplet away. Then she whirled her tongue around the head of his penis, and into the ultra-sensitive ridge of tissue under his foreskin while she held the foreskin firmly back with her fingers. As Micky pushed with increasing desperation, lifting his hips off the seat and brandishing his rock-hard cock at her, Venny happily took it right into her mouth, controlling the depth of his penetration with her hand gripped around his straining shaft. As she did so, she was sure she felt the car stop and the engine's steady, powerful note die away, but she was too involved in what she was doing to take much notice. Only when the door opened beside her did she look up in surprise, blushing with shame to be caught in such an intimate act.

'I just thought I'd check that everything met with your approval,' said the chauffeur, doffing his uniform cap and climbing into the back to sit on one of the long side banquettes. 'We're a little ahead of schedule, so I wondered if there was anything else I could do for you, to kill a little time? After all, you don't want to arrive too early.'

Venny sat back on her heels, regaining her composure. She glanced at Micky, and he gave her a grin, but made no move to conceal his tongue-reddened erection. Indeed, he seemed to flaunt it in front of the young chauffeur. Micky sat there with his legs sprawled apart and his hips tilted forward, his naked and very erect penis sticking starkly out of his black trousers. Venny thought that for propriety's sake he really ought to put it away, but if she found the situation embarrassing, she also found it very exciting. Her own sex was throbbing madly with arousal, and her nipples were rigid again under the thin red fabric of her gown. She saw the chauffeur's dark eyes drop to her breasts and blushed even harder. He was quite a handsome young man, with straight brown hair and a very direct gaze. Although not tall, he was compact and muscular, and there was something very alluring about a man in a chauffeur's neat grey uniform and black highly polished boots. It was pretty obvious that he'd seen what they were doing in the back of the car, and was keen to join in.

'Actually there is something you can do,' said Micky casually. 'You can fuck her while she blows me.'

Venny looked at Micky. Micky returned her look with a look of his own. It said: well, are you up for it or not? You say you're so relaxed now, so different from the uptight Venny you were before. So here's your chance to prove it, once and for all.

Venny looked back at the eager young man on the side seat. A gauntlet had been thrown down, and she was determined to pick it up. 'Will you do it? I want you to do it,' she assured him.

'Well, I'd be pleased to,' he said huskily.

'Good.' Micky leaned back against the seat once more. 'Come on, get on with it, Venny.' He glanced at the chauffeur. 'You join in when you like, pal. Is that all right?'

'Fine,' said the young chauffeur, swallowing convulsively as he watched Venny move between Micky's legs again.

As she once more bent to lick and suck at Micky's exuberantly upright penis, Venny was very aware of what the young chauffeur must be seeing from behind her – the low seductive back of her gown which revealed nearly the whole of her back, right down to her buttocks. In fact, she knew that he could even see a glimpse of her bumslit, the very top of it – just a teensy, teasing glimpse but a glimpse nevertheless, at the very bottom of the gown's outrageously cut back. It must be obvious to him that she was not wearing briefs – and a bra was out of the question with a gown like this, and anyway hadn't he already looked at her nipples? He knew she was naked beneath her gown.

Quivering with excitement and anticipation, Venny tried hard to concentrate on Micky's hot and horny penis, but she was also thinking about that other penis, tucked into those tight uniform trousers and soon to be released and used upon her cunt. She couldn't hear him moving yet. Suddenly she was aware that she was hungrily waiting for his movements, waiting for that first hard nudge up between the swollen lips as he strove to locate her with the head of his cock.

'Concentrate, Venny,' said Micky with a chuckle, twining the fingers of one hand into her hair to keep her head just where he wanted it.

And now, with his hand holding her head like that, she couldn't turn, couldn't look. The chauffeur could be upon her at any moment. But the feeling was good, so good that she moaned as her mouth closed once again upon Micky's erection.

Micky sighed blissfully and leaned over, fiddling with something out of her line of vision. Now what was he doing? wondered Venny. He kept her head still while he moved, kept her pinioned there with her mouth attending to his cock.

'Try this,' said Micky, straightening up and slipping something startlingly cold between her lips.

Venny nearly gulped in surprise, but she controlled it. It was an ice cube! He'd raided the fridge in search of new sensations. Venny smoothed the rapidly melting cube of ice over her tongue, then ran her chilled tongue around her lips to cool them. She repeated the exercise twice more, and then spat the cube into her hand and applied her cold lips to Micky's prick. She heard his sharp intake of breath and smiled against his shaft as her lips slid up and down it. Micky's hips came off the seat and she knew that he wanted her to take the head into her mouth now, needed her to do that.

But she held back, teasing him.

She continued to caress his shaft with her lips and tongue, relishing the silky texture of his cock, such a vivid contrast to its total hardness. She inhaled deeply, loving the gamey male scent that arose from his sex. His hand on her hair tightened convulsively as her tongue fluttered deliciously around the indentation beneath his glans – so near and yet so far.

'Jesus, Venny,' Micky groaned, and only then did she do as he wanted and close her mouth over his come-covered glans, sucking his salty juices while she pulled at his quivering shaft with her hand.

He was going to come. She felt it in his shaking thighs, his harsh breathing, the unconscious savagery with which he gripped her hair. And now she wanted him to. This, she thought, was absolute power, to have a man helpless with lust while you did this to him. But suddenly she was distracted from her goal. She became aware of the young man behind her lifting the back of her gown. She felt air on her naked buttocks, and an indrawn breath. There was a brush of coarse material between her thighs, and the chauffeur's thighs were abruptly between hers, pushing them apart. She heard his zip come down, and then a hard, warm cylinder of flesh was pushing between the soaked lips of her sex, pushing up briefly against her clit and making it leap with pleasure before pulling back and nudging into her aching, empty cunt.

The chauffeur came into her in a rush, thrusting up with such heavy desperation that she felt his naked balls slap hard against her buttocks. Still nuzzling Micky's cock but finding it increasingly hard to lavish attention on his satisfaction when she was suddenly very concerned for her own, Venny eagerly lunged back against the steady encroachment of the hard male organ behind her.

As the chauffeur thrust forwards, she thrust back, and they were soon performing a dance as old as time itself, meeting each other in a frenzy again and again, her hips pushing back, her buttocks slapping against him as his upright cock thrust up and forwards.

And then Micky came, his seed shooting into Venny's mouth like a series of shots from a pistol, creamy and full of salty savour. Venny groaned in delight and swallowed his rich ejaculation as if it were the finest, the most expensive sea-fresh oyster. Micky moaned her name. Darling Venny, she heard him say, and that was so touching, so sweet.

The chauffeur was enjoying himself too, thrusting so vigorously against Venny now that she was having to brace herself firmly against Micky's thighs to stop herself from overbalancing. His orgasm was a far more noisy affair than Micky's. He clutched at her waist and almost lifted her from the floor of the car, emitting a series of sharp cries that would not have disgraced a Tarzan movie. She felt the young man swelling and surging inside her as his seed was spilled, and moved desperately against Micky's shin like a bitch in heat, rubbing her tingling clitoris against him until she too came, moaning and gasping out her pleasure into the rich cloth on Micky's thigh.

'Well, we'd better get on over to the hotel now,' said Micky, refastening his fly.

Venny was sad to see his lively and lovely prick doing its vanishing act back inside his trousers, but he had a point. She glanced at the little gold wristwatch she wore. It was gone eight now. She turned and gave the chauffeur a grateful smile. He too was tucking his cock away. Suddenly shy, she pulled her gown back down to cover her exposed buttocks.

'That was wonderful,' she said, feeling that some sort of thanks should be expressed.

'Oh, any time,' returned the chauffeur, reassembling his clothing and stepping back out into the night.

Presently he got back behind the wheel and the engine purred into life once again. The limo started to move back into the flow of the traffic.

Venny cuddled up against Micky to enjoy the ride.

By the time they arrived at the Cranleigh Hotel in Piccadilly, the joint was jumping. Venny was quite staggered by the number of people there, even though she had been prepared for a crowd. There were restaurant critics, restaurateurs, chefs, staff, food suppliers, food writers, and sundry hangers-on and guests swelled the numbers still further.

The big banqueting hall was packed to bursting. There was a crush of people searching, most of them already clutching drinks, for their place markers at the ten-seater circular tables. Venny looked around and thought that Dani had done her usual excellent job in making the whole thing look opulent and eye-filling. She'd gone for yellow, white and green on the table arrangements in the end – yellow flowers at the centre of each table, lime-green tablecloths, white and yellow napery; the whole room looked magnificent. And up on the stage, also decorated with mounds of yellow flowers, was Jamie's ice sculpture, the centrepiece beside which the awards would be made by a well-known television celebrity.

Venny squinted up at it while Micky was busy chatting to people he knew in the crowd. She'd never been sculpted before, and she was eager to get a good look at it. She looked now, long and hard.

She quickly discovered that the woman in the sculpture wasn't her.

What the hell? she wondered in bewilderment.

She struggled closer and stared up at the sculpture. The man with whom the woman was linked in an icy kiss was recognisably Micky. It had his porcupine hairstyle, his slender, muscular grace of body. But the ice woman was much smaller than Venny, smaller in every way. Shorter and less curvy. And the hair was different. Shorter, straighter. And the profile, too. The profile, in fact, looked like Dani's profile.

'You've seen it then.' It was Dani, bustling up beside her with a tray of glasses in her hand. As always when she was working, Dani looked the very picture of respectability. The ear, nose and eyebrow furniture was all gone, and even her make-up was muted. She wore a dark dress, and a pristine white pinny.

Venny opened her mouth a couple of times but no sound came out. At last she managed: 'But it was supposed to be me and Micky.'

Dani's expression was thunderous. 'That's what Jamie told everyone,' she said angrily. 'This is obviously his twisted idea of a joke. Can you imagine the ribbing I've been taking from all the staff I've hired? It took them two seconds flat to realise it was me up there, and I haven't heard the last of it since. I am going to *kill* that little bastard.'

'I think it might be my fault,' admitted Venny with reluctance. 'I was upset that you and Micky got together when we split up, and I told Jamie about it when I went there to sit for the sculpture.'

Dani stared at her incredulously. 'For God's sake, Venny!' she burst out.

'I know, I know.' Venny squirmed. She glanced around. 'Look, I've got to go and get seated; everyone else is already in place. I'm really, really sorry, Dani.'

Dani looked up at the ice sculpture, then back at Venny, and her face softened a little. 'Oh, forget it.

Jamie's had his fun now. Let's hope that's the end of it.'

Venny found Micky among the tables and sat down next to him. The waiting staff were starting to dish up the first course. She didn't know anyone else on their table, but it was obvious that Micky did. Micky seemed to know everyone in the business – whereas she had only ever thought of her restaurant as just that. A business. She thought about that, and realised abruptly that although it would help her profits to win the award, it would mean very little to her personally. But to Micky, who loved the business, who lived for cooking and food and the whole buzz of owning a restaurant, it meant so much more.

Micky deserved to win.

And she didn't.

'Have you seen that sculpture?' Micky asked her with a grin.

Venny gulped back her bubbly and nodded when a waiter offered her a top-up.

'That's Dani up there with me in a clinch, isn't it?' Micky eyed her curiously. 'But I thought Jamie was sketching *you* for it.'

'So did Dani,' said Venny, aware that the other guests at their table were earwigging like mad. 'She's hopping mad with Jamie.'

'Sorry,' said Micky sympathetically.

'Oh, I don't suppose it really matters,' sighed Venny. 'Where is Jamie, anyway? I thought he'd be here for at least part of the evening, to see how the thing actually looks up there.'

'Well, I think it's a very good likeness of me,' said Micky, laughing. 'Particularly the cock.'

Venny glanced over at the sculpture. The male figure had a massive erection. God! Why hadn't she noticed that earlier?

Because I was in shock, thought Venny, that's why.

'Jamie's up on the stage now,' Micky pointed out, looking over with interest. 'I don't want to be alarmist, but he appears to have a blowtorch in his hand. It's probably my blowtorch, come to think of it.'

Other people at the table – and at the other tables too – were looking up at the stage, wondering what a man in a kilt was doing up there on the stage wielding a blowtorch.

A kilt? thought Venny. She'd never once seen Jamie in a kilt, so why was he wearing one now, as the Scots did on those ceremonial occasions like Hogmanay and Burns Night?

But maybe that was it. Ceremonial. Maybe Jamie was about to do something he saw as deeply significant to his Scots honour.

'Someone ought to get him down from there,' said Venny, glancing around in the hope of catching the eye of some of the bouncers who had earlier been on the door, admitting ticket-holders only. And of course they'd have let Jamie in. Jamie would have a ticket. Dani would have got him one some time ago. Before she had discovered what an all-round mad bastard he was.

Micky too was looking around, searching the room with his eyes for bouncers. There were two standing by the door. One of them was looking over to the stage, where Jamie was now strumming the microphone beside his sculpture.

'Testing, one, two, three,' he said in his deep Glasgow burr.

The waiting staff were glancing up at him too, but clearly Dani was ordering them about their duties, telling them to ignore him, to just carry on with serving the first course. The bouncers were just starting to move across the room.

'*Dani,*' boomed out over the speaker system.

Dani, at the far side of the room, looked around as if she'd been goosed.

'This is for you, Dani,' Jamie shouted, and set the naked flame from a cigarette lighter to the roaring throat of the blowtorch. A long tongue of yellow flame shot from the end of it. He adjusted the setting. Then the colour dimmed to blue.

'He isn't,' said Venny in a horrified whisper.

'He bloody well is,' said Micky.

And he was. He was melting the sculpture with the blowtorch. As soon as the blue flame touched the female figure, water started to cascade down and drip onto the stage.

Dani looked up in disbelief, and several of the waiting staff, bustling about with fully laden trays, glanced over at her anxiously, wondering if they should continue, or stop what they were doing.

'Get on with it,' hissed Dani at them, making urgent shooing motions with her hands.

The waiting staff carried on, skirting the stage. Unfortunately the water from the fast-melting sculpture was now dripping over the edge of the stage and onto the highly-polished floor beneath. One of the waiters slipped, and chilled lobster bisque went shooting up into the air and fell in a huge pink cascade, landing on several of the diners, who leapt up with squeals and shouts of protest.

'He's better entertainment value than a circus, that boy,' laughed Micky.

The bouncers were struggling to cross the huge room against the sudden chaos of people leaving their seats and making for the doors. One collapsed in a flailing heap as he neared the stage, taking three of the diners with him. One of the women who had fallen was so irate she started belabouring the bouncer with a sequinned handbag.

Venny stared, fascinated, as the sculpture quickly lost its shape. Dani was gone now; there was only Micky left, and Jamie was busy attacking the ice-Micky's erection with the blowtorch.

'Ouch,' said Micky, watching.

One of the bouncers reached the stage, and from the wings a uniformed security guard came charging out. The guard went skidding past Jamie to land with a thump on the other side of the stage, but the bouncer grabbed Jamie. The blowtorch fell to the floor and the security guard crawled to his feet, dripping and slithering about, and grabbed Jamie's ankles. Jamie's feet flew from under him, and all three of the men went down in a churning mass of flying fists, arms and legs.

'It's true then,' said Venny.

'What's true?' Micky asked her, grinning with enjoyment as he refilled their glasses. Everyone else on the table was gone, thundering towards the doors like wildebeest during summer migration.

'That the Scots don't wear anything under their kilts,' said Venny, and started to laugh.

Somehow within the next half an hour the hotel management swung into action and managed to restore order. Jamie was removed to the kitchens – but not before he'd mooned comprehensively at the diners. The sad-looking mound of ice that had been his glorious sculpture was cleared away, and the stage and the surrounding area were mopped up. Angry and offended and downright frightened diners who had been unlucky enough to be seated near the stage were escorted back to their relaid tables, and Dani got the waiting staff in order and got the main course served. There were mutterings about compensation and charges being brought, but on the whole things settled down quite quickly and a sumptuous main course was followed by pudding, then cheese and biscuits, fruit and mints and coffee and brandy, and everyone's tempers started to improve. The diners became quite mellow, so that by the time the awards were to be given people were leaning back in their seats, cigars were being puffed upon, and smiles were again the order of the day.

The television celebrity turned out to be a perky

Irish BBC weather girl, escorted onto the now pristine stage by the hotel manager. She was blonde and had improbably perfect large breasts which seemed about to burst from the confines of her black bugle-beaded gown. She handled the gold envelopes containing the Blue Ribbon awards results with reverence. Canned music boomed out from behind the stage, and as synthetic drums rolled she made a very pretty speech during which her audience, sated with food and fine wines, hardly fidgeted at all.

Venny smiled across at Micky; he winked back. And then, over his shoulder, she noticed someone who looked familiar. A thick body, dark curls, a choleric face. It was Bill Thompson. Catching her eye, he cheekily raised his glass to her. Venny quickly averted her gaze. He had grown a goatee beard, which added an edge of sophistication to his image, she thought. But he was still a bastard.

'So here we go,' the weather girl was saying with the effusive warmth she usually reserved for isobars and wind chill factors. The drum roll grew progressively louder. 'The Blue Ribbon awards, the most prestigious restaurant awards for excellence, for efficiency, for ambience, for the very best food.'

'Come on, get on with it,' urged Micky.

'The standard of entry has never been higher, and the panel of judges were faced with a terribly difficult decision when they saw how exceptional each of the contestants were.'

'Yeah, yeah,' sighed Micky.

'Hush,' Venny urged him.

The weather girl was opening the envelope, taking her time over it, building up the bated-breath atmosphere in the big room.

'And so in third place we have Le Petit Noir,' shouted the weather girl with a broad grin. 'Proprietor, Philippe Noir.'

'Who?' asked Venny, peering around heads as a spotlight caught and held the Frenchman who now rose and started down towards the stage.

'He's very good,' admitted Micky, clapping along with everyone else.

'I've never heard of him.'

'You must have.'

'I haven't.'

Up on the stage, Philippe Noir was embracing the weather girl and kissing her with exuberant Gallic charm on both cheeks. He gave her a friendly pat on the ass too, something no Englishman would get away with. The weather girl smiled, and blushed.

'Think he's in there,' said Micky.

'Shush! She's going to announce second place.'

Philippe Noir was returning to his seat clutching his prize. The weather girl steadied herself, patting her hair. 'And now for second place. Of course here the competition became very intense.'

'Oh, cut to the chase, can't you?' muttered Venny.

'So intense in fact that the judges were very divided as to who should have the honour of being runner-up this year.' The weather girl paused for dramatic effect.

Venny's fingers were digging into Micky's forearm. 'So it was decided that two restaurants should share that honour. In second place for the Blue Ribbon award, ladies and gentlemen,' she flourished another envelope and consulted its contents, 'I give you Beurre Blanc, proprietor Mr Micky Quinn.'

Micky rose to his feet with a grin as the spotlight zoomed in on him and the room erupted in a wave of clapping.

'And Box of Delights, proprietor Ms Venetia Halliday!'

Venny stood up dazedly. If they had come second, then who the hell had come first? Still, was second really so bad? And they had tied for second place, so there would be no hurt feelings or bruised egos on either side. Actually, for her and Micky, it was a pretty good result.

She went up onto the stage with Micky, and they collected their blue ribbons set in perspex. Their names and the names of their restaurants were engraved on the silver base of each prize. Flashes fired. The press were in, and what with Jamie's behaviour earlier in the evening and this surprising result, there were sure to be plenty of write-ups in the papers tomorrow, and lots of good publicity.

They kissed the weather girl (Micky seemed particularly enthusiastic about kissing the weather girl, thought Venny ironically) and went back to their seats clutching their prizes.

But who had won? Venny wondered.

Who could have beaten both Micky and herself, when she had been so sure that they had it all in the bag?

'And now,' said the weather girl portentously, 'the moment we have all been waiting for. The moment when we bestow the first prize in these prestigious Blue Ribbon awards. Ladies and gentlemen,' the weather girl opened the envelope, looked at it, paused, and then screeched: 'First prize goes to Fantoni's, proprietor Pietro Fantoni!'

The room was a solid wall of noise. The drum roll burst into a crescendo, then a fanfare sounded. The spotlight dipped and dived and spun around the packed room as a roar of approval and an explosion of clapping, catcalling and whistling went up from the crowd.

'Who?' yelled Venny at Micky.

'Fantoni's.' Micky shrugged fatalistically. 'I told you they've been getting good reviews.'

Over Micky's shoulder Venny saw the spotlight settle upon Bill Thompson. She thought it was going to pass on, but it didn't. Bill Thompson rose to his feet, waving and grinning.

'But that's Bill Thompson,' she shouted across to Micky. 'Is he going to collect the prize for this Fantoni chap?'

'You're joking,' said a sour-faced girl sitting at their table. Her restaurant hadn't even been in the top three. 'That *is* Pietro Fantoni.'

'No, that's Bill Thompson,' insisted Venny.

The girl shook her head vehemently. 'Haven't you

heard of PR?' she said bitterly. 'Bill Thompson changed his name to Pietro Fantoni. It's easy enough and it sounds a hell of a lot more impressive, I think you'll agree. I spoke to him just a couple of weeks ago, he's even started using a dummy Italian accent to convince the punters he's genuine. Then he got hold of one of the big PR consultancies in Mayfair, to launch the whole thing. I tell you, he's fooled everyone, the judges included.'

'But the food must have been good,' remonstrated Venny. She could barely take all this in. She watched in a complete daze while Bill Thompson – or, rather, Pietro Fantoni – went up onto the stage and cheerfully groped the giggling weather girl.

'Of course it was,' scoffed the sour-faced girl. 'It was good because he hired a top chef straight off the plane from Tuscany. I tell you, the whole thing was rigged.'

'Pietro' was coming back to his seat – thank God he wasn't going to turn all their stomachs by making a speech, thought Venny.

She couldn't believe it.

Plodding, useless Bill Thompson had fooled them all. He'd had the last laugh.

And stupidly, incredulously, Venny now found herself laughing too. Laughing at the sheer absurdity of the situation.

'You're not getting hysterical, are you?' asked Micky with a concerned look. 'I'm not going to have to slap you round the chops or anything drastic, am I?'

'No,' chuckled Venny. 'Don't worry. It's just all so silly, that's all.'

Micky gazed at her curiously. 'When I first met you, these awards were all that mattered to you.'

'I know. Ridiculous, isn't it?'

'You're happy with joint second?' asked Micky as the weather girl started another speech.

'Perfectly,' said Venny truthfully.

'Almost like being in a partnership after all,' quipped Micky.

'Yeah. Almost,' said Venny, and darted forwards to kiss him fleetingly on the lips.

'What was that for?' asked Micky, his blue eyes dancing with devilment as his hand slid up her inner thigh under the table. He kissed her back, lingering over the kiss, uncaring of the others at the table looking on with envy.

'Nothing, really.'

'So maybe you'd consider a partnership at some time in the future?' Micky probed gently.

'I might,' admitted Venny, moving his hand further up her thigh and opening her legs a little so that he could get his hand just where he – and she – wanted it.

'Pleasure, not business,' said Micky, rubbing her furry mound lustfully.

'Pleasure?' Venny asked just a bit breathlessly.

'Yeah. How about it?'

Venny smiled and leaned closer. 'OK,' she said happily. 'But Micky, when are you going to pay me for the damage my car sustained in that shunt we had?'

'I'll pay you in kind,' said Micky with an evil grin.

In the hotel kitchens an hour later, the staff were washing up, tidying away excess food, packing up for the evening. Jamie was sitting, head in hands, at the big aluminium prep table in the middle of the room while the others worked around him.

'You're a crazy son of a bitch,' said an irate female voice from above him. He looked up. His grey eyes stared into Dani's blue ones. She was holding a tea-towel and looked as if she was about to swipe him around the ear with it. He ran a hand through his tangle of blond hair and shrugged truculently. 'You know, you're really lucky the hotel management decided not to press charges,' Dani raged on. 'You're lucky they didn't just throw you out in the street and boot your sorry arse all the way back to Shepherd's Bush. You're lucky I was here to vouch for your good character.'

'Yeah, well, thanks a bunch,' said Jamie sarcastically, and pulled the angry and squirming Dani down onto his kilted lap. She wriggled, trying to get free. His damned sporran was digging into her hip. Or was it? God, it was his erection!

'What made you do it?' she demanded hotly, giving up trying to get away from him while her staff moved around them, listening surreptitiously. 'One moment everything was sweet, and then you start doing your Braveheart impression up on the stage, and the whole place is in uproar! You're the absolute bloody end, you really are!'

Jamie linked his arms around her waist and looked

at her consideringly. 'Shall we get engaged, then?' he asked her bluntly.

'That's a ridiculous suggestion,' said Dani frostily. 'My parents would go demented.'

'Shall we?' he repeated.

'Oh – all right, then,' said Dani, and kissed him. The staff let loose a thunderous roar of cheers and clapping, but neither Dani nor Jamie paid them any attention.